HEROES OF
TERRA

Sophie
Evans

HEROES OF
TERRA

Heir to the Throne

SOPHIE EVANS

Copyright © 2014 by Sophie Evans.

Library of Congress Control Number:		2014916760
ISBN:	Hardcover	978-1-4990-7436-9
	Softcover	978-1-4990-7493-2
	eBook	978-1-4990-7435-2

Cover Design: Ricardo Rullo

This book was printed in the United States of America.

Rev. date: 09/22/2014

To order additional copies of this book, contact:
Xlibris LLC
1-888-795-4274
www.Xlibris.com
Orders@Xlibris.com
635833

CONTENTS

PROLOGUE

Filix Lux turned quickly, dodging the boulder as it barreled by, smashing against the stone of the cavern wall. Gasping for air as the gigantic malus bellowed at her, Filix pressed herself to the cold stone of the cave. The malus's ram-like horns struck sparks off the stone above. She knew she had been lucky to survive with only a few broken ribs despite the pain shooting through her. She had been lucky to survive at all. "But it isn't over yet," she told herself.

Her keen senses told her she was in a cavern somewhere in an arid valley the humans called the Grand Canyon, the largest portal from Terra to earth. Elf kin knew it well for the old magic that resided there. It naturally drew you to it if you weren't careful. Filix hadn't been careful enough; transporting two took more finesse than she anticipated. She brought a malus with her.

The beast loomed over her, snapping his sharklike teeth, clawing the ground with his enormous feet as his bellows echoed through the cavern. Shutting out the noises, she focused on her goal: getting out. Filix knew she had to escape, or all she and others had fought for would be lost.

With a powerful utterance, she healed her broken ribs. Holding tightly to the tiny she-elf bundled in her arms, she avoided another blow from a meaty fist. Filix glared up at the beast above her, trying desperately to think of a way to confuse it so she and her young niece could escape. A plan started to form. She just hoped she wasn't too late.

"Why play with me, beast? You could easily kill me! Do it! You know that I have the elves' only hope in my arms! Or better yet, go play with someone your own size!"

She needed a way out of there. She hoped the malus, not known for their intelligence, would take the bait. And luck didn't fail her.

The giant creature grunted, befuddled his trapped prey would speak to him. The only sound he'd heard from his victims were desperate cries and an occasional plea for help but never defiance. He regarded her curiously, letting his club fall slightly toward the ground, and stepped back a pace.

"It is *because* you have the elves' only hope that I must kill you!" he rumbled. His terrifying pose now shifted to confusion, and Filix knew she didn't have a second to waste.

"Ventus! Trahe me California!" she called out to the wind. The cavern vanished, replaced by gray, howling wind. The baby squealed at the rushing sound, but her cries blew away.

Once the wind died down, Filix looked up at her surroundings: lofty palms, empty beaches, and a modest beach house. The door opened revealing a tall elf with long black hair and bright blue eyes. A gossamer dress fluttered about her, reflecting the color of her eyes.

Her gaze locked on the baby. "Filix! You brought my child back! Are you all right?"

Filix nodded. "Yes, Regina. I am, and so is the prophecy. The child is well." Filix paused to hand her the baby. Smiling at the reunion, Filix watched Regina coo for the dark-haired child. Filix turned, soberly thinking of the mess they had created in Terra. Not one princess had stayed to rule, and there were no male heirs. Filix and Regina knew the queen would be furious when she found out all her daughters had deserted the throne and run away from the fight.

Filix's sister looked up at her. "I will have to disguise myself and erase her memories of Terra. She has already had her age concealed. It's heartrending to do this, Filix, but it may be the only way to save the lives of those who live both on Terra and in this realm. I wish she could know what Elisium looks like, for it is so beautiful. But she will go back, won't she, Filix? Surely *you* would know that. You *are* the oracle."

Filix nodded, long hair spilling over her face. She silently thanked the wild auburn tresses for hiding her tears. "Yes, Regina."

In another realm, a ghostly figure, standing in a shadowy forest, chuckled darkly. As the vision of the beach house faded from the mirror in his hand, his rasping voice sent shivers through all listening.

"Well, well, well, the only hope for the elves is a wee babe. Ha! How could they think a mere youngling could even threaten my forces? Or me for that matter! How in Terra's name did the elves grow so absolutely desperate as to send their little children out to war?" He looked at the tree nearest him, and a bulbous form erupted from the trunk.

"Master Umbra, the assassin is prepared to kill the child," it said.

Umbra sighed ruefully. "I'm afraid that won't happen. The child is currently so well shielded it would be futile." He shook his head, smirking. "Besides, what could a child do to me?"

Orange bits of fiery light glowed in the dark pits of the wood dwarf's eyes as he shrugged and confessed, "Nothing to my knowledge, sire."

The evil figure grunted, "Then I will wait till she is unguarded before destroying her . . . Or perhaps I can persuade her to come to my side. Having an elf princess might certainly be useful. Besides, it will be entertaining to send horrors to torture the child until I am ready. You may leave."

The dwarf no sooner left when a bright light flashed before the dark figure, and a pearly door developed within it. A strikingly pretty blonde stepped out as the door swung wide and threw more light upon trees and grasses. She faced the shadowy cloaked man, the light not seeming to touch him. Her golden hair swept up into a loose braid, and she wore a shimmering white dress. Her bronzed skin and sky blue eyes shone like the dawn despite obvious efforts to hide it from the evil being.

"Umbra, you will not find her defeat so easy," she said calmly.

Snorting derisively, he replied, "You think so, Queen Aurora? Have you forgotten that I know you've married my younger brother Tonitrus and have knowledge of our power? And did you forget that as the Dark Lord, I know of your petty magic?"

Aurora smiled despite the threat. "Elvish is not the only way to victory." With that, Umbra growled and disappeared. The queen's lips turned into a thoughtful frown as she let her golden hair revert to ebony and her features back to her own. She had disguised herself knowing she would be seen by many of the Dark Lord's allies.

Queen Lux Aurora Vesper stood there, thinking about the child. She knew there was one more prophecy to be spoken for the baby. She teleported to the beach and waited outside the house until Filix and Regina went to another room to talk. The queen walked through the closed door and looked down at the sleeping baby. Without heirs to the throne, the elven kingdom would fail, and the only good creatures left would be murdered without elves to defend them. She knew Regina was only trying to salvage a life here for the baby and herself, away from the wars and destruction on Terra. Brushing strands of hair from her eyes, Aurora leaned down to kiss the baby's forehead. She whispered gently, "The time will come when you will stand alone. Remember yourself and accept the throne." She stood up, shoulders relaxed, and disappeared in a flash of brilliant light, just as a smiling Regina appeared in the doorway.

Regina screamed, her easy demeanor now outrage, realizing what Aurora had done. "No! You cursed my child! She was to live a simple life, away from the suffering she must now have! How could you do this to me, Mother?" she asked with tears streaming down her face as she hugged the baby girl.

Aurora's voice lingered. "She will be all right, my love."

Regina sobbed into the baby's wavy hair. Filix stood in the doorway, her gaze filled with misery. "I hardly think death 'all right,'" she whispered.

Regina's melancholy eyes, red-rimmed from crying, traveled to Filix. "I am afraid it might not be only her that will die. It could be us all."

CHAPTER 1

THE GATEWAY TO TERRA

Vanessa Nox looked out of the train window at the fading light. It had been a long time since she had seen her father. He had visited often before but not lately. Most people made fun of Vanessa because her father lived so far away. They joked around and teased her about her parents being "divorced." This, however, was not true in the least. Vanessa's parents loved each other from a distance, and whenever they met, they did so with such warmth that Vanessa knew they would never separate from each other unless they were forced. And that was what got Vanessa curious. Were they forced to be apart? Why? Many questions flowed through Vanessa, but none were answered. And that brought Vanessa's thoughts back to herself.

Vanessa was twelve, turning thirteen soon, and her sister Abigail had just turned nine. Vanessa, Abigail, and their mom lived in Southern California where Mom worked in her large garden. Their father, however, lived in the far reaches of Northern Idaho. Vanessa hardly knew of Idaho, and she was curious about what kept him there.

Abigail was now looking out of the second window of the train at the forest. "Wow, I never have seen so many evergreens in my life," she whispered in awe.

Vanessa nodded in agreement. Despite the fact that they had traveled a little, all their lives, they had lived in Monterey, California. The only time that they saw their dad was when he came for the holidays. Vanessa didn't even know what kind of work her dad did, but whatever he did, it gave them enough money to survive.

"I wonder what kind of land will be there!" her sister said to her, snapping Vanessa out the trance.

"Probably the same stuff as we see here," Vanessa replied, bored out of her mind. She looked down at the fairy-tale book in her hand. It must have been really old. It was one of the books her dad gave her. It was not the only book her father had given her on her last birthday; in fact, there was a small pile of them. Most were about elves and dragons—boring stuff like that. Suddenly, the train began to slow.

"We are nearly there!" her sister cheered. She was quite enthusiastic. Vanessa wanted to be sick. Perhaps she had eaten too much of the cheap sandwich she had bought on the train. But she felt more like something was making her feel like this, as if something was about to happen. She stood up to go to the bathroom to wash her face, but she tripped and fell on a suitcase that was sticking out of nowhere. She landed on it right where her heart was. She swore a bruise would form there within a minute and decided to skip the bathroom idea. She rubbed the spot of which the hard suitcase had struck, not feeling any better.

Abigail grinned at her. "I did that too! You OK?" Vanessa nodded uncertainly. A young female train attendant stepped out of a hidden door just as the train came to a screeching stop.

"Ms. Vanessa and Ms. Abigail, please come, for your father is waiting for you," she said formally, helping the girls out of their chairs. Vanessa groaned as she stood up, her jeans rubbing against her leg painfully. Why all the formalities?

"Why did we stop here? There is nothing but trees," she complained, getting her backpack. She and her little sister headed outside of the private train. Their father was waiting for them, his arms spread in a welcome. The girls rushed to him, hugging him tightly.

"Welcome to Idaho. How are you, girls?" he asked, smiling broadly.

"We are good, Da . . . Is that a buggy?" Vanessa trailed off, staring in astonishment at the little carriage beside him.

"A buggy! You have a buggy?" an incredulous Abigail exclaimed then turned to Vanessa to ask, "What's a buggy?" Vanessa pointed wordlessly to the buggy.

"Oh thanks, Ms. Specific," Abigail said sarcastically. And she looked over at the huge horse. "You have a horse—it's big!" she said in surprise.

Dad smiled. "I have many horses, and Mons is a draft horse—a Belgian in fact. Let's go before the gateway closes," he added thoughtfully. Vanessa looked at Dad with interest.

"What gateway?" she said.

Their father laughed as if the question was ridiculous. "The gateway that your mother taught you about, of course."

Vanessa was puzzled, but got into the buggy along with Abigail and her dad. A few hours later, they reached a tunnel of which Vanessa could not see the end. "That's a long tunnel!" she said with a note of surprise.

Dad looked at her with amusement in his eyes. "Silly, that's a gateway, not a tunnel."

Vanessa didn't understand, but Abigail did. "You mean the gateway in Vanessa's books?" she asked, slightly excitedly.

"Yes," Dad replied, a slight frown of confusion creeping up his face. With that, the buggy rolled forward.

Halfway through the tunnel, the ground around them started to shake. Vanessa grabbed her sister and started to open the door when her father locked it.

"What are you doing, Dad?" Vanessa screamed frantically, trying to unlock it.

"It's always hard on the newbies," Dad said, raising his deep voice to be heard.

"WE'RE GONNA DIE!" yelled a hysterical Abigail as loudly as she could.

Dad looked out of the window. "It will stop soon," he announced. He was right. Two minutes later, the shaking stopped, and the little carriage moved on. Soon they saw a light at the end of the tunnel which got brighter and brighter until they emerged out into the daylight.

"It's morning here!" Vanessa said with a slightly hoarse voice. Had she really screamed that much?

"Yep, time goes faster on the earth," Dad said with a grin, and then his grin disappeared. "Your mother never told you about the gateway?" he asked.

Abigail and Vanessa both shook their heads and said, "No, Dad."

Dad started to panic. "Nothing about magic and powers?" They shook their heads again. Their father seemed to be thinking furiously. His next question evoked the girl's curiosity. "Not even about her own kind?" he yelped.

"Dad, what do you mean by her own *kind*? What *is* Mom?" Vanessa asked, and Dad looked at her, his face very pale.

"Your mother is an *elf.*"

CHAPTER 2

REX

Vanessa had been gifted with the ability to tell when somebody was lying, and her Dad wasn't. She also could tell he didn't need mental help. Abigail hadn't quite received that gift yet.

"What? You want me to believe that my mom is an elf?" Abigail cried indignantly, not believing her ears.

"Abigail, listen to him. He is telling the truth, no matter how bizarre it sounds to you. I can even tell you he isn't crazy," she reassured.

Dad nodded emphatically. "Thank you. I'm glad someone can vouch for my sanity. Not even your mother does that sometimes," he grumbled. Abigail decided that her elder sister was speaking the truth and seemed to believe what Dad had said. Dad began to relax with the assurance that they believed him. They listened as their father told them that everything in the books Vanessa had gotten was true.

Ten minutes later, Dad looked out of the window and blanched. "Get out now, girls!" he barked.

Vanessa looked out and found herself staring straight at a small cliff ahead. She and Abigail tried to unlock the doors, but they were jammed.

"Stop the carriage, Mons!" their father called to the great draft horse.

Unfortunately, the huge horse had tried to turn away earlier, but his sharp move had accidently broken his attachments to the buggy. The separated carriage, now sliding off the cliff and plummeting down to the bottom of the ravine, faintly reminded Vanessa of a roller coaster ride. Such thoughts flitted away from her as the carriage slid off the edge of the cliff. Just before they hit the water, Vanessa's door clicked open. With a splash, the buggy went underwater.

Vanessa opened her eyes and grabbed her sister, and they both swam up out of the submerged buggy and into the air. Vanessa looked at the small cliff in slight surprise, for she had not expected to find water when they went over it. In fact, she had expected to die from being smashed against the stony ground below. She definitely had not expected to be nearly drowned.

Vanessa soon realized that this was a small river. She swam over to the rocky shore and set the now unconscious Abigail on it. Then remembering her father, she frantically plunged into the icy water and started to swim toward the drowned buggy. Halfway through the river, a strong current pushed her under. Something hard hit her head and left her disoriented. Struggling in the murky river, she began to swim hard, thinking she was going to the surface. The clouded water was no help, and she felt her lungs burn for air. Her hand reached silt and she realized too late that she had been swimming the wrong direction through the murky water. Despair, colder than the water, clutched at her heart. She knew that she didn't have enough strength to swim to the surface, and she was quickly running out of air.

Just as she had decided she was going to die, strong hands grabbed her waist and pulled her up to the open air, gently setting her on the rocky sand that formed the beach. She slowly opened her eyes and tried to see, but every thing was foggy. The only thing she could make out was a figure crouching over her.

"Dad?" Vanessa groaned groggily, wet hair getting in her face.

Then her vision cleared. She was staring at a young boy about the same age as she. His dark hair hung over his emerald green eyes, and his nose was a little on the big side. Vanessa gaped in awe, mouth slightly open. Then she snapped it shut with a clapping sound and brushed the wet strands of hair out of her face. She had completely forgotten that she nearly died from drowning and now felt like she was going to die of embarrassment.

"Oh, I guess you aren't Dad after all," she said through gritted teeth.

He smiled with a mischievous glint in his eyes. "Nope, its just Rex. I haven't earned *that* title . . . yet."

Vanessa felt her face flush and wondered why he lingered at the word "yet."

Then a voice from further up the beach rang out, "And you are a long way away from may I remind you!" Dad called.

Rex looked up from Vanessa. "There you are, Drake! I was worrying myself sick!" he said, smiling broadly. Vanessa had forgotten that her father was named Drake. It had been a long time since she had heard his real name; it had been a long time since she had seen him.

A small moment of hurt flashed back to Vanessa. She remembered when she was supposed to bring her father to school when she had been seven. She had asked her mother where her dad was, and her mother had responded that he was at work. Vanessa had refused to go to school without her dad, and her mother was forced to tell the teacher she was sick. Since then, Vanessa had harbored a bit of resentment toward her father. But after the gateway, that resentment had vanished. She had had no time for it. Vanessa snapped out of the reverie at Drake's next words.

"Not as worried as you seemed with my daughter," Dad said teasingly.

Vanessa scowled. "Father!" she said angrily getting up, but once she did, she nearly passed out.

"Whoa, girl! Easy there." Rex laughed lightly and helped her up much more gently.

From over the small hill came Abigail, skipping delightedly with a gray blanket over her shoulders. When she saw Vanessa, she stopped dead in her tracks, and then she charged toward them, embracing Vanessa tightly. "I missed you! I woke up as you went to find Dad! Then when the current pulled you under, Rex came from nowhere and dove in to rescue you . . . which I thought was really brave! Then Dad came and wrapped me up in a blanket! I was really worried about you."

Vanessa felt a little guilty about leaving Abigail without anyone there to protect her. In an unfamiliar world like this one, that had been a very unwise thing to do. Her father had made it out of the water without her. She should have waited. "I'm sorry I didn't think of Dad at first. And I apologize for leaving you unconscious and alone at the beach."

Abigail widened her eyes, about to protest, when Rex broke in. "I'm rather glad you did. I wouldn't have had a chance to rescue you then," he said, imitating a slurred voice with an English accent. Vanessa was surprised by his boldness and resisted a giggle as Rex continued.

"It isn't every day I get to meet Drake's daughter and her lovely sister," he added and bowed in Abigail's direction. She giggled as he kissed her hand gently.

Vanessa rolled her eyes. "Oh brother," she muttered. Abigail was in heaven. This was her dream—handsome elves, warm blankets, her sister apologizing. All they needed now was a unicorn.

Rex bowed slightly to Vanessa. "In your case, oh sister," he said with a boyish grin. Vanessa couldn't help smiling. There was something about Rex that screamed royalty, but she couldn't put a finger on what.

Drake laughed easily. "You two comedians will get along great," he said.

Vanessa raised an eyebrow. "I take it you know Rex well?" she asked.

Drake nodded. "Better than almost anyone. Rex is someone you can trust your life with. The only life you *can't* trust him with is his," he said.

Rex chuckled. "That is probably true. We should get back," he replied.

Vanessa wondered what he meant by that. "Back where? I feel pretty homeless. I thought the gateway only worked once in eight fortnights . . . At least that's what it said in one of those fairy-tale books," she said uncertainly.

Dad nodded and looked thoughtful. "You are right, Vanessa, the gateway is closed, and that means you are stuck here until it opens again. But you are scheduled to stay here for at least a month, so we should be good for now."

Vanessa could not believe her ears. "A month?" she exclaimed. Why hadn't she been told? She felt sick at the thought of staying in an unfamiliar world—one with elves and other dangerous beings too. Later, she would look back at that and laugh. There were worse objects than cliffs, much worse. But for now, she was oblivious. And ignorance was bliss.

CHAPTER 3

"EVERYTHING TALKS?"

As soon as they climbed back to the top of the hill, they noticed that the draft horse Mons had returned with a sleek new carriage.

"Where did Mons get that?" Vanessa asked. Rex shrugged and looked at Mons.

The great horse nickered. "I found some carving wood nymphs, and I asked them if they had one to spare," the horse answered in a deep male voice.

Abigail fainted again, and Vanessa almost followed suit if she hadn't been so busy trying to stabilize her fallen sister. "The draft horse talks?" she gasped in Rex's direction.

Rex laughed. "Sorry if that bothers you, but all animals talk here," he said, though he didn't look too sorry at all. "Even plants do."

"Even plants do?" Vanessa blurted, wanting to lie down and wake up from this horrible dream. She didn't like eating talking things. "*Everything* talks?" she asked hysterically, a lot louder than she meant to.

Birds flew up from the tall trees around them, and something big crashed away from the group. It did nothing to soothe Vanessa when she heard the birds speak as they flapped away. Their comments went like this: "Yikes! What was that?" and "Where's the food?"

Vanessa wanted to cry. The comfortable world she once knew was ending. Magic was cool, but this was altogether frightening. Vanessa noticed a tree move away on its roots, and a boulder hop away on tiny stone limbs.

Vanessa dropped Abigail, and covered her eyes. This couldn't be happening. Abigail came to suddenly as she hit the ground. Her little sister got up, and glared at elder sister.

Vanessa braced herself for an argument or to be reprimanded by her father for her clumsiness, but to her surprise Drake started laughing. Vanessa started to laugh as well. Abigail's face was contorted in something of a scowl as she glared at Vanessa. To them, it looked like she had bitten into a lemon.

Rex seemed to be holding back a burst of laughter and gave Vanessa a grin. She smiled back. Then another crashing sound came, and Drake turned pale. "Get into the carriage! Now!" he commanded, and they didn't argue.

"Why do we have to constantly be in a carriage? I mean, it's awesome, but who cares if a deer crashes around next to us?" she asked her father.

Drake, with an eyebrow raised in question, turned to her. "Have you ever known a deer to crash around like that?" he asked.

Vanessa made a dismissing gesture. "Well, it could have been a bear or a moose or a—" She began, but her father cut her off.

"Or a Minotaur or a dragon or even an ogre!" he argued.

She stopped. "Those things aren't real!" she said in a don't-be-silly voice.

Drake's eyes flared with a dangerous light. "Are you meaning to say that *I'm* not real? What about your mother?"

And Vanessa winced. She hadn't totally accepted the reality of the new situation. Even though she could tell her father wasn't lying, he could still believe it without it being true... couldn't he? "Well, maybe you just hit your head or some—"

But Drake silenced her with a look. "Do I look like someone who hit my head and is delirious? Do I appear as an idiot?" he asked, his voice soft.

Vanessa knew that she was in trouble. "No," she muttered, looking away from his eyes. But just as she did so, she saw them turn silver. Her gaze switched back, trying to catch it, but it was gone.

"Good," he said. Vanessa knew by the tone of his voice that the conversation had ended.

Everyone in the carriage looked at her father. He sighed. "Let's go to the castle," he said.

Vanessa heard another crashing sound from the forest.

Rex cocked his head, glancing nervously around as if something were following them. Vanessa was suddenly suspicious that those eyes she had seen were not from her imagination. Rex looked at her, and their eyes locked. He nodded, put a finger to his lips, and motioned behind him. Vanessa glanced there and saw a shadow moving slowly around the carriage.

CHAPTER 4

THE POWERS

Since Dad, Abigail, Vanessa, and Rex piled in the new carriage, they only now started to notice what was in it. The new carriage had two rows that only sat two people. Abigail wanted to sit by Dad, so Vanessa was stuck with Rex, making her very uncomfortable.

The first thing that Vanessa noticed was that the inside of the carriage seemed much bigger than the outside and, second, that it had beautiful green carved wood. The outlined figures in the carvings depicted lithe cats hunting, magnificent horses galloping, swift falcons flying, and beautiful women being chased by things that looked like goat men.

"Are those fauns?" Vanessa asked. She felt a bit queasy thinking of magical beings.

Rex looked at her and replied, "We call them satyrs here, but yes, those are." And with that, their conversation ended.

Then when Vanessa could no longer stand the awkward silence, she asked, "How old are you?"

Rex smiled mischievously. "Why would you want to know?"

"It's only a question!" Vanessa said defensively. "I don't know a lot of things around here!"

Rex looked around the carriage as if checking to see if anyone was listening. "I am around eighteen years old," he answered quietly.

Vanessa shook her head. "What do you mean you're eighteen years old? That's impossible!" But as soon as she said it, she realized that it wasn't impossible.

"No, it's not impossible. I'm an elf," he said then added, "You are eighteen too. You had your age disguised when…. Yeah, you're eighteen too.

Rex was a bit worried Vanessa had caught the slip, but the girl wasn't listening. A horrible thought had just crossed her mind: *What if my mom is a hundred?*

"So how old is my dad? And what *is* he?" Vanessa asked Rex. She was trying to make conversation, because staring at the carvings on the wall was getting tiresome.

Rex suddenly seemed very interested in the foliage outside. "Wow! That's a very beautiful birch!" he said way too quickly.

"Don't change the subject!"

"I am not!"

"Oh yes, you are!"

"And why do you say that?"

"Because you are. And you're as red as a stoplight!" Vanessa said, unable to think of a suitable answer.

"What does that have to do with it?" Rex defended.

"Everything!"

"Does not!"

"Does too!"

"Nuh-uh"

"Well, I—"

"GUYS!" It was Abigail and Dad. They were laughing, and Vanessa joined in.

Everyone but Rex was giggling and grinning. Everyone but a very frustrated Rex was finding this funny.

He had stopped his blushing but was still a little embarrassed about being teased. "Oh yeah! Just laugh all you want! he said, throwing up his hands in surrender.

"Oh, Rex, you are such a hypocrite!" Dad said and gave Vanessa a suspicious glance, smiling slyly.

Her father had only given her that glance once before, and that had been when she had been at Steven's house. Steven Johnson was his name. Vanessa remembering that incident, wished she could change into a mouse and hide in a hole. To her surprise, she felt kind of tingly, and then everything began to grow big around her.

"What's happening?" she yelped and looked down at her hands.

What she saw made her scream. Her hands had turned into furry rodent feet. Realization hit her like a blow to the head: She had wished to be a mouse, and here she was—a mouse.

"Yikes!" Rex said.

"Cute!" said Abigail.

"Help!" squeaked Vanessa in mouse form. "How do I get out of it?"

"Oh well, um, how did you get in it?" Dad asked.

"Can I name her?" Abigail pleaded, both shocked and excited.

"Yeah! Name her Squeaky," Rex encouraged.

"no!" Vanessa yelled, and Rex looked hurt, not hurt enough in Vanessa's opinion.

Dad explained patiently to Vanessa that if she thought about becoming a human again, she should revert back to normal. It worked. Vanessa looked at her father, "Am I the only one who can do that? Or can all elves do that?

"Well," Dad began, "each elf has a power. Most abilities are harmless, but some are deadly. Rex's power is to breathe underwater, talk to animals, and he is also handy with a sword or spear, among other things. Your mother can heal, shape-shift, and grow plants at any rate she would want. She can also wield a bow like a master."

Vanessa wondered for a moment and tried. "What are you? A satyr? An elf?"

Suddenly, their father's attention was riveted on Rex. "Are you sure . . .," Drake asked as he peered out of the window and sighed. "Girls, I will tell you later. We've arrived at your temporary home."

Rex grinned. "I put dibs on the tower!"

Vanessa elbowed him. "Oh shush! If you were a brother, maybe! I don't even have a brother, silly!" she said, preparing to leave.

Rex stuck his tongue out, but out of the corner of Vanessa's eye, she saw her father flinch at that comment. Vanessa felt a worm of doubt crawl into her heart. *Or do I?* she silently asked herself. There was so much she didn't know, so much she had to learn.

CHAPTER 5

THE CASTLE

The castle was even bigger than Vanessa had imagined, with a huge moat and a gigantic wall surrounding it. But the castle itself was the most impressive; it had tall towers, monstrous oak doors, steel-lined windows scattered about its large exterior, stones of gray or white color, and a silver banner with a snow leopard and a bluish platinum dragon embroidered on it. All in all, Vanessa thought that it could make the perfect postcard picture for her mom.

"Whoa, that is the most beautiful castle ever!" she exclaimed and looked over at Abigail, who had dropped her jaw at it, then at her dad. He glanced at Vanessa, and the father and daughter locked eyes.

"This is nothing compared to castles in the elven kingdom or the fairy kingdom or even, for that matter, the dragon kingdom. But I think she is still quite a little beauty. Your mother and I built it with a bit of help, and we used ideas from other castles," he told them. Then he turned and opened the door for the girls as soon as the carriage stopped.

Vanessa followed Rex and Dad to the big oak doors and was filled with a sense of awe. The interior was even more gilded than the outside; it had a large silver and oak spiral staircase, a beautiful crystal chandelier, a huge silver clock, and glass doors with delicate carvings on them, leading off to the sides.

As their dad walked off, Rex bowed as Vanessa entered. "My princess, how may I serve you? Perhaps you can dance with me!" he asked in a formal voice.

Vanessa caught his gaze as he motioned with his head toward Abigail. Vanessa understood and played along. Abigail had had a stressful time with this different realm, and a distraction was needed. "That would be delightful, sir. May I know the name of my escort?" she replied in an equally formal voice.

Abigail giggled, enjoying the acting. "Sir Squiggle!" she whispered loudly.

Rex hid a smile. "My name is Sir Squiggle," he said.

Abigail giggled harder. "Dance!" she whispered, even louder this time.

Rex winked at Vanessa, and they began a ballroom dance. Vanessa quite enjoyed it, and since her mother had taught her dancing, she moved fluidly. When they got close enough to Abigail, Rex pounced.

He tackled her, and she fell laughing and screaming. He and Vanessa tickled Abigail until their father came down.

He silenced them with a wave of his hand, and they shot one another glares until they stopped. Vanessa had a newfound respect for Rex. He could be the "cool" guy, but he could also play with a little girl with more enthusiasm than Vanessa could muster. He was also the only youth they had met in this world, and that gave him a place in Abigail and Vanessa's company.

Vanessa watched as Abigail plopped down on a couch next to the spiral staircase and slipped off to sleep. Next to her, Rex sat down and stared up at the staircase curiously. Vanessa walked over to the glass doors. They had carvings in them like the carriage.

Examining them closely, she saw that the carvings held pictures of dragons flying over misty mountains and seas. Vanessa focused on the waves and gasped. The waves were actually moving. She looked at the dragons and saw that they were actually flying. Captivated by the moving scenes, she did not notice that Dad had silently approached her. She jumped when he spoke.

"That is my favorite! It is a *speculi*," he said.

Vanessa thought for a moment then exclaimed, "*Speculi* is Latin! It means looking glass!"

Dad laughed. "Vanessa, do you know that Latin came from another language? Latin is actually Elvish, a language that all types of nymphs use, like elves, dryads, naiads, and fairies. And Latin also is Draconic, Wolfish, Felinian, and Fish. It is very interesting, and you can learn more about it in the library upstairs." Vanessa looked at the designs with new appreciation. It was starting to make sense why her mother had forced her and her sister to learn Latin for as long as she could remember.

She soon got interested in the staircase, wondering what else was up there, but her belly rumbled with hunger, and she glanced at the clock, which showed 9:56 AM. Vanessa was surprised at the time, wondering if she and her sister could eat, when, out of the blue, Dad said, "My, my! It is breakfast time! You guys are probably starving!" He was right. Vanessa heard Rex's and Abigail's midsections, which also thundered in applause. Dad guided them to the glass door, opening them to reveal a marble hall.

Vanessa walked by Dad to the end of the hall and another glass door. She studied the carvings with intent and found there were no dragons on this one; there were fairies. These were unlike any fairies she had ever seen. They were all different sizes, ranging from 2 to 10 inches tall, but each were slender and graceful gliding across the white glass with celestial beauty.

Vanessa had been used to cupid-like fairies who wore ball gowns, not ones that were so svelte, exotic, and dressed in leaflike slips. Two larger fairies about a foot tall hovered in front of them then bowed, opening the doors for them with a whirl. The doors spread apart to reveal a handsome room with a large balcony big enough for a party of twenty-five to fit comfortably. In the center of the room sat a long table laden with food.

Vanessa smelled pancakes, omelets of many sorts, broiled, fried, and scrambled eggs, crepes, toast and jam, scones, French toast, puddings, fresh fruits, and other desserts. Abigail and Rex stared in astonishment. "FOOOOOOOD!" cried the two, and then both dug in.

Vanessa settled on to the bench with much more politeness and took a plate. Putting some toast on her dish, she decided to experiment, piling scrambled eggs on her toast then delicately laying bacon on top. She rolled it all into a crepe.

Feeling as if someone were watching her, she looked up and spotted Rex staring at her intently. When he noticed her watching him, he blushed then copied Vanessa's moves and made a breakfast sandwich. When he left out the meat, she guessed he must be vegetarian and respected that. She only ever used bacon herself because it tasted so incredible. Perhaps elves had a better alternative. Her thoughts went back to her father. What was he? *Obviously, a carnivore . . .* Vanessa quit pondering when Rex finished his sandwich making. She was anxious to see how he liked it.

Rex bit into it, and then his eyes widened, and he scarfed the rest while making another. Vanessa decided that it was probably pretty good. She brushed her hair out of her eyes and took a big bite. She had never tasted a better concoction in her life.

Soon after breakfast, Abigail and Vanessa were getting sleepy. "I think I'm getting jet lag," she announced to Rex who was almost rolling off his chair.

"What is jay-lap?" he asked, and Vanessa stifled a giggle.

"No, silly! Jet lag! It is a term we use when we cross time zones on an airplane," she said then realized that Rex must have no idea what she was talking about, so she attempted to explain further. "An airplane is like a flying car, except it is very long."

But Rex simply looked even more bewildered. "What, in the name of Terra, is a car?" he asked, totally baffled. Then he smiled. "I'm joking. I've been to earth before," he said.

Vanessa was slightly offended. Resenting being tricked, she rolled her eyes.

Dad came up next to them. "Rex, we'll have a talk on teasing her later. As for now, Vanessa, you look as if you are going to fall asleep on your feet. Let's find you a place to sleep!"

Then to both Vanessa and Abigail, he asked, "Would you like separate rooms?"

Before Vanessa could answer, Abigail broke in. "Yes, please!"

So Vanessa sighed resignedly and added unenthusiastically, "I will go with whatever Queen Abigail says."

With a snicker and a wide grin, their father led them up the spiral staircase. Vanessa loved the staircase, for it too had lovely carvings. These carvings, unlike the others, had big wild cats on them. That made Vanessa curious. "How come there are so many leopards and stuff?"

Dad looked at her and answered, "Since your mother is a shapeshifter, she can turn into many things, right? Well, she likes a certain animal: the leopard."

Realization struck her, remembering the flag with the leopard and dragon. "The flag! It has a leopard on it! That is Mom!" When Dad nodded, she continued. "But it has a dragon on it. Who is the dragon?"

Dad opened a door in the hall.

"Vanessa, this will be your room," he said as she walked into it.

It was beautiful. It had ocean colored walls, handsome wood floors, a king-sized bed with a waterfall duvet, a big balcony, and a large bathroom leading off to the side. The whole room was built like a suite, and Vanessa loved it.

Unfortunately, so did Abigail. "What on earth? Why can't I have this room?" she exclaimed indignantly.

Vanessa smiled smugly. "Because you didn't want to sleep in the same room. And you also hate the color blue!"

"I do *not*!" Abigail yelled unexpectedly.

Drake smiled, "I have a room that you'll like. Come with me." He said, leaving Vanessa to inspect her room. She snuck to the bathroom and gazed in wonder at the beautiful design. She opened some drawers in a different corner, and noticed all of the clothes. They were just the right size and style. Vanessa grinned as she noticed a bowl of fruit on a table near the balcony. She picked a ripe pear from it and sat on the stone railing of the balcony, looking out at the beautiful grounds. She bit into the fruit, and enjoyed the delicious taste. After she finished the pear, she flopped onto the bed, letting her head sink into the pillow, falling into a wonderful sleep.

CHAPTER 6

MOM

V anessa woke up with a start, not knowing how or where she was. Much too suddenly, it all came back to her: Dad, Abigail, magic, elves, and Rex. She relaxed only when she remembered where she was.

"Who on earth—or this world—opened the balcony door?" she wondered aloud.

Just then, a familiar voice answered her lovingly, "Oh, I did. And you have only known me to be on earth."

Startled, Vanessa quickly turned toward the musical voice of the intruder. Standing on the balcony was a beautiful woman, who had to be an elf. She was thin, tall, with olive-tan skin (like Rex's), and long flowing black hair. She was dressed in a light turquoise T-shirt with loose green pants. But what was most startling was her face: it had wide cheekbones, pointed ears, ruby lips, and luminous blue eyes. Her face was a picture of pure joy as she said in her motherly voice, "Oh, my Filia! You are awake! I thought you would sleep for decades!" and she walked over to Vanessa and embraced her.

The only person who called her filia was—"Mom? Is that you?" Vanessa questioned.

And the elf smiled delightedly and said, "Oh! Yes, it is! I guess you could not recognize me without my disguise. And my name is Regina. Alas, you have been asleep for two days."

And Vanessa gasped, "How is Abigail? What about this new world? How is Rex?"

Regina grinned. "I think you need to see that for yourself! Come, you must be starving. Then we have to see about something for your birthday," she said lovingly.

Vanessa thought for a moment then blurted, "It isn't my birthday yet! It's not even close!"

Regina grinned. "It is different here! We have different month zones as well as time zones . . . Well, enough of that talk! We shall be gone, once you get dressed, of course!"

CHAPTER 7

DISGUISES AND TALENTS

Once Vanessa had gotten dressed, brushed her teeth, and done all her morning rituals, she followed her mom through the long hall and downstairs. When she went down the spiral staircase, she expected to see Abigail. But instead, she saw Dad and Rex.

"Regina! What are you doing here!" cried both of them. Dad looked excited; Rex, however, looked slightly queasy.

Vanessa ran down to Rex and smiled. "You look as if you saw a rotten fish! What is wrong? she said, trying to lighten his unhappy mood.

"Oh! Vanessa! Sorry, I look so unusually . . . sour," he said rather surprised and almost instantly rejuvenated. "I guess I am kind of . . . well . . . surprised."

Again Vanessa smiled warmly at the awkward Rex. "Well, if anything is troubling you, you can always talk to me about it."

She walked over to where her mom and dad were talking. Only when she had taken a few steps did she hear Rex mutter, "Nisi sit in te," which Vanessa understood as "unless it be about you." Face turning red, she walked over to Regina and her dad. He spoke with Regina in

Elvish, and Vanessa, though she could not understand much, could see that he was just as surprised about her mom being here as Vanessa was. Her parents upon seeing her there, stopped speaking.

Regina stared at Vanessa in astonishment then looked at Dad angrily. "I did not come here for that reason! It is not allowed! She is not old enough. And according to the elven law, she must be seventeen or older to rule! How could you say that?"

Dad shrugged. "You did not tell me that you were coming. It is fair. Besides, we must join our kingdoms, the elven to the dragon ones, I mean."

Regina glared at him and turned into a snow leopard, pacing menacingly. Dad was still as a stone as Mom roared in his face, "Really, I thought you had more sense than that!" she said between her large fangs. "If this was your plan, why didn't you say so. And why not ask Vanessa yourself?"

Then Vanessa stepped between them and said, "What do you mean? What am I choosing for myself? And why did you just shape-shift into a snow leopard, Mom?" Vanessa was suddenly barraged with thoughts, voices, and visions. It was if she could see in the minds of those around her, hearing their thoughts, seeing their memories, and feeling their emotions.

Mom's thoughts were a whirling mess, while Dad's mind was calm, though a bit frustrated. So Vanessa dug into Regina's thoughts more, finding memories of a beautiful land covered with rivers and dotted with forests. As she entered those, she was astounded by what she found. Concentrating on a tall person, Vanessa realized that that person was a beautiful she-elf. A white dress of silky fabric fluttered gently on the breeze, and Vanessa couldn't help wishing she had a gown like that. The elf's auburn hair flowed freely down her shoulders.

"You should not be in your mother's memories until you are strong enough to handle them," the ginger-haired she-elf chided.

Vanessa didn't answer but felt thoroughly curious. The elf seemed to sense this and continued. "I will see you again later to teach you more about your powers. For now, however, you need to be freed of your certain . . . spell, as you call it, and I will do so now. Remember one thing; wash your face." With that, the beautiful she-elf waved her hand and uttered a few verses in a language Vanessa could not decipher.

The world seemed to spin around Vanessa. Then with a flash, the whole scene disappeared, and Vanessa fainted, darkness enclosing over her.

"Vanessa!" Vanessa opened her eyes and saw Abigail, her dull blond hair flowing in her own face.

"Abigail? What are you doing here? I thought you were asleep!"

Abigail laughed. "Dad woke me up. But I saw Mom!" she said hurriedly, not wanting Vanessa to interrupt. "Oh my goodness! I've never seen anyone so beautiful in my life! Without her disguise, though, she does not look anything like us! It made me wonder if she was our real mom."

Vanessa looked around and realized it was her own room. "I am going to wash my face. Stay here." she said, and walked over to the bathroom. The woman in the vision had told her to wash her face. What kind of riddle was that? Vanessa's pale complexion was free of blemishes, so she was sure the woman wasn't commenting on her hygiene. Would water take some kind of curse away? She had to try. She was willing to do just about anything for some answers. She turned on the faucet, surprised that cold water rushed out. She didn't wait for the liquid to warm up. Splashing water into her cupped hands, she washed her face with the freezing water. The shock of it sent a ripple through her. Looking up, she gasped as she noticed what had changed. Her pale complexion was changed into an olive/tan like her mother's. She ran her hand through the once straight blond hair. Now it had dark chocolate curls that made Vanessa think of a shampoo ad. Her irises reflected the color of the Caribbean sea. She stood straight, and found herself almost a foot taller than before. She grinned, and walked out of the spacious restroom, finding Abigail picking at a silk pillow.

Looking up at her elder sister, Abigail gasped, "Where is Vanessa, and what have you done with her?"

It was more of a statement than a question, but Vanessa answered
it anyway. "I'm the *true* Vanessa! And I'm about to have a few 'words'
with those who told me otherwise!"

"I am being honest! I had no idea! It was probably your parents! I
had nothing to do with it!" Rex hastily explained, answering the same
question that he had been asked a hundred times. Vanessa thought
furiously, scowling with frustration. How had this happened? Rex
looked at her, "I always try using magic to calm myself down. It tires
me out. You should give it a try." He said. Vanessa snorted and sat down
by a bunch of flowers, thinking of a way to grow them.

"Surgo!" She tried, but finding that her growth spell did not work,
she tried others. "Nascor! Gnatus! Adsurgo! Aro! Arrgghh!"

Rex smiled despite the irked Vanessa. "I didn't know that there was
a such thing as the word 'argh' in Elvish, but alas, I guess you were
treading on new things," he commented idly..

Vanessa growled, "You're treading on thin ice."

And Rex laughed. "Maybe so, but with you, it is like ice above a
flame!" Vanessa frowned. "No, it's not!" She answered, then realized
Rex was right. She decided to changed the subject. "Anyway, I think
we need to explore."

"I thought we already were." Rex frowned.

But Abigail knew where Vanessa was going with her vague comment.
"No, Rex. We need to explore out of the grounds! We're going on an
adventure!"

It was obvious Rex could not resist. "Sure!"

Vanessa and Abigail set out to their rooms. But when they were
nearing the front of the castle, Rex stopped them. "Wait! I've got a better
idea.. If we go this way, we can get in without everyone asking questions
and all." Following closely behind him they snuck through the grounds
to Vanessa's window, which was above their heads.

"Here, I can boost you up," offered Rex.

But Vanessa had a plan. "No, let me!" She hoped this would work. Picturing a giant eagle in her mind, she willed herself to change into one. Feathers sprouted from her arms, and her lips grew into a hard beak. Before a minute had passed, she had turned into an eagle. Abigail looked so shocked and quite leary of this shape shifting but then Abigail seemed to shake it off and Vanessa turned her thoughts to the task ahead.

Hopping a few feet away from them, she found a good breeze blowing through. Lifting her wings, she glided into it and, turning in the air, flew over Rex and Abigail, snatching them off the ground. She flew them up to her room and dropped them neatly on the balcony, she let out a breath. It had worked! She imagined her normal body, and shape-shifted back into it.

Rex glanced back at her, eyes shining with admiration. "Nice trick!"

Vanessa grinned. "Thanks. It was kind of fun!"

Abigail smiled, "I am going to grab some snacks. See ya!" And she bolted out of the room.

Grabbing her large backpack, Vanessa stuffed a blanket and change of shirt in it just in case.

Rex cleared his throat and said, "Um, Vanessa? I have a gift for you and Abigail." He reached into his pants pocket, bringing out a small bag at least the size of his fist, and handed it to Vanessa. Not knowing what to think, she accepted it, thanking him cautiously.

Rex smiled at her uncertainty. "It's called a *pera*. It's a place where anything can be stored, even a *malus*!"

Vanessa was curious. "What is a malus?"

Rex blinked. "A malus is a demon. They are the brutes of this realm. I'll explain more later. For now, I think you might need to pack." And with that, Rex jumped off the balcony, climbing carelessly down a thin vine.

Vanessa thought about it for a moment longer, and then she threw the backpack into the *pera*. The mouth of the tiny back suddenly expanded, opening up, to admit the pack, then shrinking back down once it swallowed the other bag. Vanessa was impressed, and quite surprised that this had worked. She decided to experiment with it. She put several items from around the room (vases, pillows, and bowls) into the bag. It fit them all, not changing in size or weight.

Abigail returned a moment later with her backpack. Vanessa grabbed it without asking and threw it in the little bag.

"Hey! That was mine! Where did it go?" Abigail asked, shocked.

Vanessa smiled and said, "It's OK. Rex gave this to me for packing." She held up the *pera*.

Abigail frowned, "Why did he give it to you and not to me?" She asked

Vanessa smiled. "It's for you too! It can fit anything."

And Abigail gasped, "No way! Can you pack food?" she asked. Vanessa nodded, "Probably. I'll go as far as to bet it will hold perishables," she said.

Abigail squealed with joy. "I want to pack pancakes! And omelets and toast and—" She began but stopped because at that moment Rex, wearing a black coat, dropped on to the balcony.

"Hey, um, guys? We had probably better go! The more daylight we have, the better!"

Vanessa nodded supportively. "He is right," she said without meaning to. Abigail, and Rex looked bewildered.

"I am?" Rex said uncertainly. Abigail giggled, and Vanessa turned red.

"Um, I mean, sure. It's . . . sensible," Vanessa said awkwardly.

"Yeah right. 'It's sensible!' Oh! Ha! Vanessa! I know you much better than that! You don't ever agree with anyone. Even if they're right." Maybe there were more transformations happening to her sister than she had thought. She had never known Vanessa to be agreeable but she liked the idea of it. Vanessa just growled in response.

The group started off by climbing down the vine. Vanessa suddenly said, "Hey, guys! I have an idea . . ."

They listened intently as she relayed her plan. Abigail agreed hurriedly, and Rex encouraged her.

Vanessa took a deep breath and focused on an image in her mind. Suddenly, she wobbled, realizing that she was standing on four legs, not two. Vanessa turned her long neck and smiled through her new muzzle.

She was a horse. It had worked. Climbing upon her back, Rex helped Abigail up behind him. Abigail looked ready to burst. Her previous shock and fear had disappeared into pure joy. Once the two passengers had a strong hold on her white mane, Vanessa took off running. The wind streamed through her pearly fur as she raced along a stream bed, jumping a few of the fences while she went.

She galloped for hours, enjoying the fresh rush of air. The day wore on, but Vanessa felt no urge to stop her constant lope. Those on her back never told her to stop, so she kept going. She could now see why horses liked running.

They had entered a big forest made of trees of many sorts; there were tall trees, short trees, fat trees, skinny trees, and many more. Rex called a halt, for the sun was getting low in the trees. He suggested Vanessa come back into her normal state so they could talk. Vanessa turned back into elf form, realizing too late that Rex and Abigail were still above her.

Time literally stopped as she hung in the air, with Abigail and Rex on top of her. But unfortunately for her, that moment did not last. They all fell straight to the hard earthy ground. Vanessa felt as if she had broken her back. Gasping, she rolled out from under Rex.

"Are you OK?" she asked him painfully.

"The question is—are you? I had something soft to land on!" he said with a worried expression. His concern made Vanessa warm inside despite the tremendous pain she felt.

Abigail, who had just got off Rex, crouched over Vanessa. She looked at Vanessa's back and made a strange noise in her throat that sounded like a whimper. "Um, hey, Vanessa? The question is—how can you breathe? You have two broken ribs and one fractured vertebrae! Let me heal you!"

Before they could ask how she knew all of this. Abigail muttered a word and Vanessa instantly felt better.

Rex looked at Abigail with astonishment. "How did you do that?" he asked. Abigail shrugged. "Don't know. The word just came to my head. I felt a weird urge to."

Vanessa smiled. "Yeah! Like I had the feeling to shape-shift!"

Abigail nodded. Rex rolled his eyes, "If you two are quite done with realizing your new powers, we need a scout." Vanessa shape-shifted into a chipmunk sending Abigail into hysterics. Vanessa had had no idea her sister was so in love with furry little creatures! She scurried up the tallest tree and scouting the area, she found a small clearing. Vanessa decided that it was probably the best they would get. She hopped down the tall birch tree, nearly missing a sharp rock, and scurried up to Rex and Abigail. Panting, she morphed into her normal self. Vanessa explained about the clearing but that she thought they should keep going. Rex and Abigail disagreed, saying that it was better that they stop.

"Even though elves are nocturnal, we prefer to let the daylight be on us," Rex had said.

Arriving at the clearing they realized that they had not packed food. Rex taught them about foraging and how to find the right nuts, berries, and plants. They set out after their lessons, Rex going with Abigail and Vanessa going alone. Vanessa soon found some berries that she knew from Rex were edible. She gathered them up, recognizing them as thimbleberries from the raspberry-like appearance. Vanessa searched the ground for anything edible. Her eyes caught sight of a patch of sorrel, a sour but delicious plant with spearhead-shaped leaves. After picking a few leaves, she walked back to their camp. Rex was already at work building a fire. He whispered a few phrases, and the pile of sticks that he had been working on was set ablaze.

Rex looked up at her and smiled. "Hey, Vanessa! Are you all right? You look kind of tired." He reached inside his coat pocket and brought out a small bundle of cloth.

Unwrapping the cloth, Rex unfolded it so that it looked exactly like a sleeping bag. Vanessa gratefully accepted it and curled up next to the fire. She dropped the berries and sorrel next to Rex then closed her eyes and napped. Her last thought before she drifted into sleep was about her new talent and how amazing this new life could be.

CHAPTER 8

THE WHIMPER

Vanessa woke up with a sudden gasp. Only sometimes had this happened to her: she had had a dream—wait, no, not a dream—a nightmarish vision. Vanessa had been walking in a peaceful garden when a whimpering cry had permeated the serene silence. Stooping by a nearby bush to see what had whimpered, a shadow leaked out from behind her, grabbing at her legs. She started yelling and shrieking, but no one came to her aid.

Nearly in the monster's grasp, she kept screaming. She quickly wriggled and lurched to run as she saw claws grasping at her. Then it got her. Its nails pinched into her skin, ripping her flesh. Fire lapped like a wave over everything, and someone cried out, "ABIGAIL!" Her throat hurt from screaming. *That's strange, I never feel pain in my dreams!* she thought. That only gave more power to the thought that this was more than a simple vision.

She had tried to turn to see the monstrous animal that had brought the shadow but was shaken awake by some force. Only now did Vanessa realize that it had been Rex who had shaken her awake.

He looked at her with concern. "Are you OK? You were crying and saying something about whimpers. I waited as long as I could before I woke you up." Vanessa blushed deeply. She hated when she talked in her sleep. Right next to her, another big bundle of blankets stirred. A second sleepy groan split the air as Abigail rolled over and grumbled something about a dumb rock that was creating a bruise. Vanessa herself had twenty sore spots all over her body. Not comfortable. She rubbed the biggest bruise, which happened to be on the small of her back. *Stupid roots*, she thought indignantly.

Rex smiled with amusement, and Vanessa swore he read her mind with the next statement he made. "It certainly looks like you guys aren't very familiar with sleeping outside. Stupid roots and all."

As soon as the girls got up, they ate the plants, roots, mushrooms, berries, and nuts that they had picked the previous day. Rex having already eaten, walked a little ways away. He trudged to a log, sitting heavily on it. He wore a thoughtful expression, peaking Vanessa's interest. Vanessa finished picking a berry seed out of her teeth, and walked to where he was perched. She sat carefully, brushing the dirt from the old log before she sat on it.

Staring into the forest like Rex, not entirely sure what she was supposed to be looking at, Vanessa felt a little awkward. Without so much as glancing at her, Rex started to speak, "Elves used to be different," he said. Vanessa jumped a little at his almost mournful tone. She stared at him curiously, "What do you mean?" she asked. Rex now faced her, his emerald green eyes gazing into hers intently. There was a sad light in them,

"They used to roam the forest. They were like nymphs, but much more powerful. Clad in a mixture of flowing robes and armor, cutting down all evil, they looked celestial," he said. Then he straightened.

"We need to get going," he said. Vanessa followed him as he strode to Abigail. The girl was pounding a nut against the rock, trying to open it. She abandoned the project once she saw they had arrived. Rex told her that they needed to leave, and Abigail grinned at Vanessa,

"Can you change into a rhino? I would like to ride that!" she said. Rex was shaking his head.

"No. No you don't! They are hard to ride. And smelly. Sorry, Vanessa. I'm sure you would be better, but I am not getting on a rhino ever again!" he said. Abigail and Vanessa gaped at him. Rex looked uncomfortable with the stares, "What?" he asked. Vanessa smiled,

"You rode a rhino?" she asked. Abigail looked even more surprised, "You didn't like it?" Rex sighed, "I'll tell you more about it later. Vanessa? Can you be our steed one more time?" he asked. Vanessa winked,

"Yes, oh knight in shining armor," she said bowing.

As she bowed, Vanessa changed into a horse again. But instead of a white stallion, she thought of a wiser choice, one of which would enable her to move swiftly, and be much stronger. Summoning some strength, she trotted around and tested her endurance a bit then returned for the two elves. She had chosen to change into a muscular chocolate brown draft horse. Abigail loved this breed, so Vanessa had chosen it with her in mind. She was surprised changing into other creatures was not more exhausting. Rex had mentioned something about her having a bigger energy reserve than most. She enjoyed her newfound powers. As soon as Rex and Abigail clambered onto her back, Vanessa started to lope further into the woods. When she had only gone a mile from the clearing where they had camped, her horse ears picked up something from further up the ravine. Vanessa froze in utter shock, pulse racing with sudden adrenalin. It was the whimper from her dreams.

CHAPTER 9

THE OUTSIDER

The whimper came from under the same bush Vanessa saw in her dream. Rex and Abigail had nearly fallen off from Vanessa's abrupt stop.

"Vanessa! Why have you stopped? Are you crazy?" Abigail cried.

Now, however, they were silent, listening to the whining. They got off Vanessa, who promptly turned back into her elf form. Rex and Abigail were very careful to get off her before she decided to turn back into her normal shape. It wouldn't be good if she were to break her back *again*.

Vanessa stalked off toward the noise. She stopped next to the bush and bent down to see the animal under it. Instantly, the whimpering stopped, and out crawled a tiny ball of black fur. Vanessa gasped, half in relief and half with excitement as she picked up the bedraggled bundle and brushed off the dust from its dirty pelt. Examining it closer, she found that it was a pug puppy. Its nose looked like it had smashed into a wall, and its fur was clumped and slightly bloody. Vanessa wondered where the blood was coming from, but she was not too concerned as it did not look fresh.

She gently carried the puppy back to Rex and Abigail. Abigail swooned and cooed to it, while Rex tried to clean it up by brushing its little head with a small cloth. Vanessa stared at him. "What do you think? Where did he come from?"

Rex looked up at Vanessa and said, "Vanessa, you need to take the pup to your mother immediately. He will die within minutes if you don't. It has been hurt badly, and it is a newborn. Without warmth, it will soon die."

Vanessa was quite surprised by Rex's response, for she had never seen him this serious. She decided not to ask any questions as she changed into a hawk and swept the pug puppy into her new talons, gently holding him. She took off up through the trees and into the brightening sky. Swooping over the green forest, Vanessa dove for the distant castle. She spotted her mother on the grounds and flew toward her.

Surprised, Regina looked up, and then spotting the bundle of black fur, she outstretched her hands. Vanessa dropped the puppy in them and landed on the ground, changing into her normal self. Her mother put a smooth hand over the pug and muttered, "Canis Curo!" The puppy let out a last whimper, and then it was still.

Regina smiled and said to Vanessa, "He is sleeping. Now my attention goes to you. You seem to be a master shape shifter already. Great power resides in you, my dear." Regina handed the snoring puppy to Vanessa, saying, "You found him, you flew him, you can keep him. He is a runt, but he will be very loyal to you. And I expect that Abigail will be jealous, even though he is an outsider."

Vanessa was curious. "An outsider? What are those?"

Regina smiled. "Outsiders are animals or people from another world that stray into the borders of ours."

Regina never said from earth, though. Vanessa turned around to shape-shift into a horse so that she might get Abigail and Rex, but her mother stopped her. "Oh no! You are taking Mons! And I'll make you, if it's the last thing I do!"

Vanessa complied, saying, "OK, Mom." Regina smiled.

Vanessa went to Mons, who was eating grain in the stable.

Grumbling, the horse walked over to where Vanessa stood. "OK, who needs a ride? I can't stand here all morning!" he said grumpily.

Vanessa stifled a giggle beholding the bedraggled draft horse. Mons started pawing at the ground.

"Oh, I thought I would see this lovely elf again. Well, get on," he whinnied and Vanessa swung onto him. Who needed a saddle and/or reins when your horse could talk?

She brushed her hair behind her ear and urged him onward. He started trotting, making Vanessa bounce a bit. Then Mons went into a canter, and Vanessa let her hips swing with his movement. She was grateful for the horseback riding lessons from her mother.

Vanessa loved this time of day, and she watched the amazing evening in awe as she rode on Mons. The rosy clouds and fiery skies were bright and even more vivid than on earth.

They rode towards the dark forest, the orange sun at their backs. Vanessa knew she would enjoy this realm despite its dangers. Unfortunately, the dangers were only the beginning.

CHAPTER 10

THE LIBRARY

After rescuing Rex and Abigail from the woods, Vanessa retired to her bedroom. She waited for her strength to return, but sadly, it didn't. Shape shifting so much had taken tremendous energy and she realized she needed to be more careful next time. She soon fell asleep while listening to the puppy snores in the basket next to her bed.

Vanessa found herself in a forest of pines. The dark trees gave off a spicy scent, and they blocked the view of the sky, making the interior dark and damp. The same beautiful auburn-haired elf was there.

The she-elf smiled at Vanessa's apprehension. "Come now. You can't treat me like I am *vecors* (crazy)! Aren't you used to these dreams, yet?"

Vanessa didn't want to go down that road. She had had many dreams, mostly nightmares all of her life. It was a touchy subject for her. "Why are you here?"

The she-elf smiled and said, "To train. There is much that you must be taught."

Vanessa thought about it for a while. She then said, "Scire quid ultra?" What more is to learn?

The she-elf smiled knowingly. "Ipsum!" Very much!

Vanessa awoke with a start. She felt amazing, but her mind, however, did not. She noticed that the sky was still dark. Without meaning to, she fell asleep again. Vanessa felt a prickle of whiskers against her face. Then she felt a not-so soft spray of liquid as the animal snorted on her.

The puppy! It's him! she thought, wiping off her face. Vanessa reached down and stroked the pug, smiling as he rolled over, exposing his undersized belly. *We'll have to fix that!* Vanessa thought.

Picking him up, Vanessa went downstairs for breakfast. Once she got to the dining area, the puppy, upon smelling the food, jumped out of her hands. With a shriek, he landed and though Vanessa thought he was injured, his next actions discouraged those thoughts. The second he landed, he ran. He pounced on to the breakfast table, surprising everyone around it. Rex and Abigail laughed, Regina and Drake raising their eyebrows in unison. The puppy burrowed his way into the tall pile of scrambled eggs. His little black head poked out of the food curiously at Vanessa's gasp.

The only one not laughing was Vanessa, who was practically dying of shame that she had let go of the dog. He was just so squirmy! "I am so sorry! He jumped out of my arms!"

But the only one that heard her was Rex. He grinned even wider, exposing his white teeth. "That is why you *hold* him!" he said, which earned more chuckling from the others.

Vanessa guessed that it was not something she could've helped, and she started to eat. Once finished, she grabbed the pug puppy and started to climb the stairs, but Regina stopped her, "How about going to the library? I will bathe this pup for you" she offered. Vanessa perked up at that, "You have a library?" she asked. Regina smiled, "Of course. You will like this one. Go on. I will take care of the dog."

Vanessa gratefully accepted the generous offer. She followed an odd Latin sign that read *Library* and followed it through several passages. She tramped up the last bit of stairs to the library. Opening the door, she saw a silver plaque that read

The Library of Drake the Dragon

Vanessa gasped at the breathtaking interior, for it must have been larger than a football stadium. Books covered every wall. Vanessa inhaled and felt blissful. The scent of books and the feeling of standing in a library were calming to her. She really loved books, especially their smell. Vanessa gaped as she beheld the roof; it was a perfect replica of the sky, except for the fact that it was glass. Not clear glass but light blue with white clouds.

She knew that the exterior roof was stone and shingle, but the picture was so real. It even had a slightly glowing sun that changed directions. Vanessa was so intent on the roof that she bumped into a bookshelf. Several books thumped to the floor, and Vanessa hastily put them back. On the spine of one of them, it read *Ten Ways to Trap a Gorgon*. She muffled a giggle, thinking about how far she had come. Before, she would have dismissed the books as stuff for toddlers. Now she actually knew these things were real. The next one read *Shadow Titans and Their Kin*. Yet another spine said *The Difference between a Naiad and a Nereid*.

Moving around the bookshelf, she found herself looking at the center of the room. It had a large round table of stone surrounding a circular map featuring a castle. Moving closer, she saw the map had great detail, unlike any map or atlas she had seen before. It was obviously the handiwork of elves. She tried to shift her position to see better but tripped. She accidentally put her hand on the castle in the map. She quickly removed it and gasped. When she had touched it, the castle had shifted. It had zoomed in... Vanessa had an idea. She placed a finger on the tallest tower where, in real life, she was. It easily zoomed in and, surprisingly, through the roof to where she was. A little picture of her standing in front of the map made Vanessa stumble back in surprise.

She was even more startled when a deep male voice came from behind her. "Ah, so you are the one."

Vanessa whirled around to face a short man. His flat face was bearded, and his nose was large. He had had a merry smile as he spoke despite his serious words. His smile widened at Vanessa's confusion.

"My name is Gedrin. I am a book dwarf. You might have read about me . . . or not."

Understanding hit Vanessa like a brick. She had read all about the dwarves from a book her dad had given to her, but she knew little of book dwarves. "Oh! A book dwarf! I thought they were extinct!" she said to hide her lack of knowledge on the subject.

Gedrin smiled with a hint of pride. "I am the last. Well, perhaps not the last, there may be a few left, I suppose."

Vanessa needed answers, and she thought that this was the best place for them. "So um, what did you mean by that 'you're the one' comment?"

Gedrin laughed kindly. "Do you not know? Maybe you should research that. There are many books here to help you. It gets so lonely here. I am glad to have a new friend."

And Vanessa knew that that was the best answer she would probably ever get. "OK, thank you," she said.

Gedrin nodded. "It is my honor, milady," he returned. Vanessa felt a slight glow of pleasure at being called "milady," but she managed to keep her pride to a minimum.

Vanessa turned to a bookcase, selecting a book randomly. It was a dark leather book with a silver title of which read

The Book of Prophecies (Fulfilled and Unfulfilled)

Interested, Vanessa Nox opened the ancient text and read:

The Book of Prophecies

CAPITULUS I (Chapter 1)

By oracle MIRIAL RYORA
To hero(s) JOHN KNUDSEN
(Fulfilled)

Wherein lithe shadows sleep,
They might have your soul to reap.
The dark spirits among a spark,
On a quest should you embark.
Fight this mighty king of night
And forever rule with light.
But if your heart is too inward curled,
It will end your precious world.
And if you are still filled with pride,
All your love shall be denied.

CAPITULUS II

By oracle LILIA PACINI
To hero(es) PETER WALKER and GRACE GALA
(Fulfilled)

Where once the youth abode,
This ancient man has rode.
To seek him out must you,
To capture him shall take two.
The dark king will come to a short rest,
And then your faith shall have a test.

CAPITULUS III

By oracle SIFF PALINIA KIALNIA
To hero(es) TONITRUS NOX and LUX AURORA VESPER
(Fulfilled)

The sun will give his first light
For the rightful heirs of day and night.
The blinded king with his last breath,
Ends the curse of eternal death.
The daughter of the young world, Terra,
Entwines good into a new era.
The son of shadow and right
Will see to the darkest knight.
To battle with daughters of the sea,
Forever will they together be.

Vanessa read a few more "fulfilled ones" then skipped to the end. Her heart stopped when she read the hero's name. She could not take her eyes off the script.

There, it read,

CAPITULUS LXX

By oracle FILIX LUX
To hero(s): VANESSA NOX
(Unfulfilled)

When all elves weep and mope,
You will be their only hope.
The touch of the Healer's last breath
Will summon the malus to eternal death.
Of the leopard and of the dragon,

The dark king's blood will fill Moon-flagon.
The one that you may call a friend,
By betrayal might see to your end.
The idea of life the young man will give,
To make your most beloved live.
At the cost of your hardest strife,
The Olive will return to life.
Time will for you subside,
A moment still might turn the tide.
The son will uncover his father's light
And then become the chosen knight.
You will sacrifice the one you love
To gain life from above.
The giants will win Terra's battle
Unless Umbra's mind to addle.
And allow the two kinds, broken in pieces
To join together so the battle ceases.
Confront the devil who brought this doom,
Sentence him to the timeless room.
Room is translated to a pit,
A dark room by a candlelit.
The young man shall find his Jewel.
Then you both will together rule.

Vanessa stared. A million questions raced through her brain. Her name? Her prophecy? Who was the young man? Was that "Dark Lord" the same one in most of the prophecies she had read? Why hadn't he died yet? Betrayal? Olive? (Wasn't that something that she ordered on her pizzas?) Who would be the one to betray her?   G r o w l i n g , Vanessa grabbed the book and fled to her room, where she found her mother drying off the newly washed puppy with a towel. Her mother looked up. "Filia! How was the . . ." Regina trailed off as Vanessa held up the book.

Taking a deep breath, Regina regained her composure. "Vanessa, where did you find *that*?" she said sharply, though Vanessa didn't flinch.

"In the library, where else?" she answered swiftly.

Regina scowled angrily, "Well, I—"

She was interrupted, much to her dislike. "I'm sorry! I wanted some answers! Nobody has explained anything to me lately! Gedrin was the only one kind enough to say that *I had a prophecy*! Who is Filix?" Vanessa blurted.

Sighing unhappily, Regina said, "Filix is a pretty she-elf with ginger hair and green eyes. She is a powerful Elvish speaker. She is also an oracle. She made a prophecy about you because . . . *because you have a destiny to save Terra*."

Vanessa wondered for a moment then asked, "Who is *Terra*?"

Regina answered, saying, "Not always *who*. Most of times it is *what*. Terra is our world. In Latin, it means *earth*. Anyway, you should know that you alone are not the only one that will save us, for there are three. You have met them already. One is Abigail, the other is . . . Well, I trust that you will figure that out later. For now, I think you need to name your dog! He can't be called 'puppy' all his life!" she scolded.

Sheepishly, Vanessa thought for a name. *Bob? Definitely not! Roger?* Was she insane? *No, a good Elvish name—Altus* (high)? Nah. *Nobilis* (noble)? Maybe . . . *Lupus* (wolf)? *Niger* (black)? *Peregrinus*? Too long. What if she could shorten it. . . . Vanessa made up her mind.

"I will name him Peregrin!" she proclaimed triumphantly.

Regina looked pleased. "Peregrin? Yes, that is a fine name indeed for a black dog!" she said, approval clearly reflected in her luminous eyes. Vanessa was just beginning to feel better.

Then Regina sobered, and Vanessa knew something was very wrong. Before she could ask, Regina said something that would change everything.

Regina sighed, "Vanessa, I know you will not like this, and I am most assured that you will protest, but it is for your own good. Your father and I feel that it is necessary for you to continue your education. It is time you returned to California."

CHAPTER 11

RETURN AND RESCUE

Vanessa sat in the classroom, watching the clock. It had been more than ten days since she had returned from Terra. She had kicked and screamed when they tried to take her home, but it had happened anyway. And worse was that Abigail had been allowed to stay behind. Now Vanessa was in her regular school with regular people. Everything was normal. Everything was not dangerous at all. Nothing could or would surprise anyone.

Vanessa hated it.

The teachers had not recognized her, so they had labeled her as "new." Boring. Turning her pencil over and over, listening to the teacher drone on about diagramming sentences. Boring.

Then a familiar male voice next to her whispered, "Vanessa! Duck!" Not so boring.

Startled, she complied, nearly getting hit by a spitball. The school bully named Tom had been the one who had fired on her. He was the least smart of all the kids and only stayed in school because his father was rich and bribed the teachers to give him good grades. He now sat there looking at her with surprise. "How did you do that? You just missed it by—"

However, he was interrupted. Ms. Carafe, the new female teacher, was calling his name. She was the only one who hadn't been bribed, and Tom had received an F the whole time she remained as teacher.

"Thomas Robert Johnson. Don't bully a girl! In fact, don't bully anyone. Now can you explain to me where to put the those modifiers in that sentence?"

Tom was furious and wordless. It was priceless. But Vanessa wondered who had been the one who had told her to duck.

Ms. Carafe asked for Vanessa to see her after school, explaining that while she had aced her tests, she still needed a lesson or two. As Ms. Carafe led Vanessa into her office, she studied her every move. Vanessa studied her back, realizing that the teacher had extreme beauty and seemed to be only in her twenties: dark blue eyes, flawless creamy skin, and, the weirdest of all, pure white hair tied up in a bun. Vanessa had always believed she had dyed it, but after Terra, she wasn't so sure.

Ms. Carafe sat in her chair. "Well, I was not lying when I said that you aced your tests, but that is not why I asked you to come to my office," she said in a serious tone.

Vanessa frowned. "OK."

The pretty teacher sighed with annoyance. "I hate it when you elves—and humans—get so jumpy. I only want to talk!" she complained.

Vanessa froze. "Did you just say *elves*?" she asked.

Ms. Carafe rolled her blue eyes. "Did I? Well, no matter, your little secret is safe with me," she said.

Vanessa wanted to ask her if she was an elf, but something stopped her. Instead, she just asked, "How do you know?"

The teacher chuckled. "You smell like an elf. Elves smell like flowers, forest, water—like how my old home smelled. Anyway, you need to be off. PE, or whatever you call it, will be waiting. What does that stand for? Pesky Entertainment? No matter. It is waiting, and so will a surprise. Oh and, Vanessa, please keep our little meeting a secret too. I would hate for the malus to find you too soon. This may sound old, but don't trust anybody."

Vanessa nodded, a little shell-shocked, and walked out of the office. Behind her, Vanessa caught sight of the teacher smiling at a being, unseen to humans, as it passed through the door.

Vanessa really liked her teacher and trusted that she was not making a terrible mistake. Ms. Carafe may or may not be who she said she was, but like Vanessa, she hated bullies like Tom. And Vanessa was resigned to the thought that nothing was going to stop him in the gym. Fortunately for her, she was sorely wrong.

At PE, all the kids came together for exercise. Here, that also meant games, weight lifting, and dance. She had wondered why they added the last few things but just went with the flow. There were very few things that irritated Vanessa; however, a basketball to the back of the head did it.

Whirling to face him, Vanessa grabbed the ball from off the ground and threw it into Tom's face with all the muscle she had grown in elf form. The bully stumbled back, his cheeks already swelling. Vanessa felt a bloom of pride blossom in her heart. She glanced at the corner where Ms. Carafe was sitting. Her teacher winked. Then she lifted her nose, apparently alarmed, and left the room.

Vanessa suddenly noticed that Tom had a forty-pound weight in his hand. Unfortunately, Tom noticed it too. Growling, he lifted it with his might and threw it at her. Closing her eyes, Vanessa waited for impact. Amazingly, it didn't come. Opening her eyes, Vanessa shrieked. A young boy with black hair and olive-tan skin stood in front of her, the weight in his hand, holding it as if it was a twig.

Glancing at the bully, the boy smiled and said something to Tom that Vanessa didn't catch. Then he launched the weight back with enough force to send it through the wall but it wasn't the wall it hit., Tom would sadly have to spend a few days in the hospital. He would not die, but Vanessa yelped in sympathy. She turned to see who had come to her aid. He grinned at her. "Vanessa Nox! You look a bit surprised!" Rex said.

CHAPTER 12

THE QUEST FOR HOME

A bramble scraped against Vanessa's arm, causing a red line to form on her skin. Dappled light from the tall eucalyptus made her seem part of the forest, and she moved as silently as she could. For the moment, all she needed was to be silent. She remembered yesterday when she had refused to come back to Terra with Rex. He had begged her once they left the school, and though she was tempted, she had refused. Vanessa didn't exactly know why she had said no to leaving, and after a night of dreaming about Terra, she had changed her mind. Wildly dashing outside in the dark, she had gone in one direction. She remembered reading somewhere that elves always were drawn to portals on earth. She had gone as quickly as she could, eventually catching sight of Rex's camp. He hadn't noticed her and she was now waiting for the perfect time to surprise him. Sneaking up on the tired and defeated Rex, Vanessa playfully shoved him, sending him into the creek.

Spluttering, he laughed and pulled her in too. They brawled for a few seconds, Rex always having the upper hand because he could breathe underwater. Finally, Vanessa shape-shifted into a minnow and slipped through Rex's outstretched fingers. After a while, they came out of the rushing stream.

They sat there in companionable silence, drying for several seconds. Eventually, Vanessa said, "Did you see Tom's face? Priceless! I have never been so happy to see you ever!"

Rex glanced up at her, grinning. "Really? Well, I have a question. What was that wet object that this Tom person shot at you earlier?"

Vanessa answered through mock gags. "Yuck! They're called spitballs. How would you know about that?" she grumbled.

Rex smiled knowingly. "I was the one that told you to duck, obviously!" That earned laughs. Smiling, they both walked on, stopping only when a sorrel clump or fruit tree came into sight. They had been walking for a while. Now they were returning home—the real home, that is—where elves and dragons roamed, where satyrs danced with nymphs, where they both belonged.

Rolling over, Vanessa awoke. She smiled at Rex's sleeping form a few feet away while packing the blanket Rex had brought for her. Vanessa remembered how tired Rex had been, so she decided to appease him. Walking over a game trail, Vanessa noticed a compact tree growing orange fruit abundantly. She grabbed a few off it and walked back, stopping occasionally to snatch fruit and nuts off trees. Returning to camp, she smiled. She was loaded with fruit, roots, leaves, and nuts. Rex greeted her after she awoke him.

They sat there eating for a while when Rex said, "I think we should store more food in my *pera*. We will need it soon . . ." For over a half hour, he explained plans until they could both finally agree on something.

The *Sunrise Express* was an old train. She had transported many people through many places, but never before had she passaged two elves, or even one for that matter. Vanessa eyed it unhappily; she had never wanted to be a hobo. Rex had been the one to suggest jumping trains. Vanessa had only agreed because it was the fastest way.

She now sprang onto it, clinging to the doorway to stay on as the old train lurched forward. Where was Rex? He had to be there. He might miss the train. Searching the surrounding area, Vanessa spotted Rex sprinting toward her.

The train was moving as fast as a horse in a lope, but Rex outpaced it with a jump. He leaped on the train with a gasp for air and a cocky smile. Greeting her happily, he sat down on a feedbag inside the old train car. Fishing inside his *pera*, Rex pulled out two oranges and a clump of edible mushrooms, splitting his store between them.

They ate in silence for a while, listening to the train as it moved north. Vanessa quietly sucked on some pulp, enjoying the tangy flavor, and cracked the shells of a pecan to get to the nut meat. Rex quickly ate his part and stood staring out the open door, no fear for the rushing land as the world raced by. Soon they were out of California and racing through Oregon.

Vanessa could stand the quiet no longer. "Remember when we first met? I was actually scared of you! Isn't that crazy?"

Rex looked hurt. "What? I'm not scary anymore? That is *rude*!" he said, frowning in mock disappointment.

Vanessa giggled and swatted at him. "No! What I mean to say is that you are not scary to *me* anymore, but I bet that you were scary to Tom!"

Rex smiled at that. "Well, perhaps, though I think he was much more scared of that weight in my hand. Now I feel like I'm losing my touch!"

Grinning, Vanessa gazed out at the scenery. "I wonder if we will meet any magical creatures. Let's hope we have avoided the bad ones. Perhaps we might have even missed a malus or two."

Suddenly, an earth-shattering roar sounded from behind the train, and Vanessa felt the train wobble at the bass of that bellow. She sensed a powerful presence close by and regretted her words. She had a feeling her companion did too.

Rex grew very pale. "I think you spoke too soon!"

CHAPTER 13

NEAL

After Vanessa got over her very first jump out of a moving train, she had to roll on the ground away from her transport, an act that saved her life despite the myriad bruises she acquired while executing that stunt.

Both Rex and Vanessa had jumped just in time, for at that very second, the train car they had been in exploded. It was replaced by a huge roaring beast the size of an elephant.

The creature had the head of a ram but with a muzzle like a lion's. His body had the shape of a man, but instead of skin, it had scales and fur. The demon's tail was like a crocodile, and his feet were those of a dog's. Thorny spines ran along his back muscular back.

Great, Vanessa thought, *just what we need—a malus.* The beast noticed that Rex and Vanessa had escaped and started shuffling toward them. With an improvised wooden spear clutched in one hand, Rex dashed toward the lumbering beast. They attacked each other with such ferocity that all the birds that had remained in the trees flew up in panic. Poor Vanessa was caught unarmed and unprepared.

Terrified but knowing she needed to do something to help, Vanessa shape-shifted into a bull and rushed into the fight. She was glad that she always had a weapon: herself. Of course, that was true for anyone. The moment she clashed into the malus's leg, he roared and twisted with fury, sending Rex flying; then the beast wacked Vanessa out from under him. Fortunately for Vanessa, she had a few hundred pounds to cushion her fall. She turned back into herself and got back up. Too late, she realized that the malus was above her. With a mighty bellow, it drew back its hand for a killing blow.

Vanessa waited for it, knowing that she would never be quick enough to roll away, but the deathblow never came. The malus's hand kept going backward till the whole thing fell back with a crunch, a black-feathered arrow sticking out of the beast's chest.

A chuckle came from behind them, and turning around, Vanessa came face to face with the figure of a tall handsome man. He laughed again, though this time in humor of the two's countenances, his longish black hair partly covering his face in his face. Even so, Vanessa felt as if she knew who this was but couldn't put a finger on it. She realized her mouth was hanging open at the ease with which he had killed the beast, and she quickly shut her mouth. The man must have been in his early thirties having the coloring and physique of an elf.

Hefting the huge longbow in his hands, he said, "Well, I did not expect you to be here, Rex, especially with such a nice catch! Hello, young lady. My name is Neal. I am an elf, and by the looks of it, you are one too." Neal laughed charmingly.

Rex smiled lopsidedly, greeting Neal as if he was an old friend. Rex decided he should use his manners, and he introduced Vanessa to the elf warrior. "Neal, meet Vanessa Nox."

At that, Neal's smile faded, replaced by awe. "Vanessa Nox!" he repeated reverently, and he bowed. "Hail, Lady Vanessa Nox, princess of the elves. Thank Terra you have been found!"

CHAPTER 14

THE SECRET PASSAGE INTO TERRA

Vanessa had not believed it at first. She, a princess? How come nobody had told her about this? It would take some time for this to sink in.

In the meantime, Neal had decided on coming with them. He thought he might add more protection. Neal had a better command of the area, not to mention more experience navigating and they were grateful to have him on their journey. Vanessa noticed Rex cut a staff from a newly fallen branch. It was green wood, and he carved it with a dagger from Neal. Neal set out to scout the forest while Rex shaved the thin bark off his stick, sharpening the point. Vanessa watched him, finally breaking the silence, "So how did you come to know Neal?" she asked. Rex glanced up at her, then back down at his staff, "Oh… it's a long story," he said. Vanessa regarded him curiously, "It's a long journey," she responded.

A few hours passed in silence when a piercing howl came from a clump of trees next to them. A coyote-like dog pounced out of the woods and onto Neal, licking his face.

Vanessa noticed the dog was a pretty female a little bigger than a Labrador.

Rex laughed and said to Vanessa, "This is Juno. She is an elf hound. Her kind are the ancestors of Norwegian elkhounds. Juno is the strongest elf hound we have and the only one on this realm that we know of."

Vanessa knew this was the only time she might get a chance to ask. "Who *is* this Neal guy?"

Rex smiled as he answered, "Neal is a hunting elf. He used to be the captain of the elven army. He made a mistake and they banished him. He is still very loyal and would sacrifice his life for you and your family and friends."

But before Vanessa could ask what mistake, Neal himself came up to them with a grin. "I can see, Your Majesty, that Sir Rex has explained about my little love Juno! How did you come to meet Rex? Pray tell."

Vanessa smiled kindly at Neal. "Well, it is a long story. May I tell you later?"

He nodded vigorously. "Yes, my lady! Sorry for the intrusion! And what is our goal in this quest?"

Vanessa's smile broadened. "We need to get back to Terra. My mother sent me back here to go to schoo for she thought it was too dangerous in Terra. How did that turn out? I got attacked by a malus and nearly killed!"

Neal nodded with understanding. "Perhaps she thought you would need a break, Your Highness."

Vanessa grunted and said, "Maybe so. Now all I want is for you to stop acting like I am a royal! I don't want to cause too much attention, no matter how loyal you sound!" She smiled to take any possible sting out of her words.

Nodding, Neal smiled back, and they started walking north again, Juno bounding at their heels.

They soon came to a old horse farm. The run-down place looked poor, but they needed horses, so Neal knocked on the door and asked. The old man that lived there said he didn't care which horses they took as long as they paid. Neal gave him three *auri*, the pure gold coins of the elves, for each horse.

The old man gladly accepted but gave a piece of advice to Vanessa. "Be careful around the black one. She is quite feisty. Made me old and grey," he muttered.

Vanessa frowned but thanked the man anyway. She knew that the old man that lived there would not get half of that if he sold all his horses.

Neal picked a sturdy brown mare, and Rex picked a golden stallion. Vanessa had yet to pick one. Browsing through the long stalls with Neal, Vanessa spotted a tall black Arabian mare munching on hay.

Pointing to her, Vanessa said to Neal, "That one."

With a silly "Yes, Your Majesty," Neal rounded the black mare up. But before he could give her to Vanessa, the Arabian bucked him away with a kick.

Vanessa stopped the mare. "TRANQUILLITAS!" she said forcefully, quickly thinking of the command for "calm," and the mare stopped.

"You could just ask nicely!" said the Arabian. Vanessa and Neal froze, staring at the mare in astonishment.

"How—" began Neal, but the mare interrupted, "And second of all, *do not* try to round me up like I am a stupid gelding! I am wild! Wild creatures deserve dignity."

Smirking, Vanessa asked the mare's name. The answer came in a huff. "If you don't know who I am, then I won't bother!" she said.

Vanessa rolled her eyes. "Fine, but can you at least give me a ride, horse-with-no-name?" she asked with sarcasm.

The spirited mare snorted, unable to resist coming. "If you insist on being—wait a minute! You are the daughter of Regina and Drake Nox! I can tell by your eyes! It would be a pleasure to escort a royal. Your mother saved me from captivity once. I would be grateful if you could do it now. By the way, my name is Ventus Queencrow."

Neal gasped and was about to say something, but Ventus glared him into silence. "If I wanted my full identity revealed, I would have revealed it on my own. Now let's get started."

Dark clouds began to form as they set out on their journey once again. Juno scented the storm that now paraded around them and they began to seek a suitable shelter for them all. Soon they happened upon a cave large enough to accommodate the group and settled in to ride out the storm. Neal was foraging through Rex's *pera*, while Rex attempted to teach Vanessa a Draconic command.

"OK, exert your will . . . Good. Now say 'ignis.' It means flame . . . Good. Now do both." He tried. At first, Vanessa could not light the candle, and she felt frustrated. Finally, after an hour of practice, Vanessa lit the candle in Rex's hand, setting it ablaze. Even Neal came over and cheered for her.

After a while, Rex taught her a few more words in Draconic like grow (*adsurgo*), divert (*deflecto*), and bone (*ossis*). Soon Vanessa had learned enough to survive. The storm soon stopped, allowing the restless travelers to continue their journey.

When they reached a river, they stopped to drink and discuss plans. Vanessa, instead of staying with the others, went to a calm part of the river to drink. Looking into the reflection, Vanessa screamed. Her face—she looked like she was *older*. Then she realized that in elf years, she was a lot older. Upon reaching the prime of her life, she should start slowing down.

Suddenly, Rex and Neal burst out of the undergrowth. They each had weapons drawn. Rex relaxed, and Neal to put down his longbow letting out a relieved sigh, and walking away, while Rex put a comforting hand around Vanessa. "Hey, I know it's freaky, but it is normal. You must not be used to it."

Vanessa pushed away from Rex. "Oh yeah, right! You are used to it! 'I know' doesn't help! I look like I am fourteen!"

He looked hurt and said, "Do I not look different too? I look the same age as you!"

Vanessa looked up at him. He was right. His face had changed like her face had: his hair was a bit longer, his face was more oval rather than round, and he, well, he just looked older.

Nodding, Vanessa grinned. "I guess you are right. I just feel like I don't know my body."

Rex smiled. "You'll get used to it. Believe me!"

As they traveled on, Neal led them through diverse trails. They stayed away from roads, and were often pushing through thick bracken and brambles. Neal had told them about a portal to Terra, and now he was leading them in that direction. Supposedly, there were mountains far ahead, but Vanessa couldn't see beyond the tall trees surrounding them.

As they walked, Rex would point out animal tracks and certain vegetation. He seemed the expert, and Vanessa trusted he knew what he was doing. Often times, they would catch sight of magical creatures. Vanessa glimpsed a white stag with golden horns before it bounded away, and Neal had showed them a cave with griffin cubs in it. Vanessa and Rex talked a bit as they went. She enjoyed hearing about Rex's adventures, and they seemed endless. Finally, Vanessa noticed the trees thinning and could see mountains looming ahead. She glanced at Neal,

"I'm guessing we're at our destination?" she asked. Neal gave her a crooked smile, "Not yet," he said. They started climbing a steep path. No. Not quite a path. It was more like a landslide waiting to happen to Vanessa. After around thirty minutes of climbing, they came to the top of a mountain. The path they were supposed to be following had split, making a small chasm they would have to jump. Rex looked down to the bottom of the chasm, "Please mind the gap," he quoted. Vanessa was too tired to smile. She must have been out of shape, and it was starting to bite her in the butt. She looked up to a high cliff above their heads.

Sighing, Vanessa asked, "Do we really have to climb up there?"

Neal smiled. "Yep. But look on the bright side! We would have to walk twice this if we were to take the usual path."

Vanessa frowned. "Yeah, bright side," she muttered sarcastically.

Rex tried to look brave. "Hey! I was thinking of a name for this ridge . . . Have any adds?" he asked. Vanessa massaged her head, "How about suicide mountain?" she offered.

Neal's smile broadened. "I don't know the name of the one that we are on. But I do know the Dwarven term for the one we need to get to: Swarventerkally."

Vanessa smirked. "Bless you," she murmured.

Neal caught the mutter and scowled. "In English it means 'eagle peak.' Don't disrespect the name." They began climbing again, and Vanessa found it was easier going. She wasn't sure if the path was easier, or the cold clean air filling her lungs was making her feel stronger.

When they finally arrived at Eagle Peak, they found Juno there with three brown rabbits for them and was wolfing down a fourth.

Vanessa was surprised. "I thought elves were vegetarians."

Neal and Rex chuckled, and Vanessa was confused. Rex explained, "Elves *are* vegetarians, but when we must, or when we are starving, we eat meat. All the plants around here have been enchanted to be poisonous. Besides, we are with Neal! He hasn't listened to that rule one bit!" At that, Vanessa nodded and started collecting sticks for a fire.

Once finished, she brought them to a shallow cave, where she arranged them and whispered, "Ignis," and a burst of flame sprouted from the brittle sticks.

Rex came over to the fire and sat down next to her. He smiled. "You learn fast. So have you heard any elven jokes?"

Vanessa shook her head, and Rex continued. "Well, here are a few corny ones . . . What did the grass say when a herd of deer started to eat it?"

Vanessa wondered for a while and finally shook her head.

"I am having a hart attack!'" Rex said, giggling at his own joke.

Vanessa snorted with mirth. She was beginning to really enjoy Rex's humor. "OK, that is pretty funny. What are the rest?"

Rex grinned. "I tried to catch fog, but I mist."

It took Vanessa a little while to get it, but when she did, she cracked up. Then she realized she had heard that one at her school. She still laughed.

Rex continued. "I made this one up myself, but . . . well, I had a little help. What did the broken branch say to the tree?"

Vanessa shrugged. "What?"

Rex gave the silly answer, "I tried to put myself back together, but I wouldn't stick!" he said. That one earned uproarious laughing from both of them. Feeling a little sleepy, she rested her head on the stone behind her. She smiled at Rex,

"Okay, here is one from me: knock, knock," she said. Rex grinned, "Oh, no. Who's there?" he asked. Vanessa snickered, "Ach" she responded. Rex furrowed his eyebrows in thought, then he realized the 'ach who' joke.

"Swarventerkally!" he responded instead. Vanessa laughed,

"Bless you!" she returned. Suddenly Rex caught sight of something behind Vanessa, and his shoulders shook with mirth as he slapped a hand over his mouth. Vanessa thought that was odd, and she turned around. Neal stood, arms folded, looking cross,

"Very funny," he muttered. Vanessa sniggered while Rex tried to get control of himself. After a bit of small talk, they bedded down. Using her coat as a pillow, Vanessa fell asleep. For once in a long while, she felt as if she belonged.

Vanessa woke up. Neal was shaking her gently. As she sat up, he pressed a metal plate of cold roasted rabbit into her hands. She ate hungrily. Neal cleaned the plate with a handful of grass, then put it in his pack. Vanessa stretched, trying to wake herself up. She looked around and noticed Rex playing with Juno. He would slap his hands on the ground, and she would dart in and try to lick them before Rex pulled them away. Neal then called them together, "Okay, see that cliff?" he asked. Vanessa frowned, "I'm not liking where you're heading!" she muttered. Neal continued as if she hadn't spoken, "We need to jump off it to get to Terra," he said.

Vanessa was startled. "Wait a second! The ground is way beneath us! It's like a million feet! And there is another cliff under us too! When my parents do find me, I want them to be able to distinguish me from the ground!"

Neal smiled. "We need to jump. The gateway is right below us. We will land in it before we smash against the rocks."

Though Vanessa was not too sure, she went along with it. Approaching the edge of the cliff, Neal grabbed Juno and jumped.

CHAPTER 15

THE AMBUSH

A bigail sat on her bed, listening to birdsong. She was so lonely and sad with Vanessa gone. Sighing, she stared at the pink ceiling. She was so bored. A knock summoned her to the door. Opening it, Abigail found it was Regina.

"Hey, Mom. Whatcha need? I thought you had gone to California."

Regina glanced down when Abigail said the word "Mom" but quickly regained her composure. "I had. But seeing as how your sister Vanessa escaped . . . well, I had to check on you."

Abigail's heart stopped for a second. "She escaped? That's great!" Then she saw the disapproving stare of her mother. "I mean . . . That's absolutely terrible! How did it happen?"

Regina sighed. "I don't know. But I have a sneaking suspicion . . . Wait a minute! Where is Rex? He was sent to guard you!"

Abigail shrugged. "He did guard me. For a few moments, that is. He said he was tired, so I let him rest," Abigail confessed.

Regina's hard expression softened. "He must be missing seeing you interact with Vanessa. He confided in me last night that he was unhappy you two had parted. The last time he saw two close sisters part was—well, never mind."

Abigail wanted something to do. "How about we find Rex! I am really bored!"

Her mother smiled. "Very well."

"Rex! Open up!" Regina called again. They had gone made their way to another corridor like their own. Abigail was impressed by Rex's door. It was a thick oak lined with some kind of metal. She thought it could withstand a tsunami.

Regina was now banging on it hard. "Rex is a deep sleeper, but he would have opened it by now."

"Can you open the door?" Abigail asked.

Regina frowned. "No, it is locked."

Abigail thought for a moment. "Can you use the Latin magic thingy to open it?"

Regina's frown deepened. "Elvish is not the only way to victory," she said. Then she kicked the door hard. The kick must have been hard enough to blast a hole on a tank, for at the moment, the door fell open.

Abigail gaped at her mom. "How did you do that? You have to teach me!" Regina smiled. "Maybe later." Then she called into the room. "Rex! I know you don't like it, but you have to come out now!" No answer. Just then, a growling sound came from a dark corner in Rex's room.

Regina froze. "Oh no," she whispered then said quickly, "Deflecto!"

Instantly, a magical wall of blue mist surrounded them. It was not a moment too soon, for at that second, a thousand little black darts were shot from the corner. Regina whispered a counterattack. Thorns sprouted from Regina's hand and flew toward the attacker. They stopped inches away from the shadow. Abigail choked a scream.

A dark figure pushed its way out of the shadow. "Well, well, well, the little want-to-be-princess Regina. How wonderful it is you survived! Now you will see the downfall of the elves. How lucky," the Dark Lord said.

Then Regina uttered a word that sounded like "pater," and everything turned utterly black.

CHAPTER 16

TRUNCUS'S STORY

Vanessa opened her eyes, expecting darkness. In its stead, though, was a forest of trees. Someone cleared his throat right above her head. Looking up, Vanessa saw Neal. "Hey, Vanessa. How are you feeling?" he asked.

Groggily, Vanessa lifted her head. "Fine," she lied. The truth was she felt terrible. Neal seemed to know what she was thinking.

"It's OK. I will get you some herbs. Perhaps you need a Rosebel and mandrake. There are bunches of them here..." Neal muttered to himself as he walked off in search of them.

When Vanessa was alone, a voice came from the trees behind her. "Vanessa? How did we get here?"

Whirling around, Vanessa spotted Steven, a tall blond boy from her class. She used to hang out with him because she enjoyed his dry wit and the fact he loved standing up to bullies.

Vanessa gasped with surprise, "Steven! How did you get here?"

The boy rolled his dull brown eyes. "That's what I asked you! Who is this Neal guy?"

Vanessa retorted, "You wouldn't need to ask those questions if you had not came to Terra! And how *did* you get to Terra?"

Steven scowled, "Vanessa, you didn't answer the question!"

Impatient, Vanessa glanced at the stream behind Steven. An idea started to form in her head. Blond hair? Dull brown eyes? Hadn't she seen—or been—that before?

"Oh, you want answering? Then get it!" she yelled and pushed Steven into the stream.

A shout came from behind her, and Vanessa turned around to see Rex pointing at the stream. "Look!" he cried.

She turned to the stream and nearly fainted. Where Steven had been before, now there was a strapping, young, and rather mischievous-looking elf. He had jet-black hair and dark blue eyes.

Rex smiled and ran to him. They embraced tightly, and much to the surprise of Vanessa, Rex said, with a grin seemingly made of pure joy, "Welcome home, Septimus!" He then turned to Vanessa, "Septimus is my elder brother!"

Once Septimus had been properly introduced, he began to help get things ready for the trip home. Rex volunteered to go with Vanessa forage for food to take on the journey.. They were deep in the forest when a voice called from ahead. "Good day to you, folks."

Vanessa yelped. Looking up, she saw the voice had come from the tree.

Rex grinned. "Hello, Truncus!" he said to the branch.

A flicker of movement caught Vanessa's eye, and a moment later, a figure dropped to the ground. She nearly shrieked again, for when she saw a beam of light rest on the figure's face, exposing his features, it was a wood dwarf. His skin was of bark, and he was very short. His round belly and bulbous features made him almost endearing. Though his eyes were tiny and hollow there was just visible a slight gleam of orange. It took Vanessa a while to realize he was part of the tree.

Rex seemed to have no trouble at all at taking in the wood dwarf; in fact, the young male elf was grinning ear to ear. "Vanessa, meet Truncus.

Truncus, meet Vanessa. Truncus is one of my most *trusted* friends. He is also a great help in a fight. Rumors have it he can hypnotize big beasts. Truncus, Vanessa is the rightful heir to the elven kingdom," Rex said this so jubilantly that Vanessa felt a small glow inside her.

Truncus's tiny eyes widened to their full extent, showing more brightly the glowing bits of orange inside them, and he bowed with a flourish. "I am most pleased to meet you, milady. You must be very startled to see one so repulsive," he said.

Vanessa shook her head. "Not at all! It is just the fact I have never seen a wood dwarf before!" she replied, guessing what he was. Obviously, she had got it right because Truncus seemed surprised that she knew what he was.

"You know what I am? That is wonderful! Not even the most educated nobles know what I am these days. So, Rex . . . I would love to come with you! Where are we going?" he asked.

Rex answered with a wink. "Well, you might not want to come if I tell you, but . . . we are going to Dnal."

Truncus sighed ruefully. "I had a feeling it was true. Alas, I will still come."

Vanessa frowned. "But I thought you can't go far from your tree," she said, motioning to the huge juniper from which Truncus had sprung.

Truncus smiled broadly. "That's only true for tree nymphs. I am a wood dwarf. I am not attached to the tree. In fact, I can travel anywhere I want *besides a fireplace*. That's one place I never need go," he proudly proclaimed.

Vanessa giggled with joy she had not sported in months. "OK, I get it," she said.

Rex and Neal were deciding which route to take to Dnal, and Vanessa didn't want any part in that conversation. It was nighttime, and she wanted some fresh air. As she walked between the trees, watching their leaves glisten with moonlight and basking in the silver rays, she felt peaceful. Her attention turned to an oak tree, and she noticed two round amber eyes staring at her. The owl let off a low hoot and flew off, silent wings making no noise.

Vanessa got an idea. She thought of and animal, and she began to change, her mouth grew hard and curved, turning into a beak, and she began to shrink. Her arms sprouted feathers, and her legs grew into scaly feet with claws. She had changed into a snowy owl. Her mind didn't change, and she could still speak, thankfully. But there was no need for speaking tonight.

She hopped to a branch, and leapt off. Spreading her wings, feeling the cold night air ruffle the feathers, she could not feel more alive. She wove between trees, making mice and other small animals scuttle away. Flapping her beautiful wings a bit more, she gained altitude, soaring into the sky. The full moon was bright and welcoming, and Vanessa basked in its silvery light.

She looked down, her eyesight somewhat changed in owl form. She could see a fire burning in a small clearing. With her night vision, she could make out huge shapes lumbering around the flames. She dared not go closer, instead, tucking in her wings and going into a nosedive. As she plummeted to the ground, the wind rushing against her face, Vanessa sighed. This was perfect. Just before she hit the ground, she spread her wings. Her belly dropped as she came out of the dive, and she flapped her wings as if to fly backwards, spreading her tail to stop as she alighted on a low branch. She tucked in her wings, quite satisfied with her neat landing, and changed back into an elf.

As soon as she had dropped to the rocky soil, a slightly accented voice sounded from behind her. "Doing something you are not supposed to do? Again?" it said.

Vanessa whirled to face the speaker. An attractive she-elf with ginger hair and bright green eyes was leaning on a tall oak, smiling slyly. Vanessa instantly recognized her as the auburn-haired elf from her dreams.

"Who are you, and what do you want?" Vanessa asked.

The she-elf smirked. "You really don't know?" Vanessa shook her head wildly.

The pretty she-elf sighed forlornly. "I guess your mother Regina did not tell you about me?" she asked.

Again, Vanessa shook her head. "My mom didn't tell me a lot of things," she replied.

The elf glanced at Vanessa with deep sadness in her beautiful verdant eyes. Then the sadness dropped like a rock and was replaced with annoyance.

"She could have, at least, told you about me! She *should* have told you about her own sister!" she complained mostly to herself.

Vanessa's jaw dropped. "My mother definitely didn't tell me she had an awesome looking sister!" she exclaimed.

The pretty she-elf's annoyance melted away, and she giggled. "Oh stop! Flattering is evil! Now if you will follow me. I don't want that camp of ogres to get you!"

Vanessa's smile melted. "What ogres?" she asked.

The she-elf ignored her and turned to walk toward Vanessa's camp.

Vanessa wanted to get in one more question. "What is your name?" she asked. The she-elf turned around to look at her. "Filix."

Vanessa froze. "FILIX?" she exclaimed. "That was the name of the oracle who prophesied about me!" she said even louder.

Filix smirked. "Yes. She prophesied about a lot of Elven Heroes. She was a real looker. You might even call her an awesome looking sister," she hinted.

Vanessa gasped in utter shock, realizing what she meant by that.

"You are her! I mean, you are the oracle!" she cried.

Filix rolled her eyes, glimmering green eyes, and said "Well, duh!"

Once they had walked back to camp, Vanessa sneaked out an extra sleeping bag for her aunt Filix. It turned out Filix didn't need a sleeping bag though. She just reached into her leather satchel and took out a handful of some tufts of dried moss. She then sprinkled the tough bits around the place she wanted to sleep and waved her hand over it. Almost instantly, the stiff little sprigs sprouted softer, more comfortable bits until there was a perfect mossy green bed.

Filix offered to do the same for Vanessa, but Vanessa declined, saying, "No, thank you! I am going to sleep on something *not* living." So Filix had kept the extra moss. Vanessa crawled into her sleeping bag and made a pillow for herself out of her jacket. Closing her eyes, Vanessa drifted into a perfectly dreamless slumber.

It felt as though she had only slept a few minutes when she heard a girlish scream. Opening her eyes, Vanessa beheld Rex scrambling away from Filix. He noticed Vanessa staring at the scene and gestured wildly at Filix. "Do you have something to do with this?" he asked suspiciously once he had regained a little of his light composure. "'Cause I hate it when you do stuff like this!" he added.

Vanessa smiled innocently. "What do you mean, Rex?" she said, still trying to figure out what on Terra was going on. Truncus had sprung up from the little pile of oak leaves he had bedded in, waving a gnarled club in his gnarled hand. Vanessa noticed the little club was gilded with golden spikes.

Next to Truncus stood Septimus who was holding an elegant sword and shield. Last was a bedraggled but still very handsome Neal. Neal held his longbow with an arrow notched in it.

Truncus stepped forward, setting his club down. Seeing his signal, the others sheathed their weapons.

"Rex, we heard a scream. What lady is in trouble?" he exclaimed confused.

Rex smiled sheepishly. "Um, that was not a lady. That was me—" But before he could finish, a gasp came from Neal as he spotted Vanessa's aunt.

"Filix!" he cried happily and dashed toward her. They met with a kiss, and Neal twirled Filix around. The pretty green-eyed she-elf laughed joyfully.

"Neal! How are you? How are Juno and Venus? Where are they?" she asked lovingly.

Neal's smile broadened. "We are all well, and I will explain about their leave of absence later. But for now, how is my wife?"

Vanessa and Rex gasped. "WIFE?" they blurted in unison.

Now it was the couples' turn to be sheepish. "Well, it was a private affair. We didn't want any interruptions 'cause we had just had a stressful war," Neal explained patiently. "But that was a long time ago," he added.

Truncus raised a wooden eyebrow. "Indeed," said he.

"We even had a child," Filix added.

Vanessa was startled. How much of this had her parents known? Vanessa shook off that thought and focused on the quest for home. "Hey, guys? I think we need to get going. Don't we need to get to Dnal before afternoon?"

The group agreed and started to leave. As they went, Filix would forage for berries and nuts, bringing them to the group as breakfast. Filix found a colorful plant that could heal broken bones, heal headaches, and make some powerful potions. Ordering the group to stop so she could preserve the plant properly, she explained the plant was called ossis or bone plant.

Vanessa was curious. "Why don't we just use Elvish?"

Filix frowned deeply. "Has not your mother told you our most used proverb?" she asked.

Vanessa frowned too. "No. What is it?" she answered.

Filix sighed. "Elvish is not the only way to victory." Then she looked back at the bone plant. "All I want right now is you to memorize the ossis. The leaves are the ones that can heal broken bones . . ."

It had broad hairy leaves and small bell shaped flowers with a delicate purple hue. Vanessa examined the delicate flowers and noticed stripes on the petals. Filix also explained if she broke off a stem and planted it, it would grow another bone plant.

After the botany lesson, they set off again. Truncus and Neal started planning what the group was going to do after Dnal. They asked Vanessa if she would join them, but Vanessa declined and made her way up to the front of the group where Septimus was. She smiled at him, and he smiled back, his jet-black hair blowing in his face. Then he looked away.

"I am sorry I followed you to Terra," he said shamefaced.

Vanessa was surprised. "But I thought you loved it here! You have your brother and your memories back! I have no recollection of what happened before I came to earth," she exclaimed.

Septimus glanced at her. "But that doesn't make it right. I do like it here in Terra. It's only the fact I remember, some very . . . unpleasant things. And by the way, why you can't remember life before earth is because you had your memories *erased*."

Vanessa stumbled back in so much surprise that she accidentally knocked Truncus to the ground. She yelped and pulled him to his feet. He murmured his thanks in a strained voice. Vanessa thought that he was angry with her until she saw the loathing look that Truncus gave Septimus.

"What did you tell the princess? I told you to stay away from her, traitor," Truncus said lividly.

Septimus looked furtively at Vanessa. "Shhh! Truncus, not so loud! You don't want to get into trouble!" he whispered.

Vanessa was very suspicious. "What do you mean by 'traitor,' Truncus?" she asked.

Truncus took one look at Septimus's pleading stare and sighed. "Nothing, milady," he replied unconvincingly.

Septimus looked relieved and stalked away. Once he was out of earshot, Truncus grabbed Vanessa's hand and pulled her into a nearby bush. She tried to cry out, but Truncus clapped his wooden hand over her mouth.

"Wait! I must tell you something!" he said in a hushed voice.

Vanessa stopped squirming and listened.

Truncus took a deep breath then began with slow intriguing reluctance. "It all started when Septimus was a youth. He loved to help out and was an obedient child. But one day, a little after his thirteenth birthday—he is fifteen now—he started looking shifty. He was always taking naps but had bags under his eyes like he had not slept well. One day, I caught him sneaking off toward the forest at night. I was one of the elven guards back then, as most noble wood dwarves are. So of course, I followed him.

"He went to the dark part of the woods where no elf in their right mind would go unless it was important. An elf has sharp hearing, but wood dwarves can sneak up on anything. I was planning on jumping out of the bush and scaring him half to death when he stopped. He looked around, and then he stared at a dark shadow at the base of an oak tree. I was so curious that I didn't show my presence. I was beginning to think Septimus had gone crazy when the shadow he was staring at . . . moved." Truncus shuddered.

Vanessa was unnerved. "Well? What happened next?" she asked.

Truncus sighed and continued. "I was scared half to death myself! Then a voice came from the shadow. It said in a raspy voice, 'You have served me well, Septimus. The time of the elves is about to end.' Septimus looked really startled. He almost screamed out his words when he said them, 'What? That was not what I wanted! I told you I wanted *one* dead! Not everyone!'

"I was so scared I could not move! Then the shadow spoke. 'I know you wish to have your revenge, but you must wait. Who do you want dead?' he asked Septimus. That rat Septimus whispered the name. 'Luna Flask. It was her fault that my sister died,'" Truncus said.

Vanessa frowned in confusion. "Rex and Septimus had a sister?"

Truncus nodded without enthusiasm. "A long time ago, yes. A Kapacki killed her."

Vanessa's frown deepened. "Why is she called 'Luna Flask'?"

Truncus exhaled again. "Some Kapacki have avatars—like a elf body. Luna's avatar is a tall, beautiful, very talented lady. She has dark blue eyes, sharp features, pale, flawless skin. She has pearly white hair, even though she looks like she is in her twenties. Though they greatly resemble elves, their ears are pointed like a wolf's—not like an elf's. No one knows her real name. Luna Flask is just her avatar's name."

Vanessa nodded. "OK, go on."

"Once Septimus had said that, the dark figure continued. 'Very well, on your sixteenth birthday, you can kill her—if she does not drink your blood first, that is!'" Truncus said and shuddered. "Have you read

that Kapacki drink the blood of their foes?" Vanessa shook her head
but stayed silent.

Truncus resumed soberly. "So after the figure said that, Septimus
bowed respectfully. 'Yes, oh great and mighty Dark Lord.' It was
terrible! I thought at that moment the Dark Lord would crumble him
to ashes, but instead, he just vanished! After that, Septimus ran toward
the elven kingdom. As he was about to exit the dark woods, I sprang
out in front of him and inquired, 'Where do you think you're going?'
Septimus nearly jumped out of his skin. 'Oh! Nowhere, sir!' he said in
a shaky voice. I answered Septimus and said, "I know where you have
been!' Septimus replied nervously, 'You mean that you *followed* me?' I
nodded and said, 'I wonder how the queen will react to discover that
her own people have betrayed her? Maybe we should punish you and
Rex!' Septimus looked scared. 'Leave Rex out of this! He had nothing
to do with it!' I nodded. 'I will not tell the queen because I trust that
you will choose better than this!' Septimus grunted and said, 'I cannot!
Luna Flask killed my sister Gemma!' Then Septimus returned to the
castle," concluded Truncus.

Vanessa nodded and withdrew from the bush. To her surprise, the
group had not noticed their absence. They just walked on as if nothing
had happened. Truncus emerged from the bush also, and both of them
set off with the group. Septimus started to walk toward Vanessa, but he
was stopped as Neal called his name, "Septimus! I need you to help me
with this map I'm trying to make." He said. Vanessa breathed a sigh of
relief as Septimus grudgingly followed Neal to the front. It was hard to
think of him as a traitor. Vanessa didn't realize she was nowhere near
the truth.

CHAPTER 17

THE FEAST OF DNAL

At around afternoon the group reached Dnal. Vanessa didn't know what she had expected before, but what she saw was certainly not what she'd envisioned. A tall dark wall rose up, concealing what was behind it. In front of the group were large oak gates. The gates opened, and out poured little men. Most wore beards and were either beefy or downright tubby.

As the group entered the city walls, they notice two dwarves seated in the center of the courtyard on a small golden stage. One of the dwarves was young and would almost be handsome if it weren't for the crooked nose and bushy black eyebrows. His black hair and beard were shorter than that of other dwarves, and his jutting features made him have an ageless look. The older dwarf looked quite like the younger dwarf, except the elder's beard trailed of the edge of the stage, and his face was covered with wrinkles and scars.

Then the younger dwarf stood up with a broad smile on his face. "Welcome, friends! You must be weary. Please join us in celebration. We will have a feast in your honor." Looking at Vanessa he said, "My name is Prince Orrin and this is my father, King Vark."

Vanessa was startled at Orrin's voice. She had expected it to be squeaky, rather it was rich and deep. Orrin jumped off the golden stage and made his way through the group. Vanessa noticed that the dwarf prince was especially enthusiastic to see Truncus. Orrin was much taller reaching Vanessa's chest and not her waist like most of the others dwarves.

Orrin smiled at Vanessa and Rex with pearly teeth as he greeted them. "Hello, you two!" he said cheerfully. "I suppose you have traveled far. Are you well?"

Rex smiled. "Yes to both questions!"

The prince laughed. "I see that you finally have a *nenack*!" Orrin said slyly.

Rex blushed a little, and then realizing Vanessa had no idea what Orrin had meant, his blushing stopped. He glanced angrily at Orrin.

Vanessa was interested. "What does *nenack* mean?" she asked.

Rex gave Orrin the if-you-tell-her-I-swear-I-will-kill-you look and said to Vanessa, "Nothing." Then he grabbed Orrin and left, leaving Vanessa standing there alone.

"I suppose I will take you to your room," called a voice from behind her. Vanessa turned around to see a pretty dwarf girl who curtsied and said, "My name is Nalla. We have awaited you. My sisters are showing your friends to their rooms. May I ask if you would like to share your suite with your aunt?" she asked.

Vanessa nodded tiredly and the two women followed Nalla to the suite. Vanessa was impressed with the elegant room's marble floors and golden buttresses. It also had two king-sized beds with soft, silky sheets and furry pillows.

Nalla smiled at Vanessa's awe. "This room is for our honored female guests, like you. May I answer any of your questions?"

Vanessa was about to ask a few, but Filix said softly, "No, thank you, Lady Nalla." So the beautiful dwarf girl left.

Vanessa glanced over at her aunt. "I want to ask *you* a question. May I?"

Filix nodded. "Of course, you can! What is it?"

Vanessa thought for a moment then asked, "What does *nenack* mean?"

Filix giggled. "Oh! I can see that you have suffered from Orrin's teasing!"

Vanessa was bewildered. "What do you mean? Orrin was teasing Rex! Not me!"

Filix's eyes widened understandingly. "Oh, that would make much more sense! Well, *nenack* means girlfriend," she answered with a smile.

Vanessa felt her pulse pound with embarrassment. "*What?* I'm not his girlfriend. We haven't even been on a date!" she yelled a little too loudly.

Filix smiled with amusement glimmering in her green eyes. "With us elves, you don't need to 'date.' You only need to have the right feelings for him and hang out with him in the right way, for instance, when you are both on a quest. It does not need to be romantic. Or it might even mean a way of being friends during a battle."

Vanessa was outraged. "I HAVEN'T HUNG OUT WITH HIM! I DON'T EVEN HAVE FEELINGS FOR HIM! she yelled and then stomped around the room, muttering to herself. Filix tried to keep a straight face but failed. In fact, she nearly doubled over in laughter.

There was a knock on the door, and Rex poked his head into the girls' room. "What is going on in there?" he asked. Filix had a feeling he had been listening but kept the thought to herself.

Vanessa yelled in both embarrassment and anger, "NOTHING! YOU HAVE NOTHING TO DO WITH IT, SO KEEP YOUR NOSE OUT OF IT!" And Filix burst into another round of laughing.

Rex looked confused. "For your information, my room is right below yours, so try to *pipe down*!" he said with a hurt expression and shut the door roughly.

Vanessa's anger shifted to alarm. Rex had never yelled like that, especially at her. She realized she had snapped at him unfairly and would need to apologize later. Filix still found the entire situation humorous for some reason unbeknownst to Vanessa. A knock at the door startled them. Thinking it might be Rex again, Vanessa hurried to open it and apologize but was met by Nalla instead. The dwarf handed them two silky dark green gowns. After well needed baths in the enormous claw footed tub, they changed into their fancy gowns. Standing in front of giant mirror Vanessa hardly recognized the image reflected. The chest and torso of the dress was well fitting, while the sleeves and the skirt were flowing and loose. Vanessa studied the designs on the green fabric. The embroidery depicted a Chinese-looking tree with delicate roots.

Filix smiled kindly at Vanessa. "You look wonderful! Absolutely lissome! You look just like the princess you are! Now about your hair . . ." she trailed off. Filix swept over to the bathroom counter and rummaged in the drawers until she found what she wanted. She brought out a brush and a globe of silver yarn-like string. It took Vanessa a moment to realize that the ball of light silvery string was actually spiderweb.

"That must have been a big spider!" she blurted while Filix did her hair.

Filix grinned with a knowing look. "Yes! The spiders are huge. They are called magna arachnid. They are blue, black, and gray. They're usually as big as a bag ball. The oldest can get to the size of a truck. Good thing they are friends to us!"

Vanessa frowned. "Bag ball?" she asked.

Filix was silent for a while, and then she laughed. "Oh! I mean a basketball! My bad!" she said.

Vanessa absorbed that for a while. *A spider as big as a truck?* Now *that* was a scary image.

After a few minutes, Vanessa looked up at her reflection and gasped. Her hair was amazing. Filix had brushed it and tied it up into a bun. She had released two front strands and let them hang. A few strands of spiderweb were crushed together, making a sticky, silvery, lotion-like solution, which she rubbed into the two front tresses, making them stick. Filix had pulled the bun apart and separated the hair into halves. She plaited each half and bound the braids with the spiderweb. With the last of the silvery solution, Filix attached the ends of the braids together and swirled it into another bun.

The end result was that Vanessa's hair shone like the moon and went flawlessly with the dark green dress. Filix went to work on her own hair, tying it up to look like a stylish ponytail. Vanessa was just about to suggest that they leave when a knock sounded at the door. Vanessa answered it and was not surprised to find Neal standing in the doorway.

He widened his green eyes and bowed in mock reverence. "Milady, how pleasant that you are awake. We have been waiting for ages! I was about to see what had gone wrong!"

"Oh my! I must not keep my maddening uncle waiting!" Vanessa laughed.

Filix appeared behind her and laughed as well. "That 'maddening uncle' of yours is my exasperating husband!" she replied.

Septimus popped out behind Neal. "Do I get a title?" he asked. They all laughed. Neal took Filix's hand in his and gestured to Septimus that he should do the same to Vanessa. Septimus obeyed, walking Vanessa behind Filix and Neal.

The men walked the ladies to the courtyard. The golden stage that had been in the center was moved off to the side and replaced by a blazing bonfire. A trio of skilled musicians played a jovial song while dwarves joyfully danced and ate around the fire. Vanessa saw Orrin and Nalla dancing together and smiled. She also recognized the bulbous form of Truncus.

Vanessa frowned. "Where is Rex?" she whispered to Filix.

Her aunt Filix shot Vanessa a crafty glance and nodded to a shadowy corner of the courtyard. A lone figure leaned broodingly against the wall, staring at the festivity. Vanessa nodded back and excused herself from Septimus's grasp, which seemed to relieve him. She walked along the shadows until she reached Rex. Vanessa noticed that Rex was wearing a dark green suit, just like Septimus and Neal. She cleared her throat, startling the sullen Rex.

He looked over at her, and his jaw dropped. "Um, hi. My name is Rex. What is yours?" he asked. He spoke very quickly, making Vanessa resist a snigger.

Vanessa punched him in the arm playfully.

"Hey!" he yelped. "Watch it! Who are you? Next time . . . W-wait a minute! Vanessa? Is that you?"

Vanessa gave him the don't-play-coy-with-me glance. "Duh!" she said with a smile.

He cringed with embarrassment. "Um, sorry. It's just that you look . . . well . . . beautiful. Not that you don't look beautiful all the time… but you look… fancy!" he said, stumbling over his words.

Vanessa bet she was blushing but didn't care. Rex had just said she was beautiful. Vanessa didn't want her embarrassment to ruin a perfect night.

"Well, you look quite handsome too! So is it the girl who has to ask the boy to dance?" she said, then added, "'Cause Filix told me that it was the other way around."

Rex took the obvious hint. "Lady Vanessa, will you join me in a dance?" he asked quickly.

Vanessa smiled. "Thought you'd never ask!"

Rex took her hand and led Vanessa to the bonfire. Rex held up his left hand and motioned for Vanessa to do the same. They clasped hands and began to dance to the rhythm of the song. Rex moved clumsily at first, while Vanessa glided gracefully around him. Eventually, though, he got the hang of it. They stepped into a pattern, and Vanessa found it similar to swing dancing. Vanessa was surprised to find that she had no trouble dancing; it seemed as though she was born for it.

By the end of the lovely song, the two were like swans, dancing flawlessly. Vanessa was so lost in the moment that she didn't realize that all the dwarves had stopped dancing and were watching them as they twirled around. Rex and Vanessa finally stopped, and the spectators clapped at the preformance. Vanessa felt dizzy, but managed a smile. She and Rex bowed, and gradually, the observers went back to dancing.

Rex grinned, took Vanessa by the hand, and led her to the large table that was piled with food. Vanessa noted that while most of it was meat, there were some delectable fruits and vegetables. Rex grabbed a wooden plate from the stack and started picking fruit and placing them on the plate.

Vanessa grabbed a deep blue fruit with bright orange specks that was rounded. Rex told her it was called a mandarblue. She cautiously took a bite. It was spicy. Almost sour, the fruit made Vanessa feel like her senses were being sharpened. Suddenly, she felt like all the moisture had been sucked out of her mouth.

Vanessa glanced around and found that two dwarves had moved a smaller table next to the bigger one. This one contained beverages. At first, Vanessa thought that one of the large jugs was filled with beer. But when one of the dwarves filled a glass cup with the liquid inside, Vanessa realized that the liquid lwas a glowing silver fluid.

When she asked Rex, he answered with a smile, "Oh, that is *argentum aqua*. It is from a stream in the Tnaig Mountains. We just call it argentum though. Try some. It is a specialty."

Vanessa eagerly took a glass cup, struggling not to get too excited at sampling something different. She filled it with the argentum and sipped at it experimentally. It was wonderful. It had the texture of water and tasted like root beer with more wintergreen and other spices that made it especially delicious.

Rex tasted his and sighed contentedly. "This is the life! Dwarves always throw awesome parties."

Vanessa nodded. "This is the first party/feast, I have been to, and it is amazing, though I think parties on earth are more . . . riotous."

Rex laughed. "Yeah. But this isn't a party! You should see Dwarven parties! They are more riotous than anything on earth!" he pointed out laughing.

Vanessa had a riot of feeling coursing through her. She thought about her sister. "If only Abigail could see this! She loves these kinds of things. She would love my dress and my hairdo! I miss her," she confessed.

Rex slipped his hand into hers. "It's OK. I promise on my life that you two will reunite," he said. "Sisters like you are not easily parted."

"What do you mean 'like you?'" Vanessa asked.

Rex glanced up at the sky. He was obviously thinking of some past event in his life that he was not inclined to share.

Vanessa frowned at the stars. "Fine," she grumbled.

The musicians started playing a soft, smooth tune, soothing Vanessa's anger. She felt embarrassment at her behavior and gave Rex an apologetic smile. The stars shone bright overhead, and Vanessa enjoyed the smell of pine and cedar. This was just like their home in the mountains of California. This was the smell of her childhood. She wondered what her mother Regina was doing with Abigail. And what was Drake doing?

Vanessa glanced at Rex, who was watching the stars. He looked over at her, his green eyes glinting in the starlight. Then he asked something that Vanessa was not quite expecting.

"Um, Vanessa? I want to know . . . are you my friend?" he asked hesitantly. There was no hesitation. "Of, course," she answered. Rex gazed at her intently, "Even if... someone in my family was evil, or something?" he questioned. Vanessa thought back to her conversation about Septimus. "Absolutely. I don't care what your family is like," she said. Rex seemed relieved, "Thank you." Vanessa looked up at the stars, "Don't mention it. I am just glad I have a friend. After today, I'm not sure who I can trust."

CHAPTER 18

I LIKE MUSHROOMS BEST

Filix woke Vanessa early so they could get ready for the journey. Filix brought out a bundle of dark clothes. Vanessa dressed in the dark bundle of clothes Filix handed her. Her traveling clothes, as Filix called them, consisted of stretchy, dark brown pants with slashes of light brown. The shirt was long in the waist and had long sleeves. It was dark, forest green with slashes of dark brown. Vanessa noticed that it was made of a fabric that she didn't recognize. Filix explained that the travel clothes would keep her cool when it was hot out and warm her up when it was cold, as well as providing a degree of camouflage.

They stepped out of the bedroom and met up with the boys. Each was dressed similarly, with dark brown pants and dark forest green shirts.

Vanessa noticed that Truncus was not there. "Where is Truncus?" she asked Rex.

He frowned. "He decided that he was not needed here," he grumbled.

Vanessa nodded and slipped her hand into his. "It's OK. I will miss him, but I'm sure that he will be fine," she comforted him.

He smiled at her, and she smiled back. Rex walked over to Septimus, helping him with his pack before they headed down to the gates, trying not to wake any dwarf there.

A few minutes passed once they had gotten into the surrounding forest. Suddenly, a shout came from behind them.

Prince Orrin came trotting up to them. "Hello! Mind if I join you sorry bunch of souls?" he asked cheerfully.

With their new companion, they tromped up north, laughing and joking. Orrin walked beside Vanessa and Rex. "Well, I suppose I should apologize for teasing you when you first came to Dnal, Rex. But of course, I am only saying sorry because Filix would have my head if I didn't." he said ruefully.

Rex shot a grin at Vanessa. "Well I noticed you have a *nenack* Orrin," he said.

Orrin blushed. "What? I do not!" he yelped.

Vanessa knew where Rex was going and knew that Orrin deserved a bit of trouble. She happily joined in. "Oh yeah! I saw you dancing with her last night. What is her name? I think it starts with an N," she teased.

Orrin went red. "DON'T YOU DARE!" he said.

Rex and Vanessa snickered. "Oooh! I remember!" Vanessa said.

Rex nodded. "Me too!" he said.

Orrin glared at them and was about to say something when Vanessa and Rex chorused, "IT'S NALLA!" Orrin folded his arms and stalked away.

Apparently, he wasn't looking where he was going because he promptly ran into a tree. Filix gasped and ran toward him, while Rex and Vanessa laughed.

Filix shot them an angry glare. "Will you two pipe down? If you haven't noticed, we are deep in the forest—the *Silva Forest* in fact. It houses some of the most dangerous animals in Terra!" she whispered fiercely. They slowly stopped giggling, shooting each other sharp glances until they were all silent.

After a while, the group came to a rest in a mossy bit of trees. Several mushrooms and tree stumps surrounded them, making a nice little clearing. Moving a little ways away from the group, Vanessa sat down and was about to drink from her canteen when she heard a giggle from behind her. Vanessa turned her head around but saw nothing. She was beginning to suspect that she had imagined it when she heard another giggle. Vanessa caught a flicker of movement.

"Wow! More victims! This is going to be fun! What do you think I should do with her? Make her drown?" said in a male voice.

"Thorn! What have I told you? You are supposed to bring the intruders to see the queen first. *Then* we can torture them!" said a feminine voice.

Vanessa smirked and turned around to where the voices came from. "How about neither?" she asked, hiding her surprise at the tininess of the figures. The figures where about six inches tall and were dressed in leaves. But the most startling fact about them was that they hovered in the air—without wings.

The fairylike beings didn't hide their surprise as easily. "You can speak Impish? Impossible!" said the one that must have been Thorn. He had messy black hair and had a bronzed tan.

The female was much prettier. She had dark brown tresses that were tied up into a ponytail. She also had bronzed skin and beautiful crystal blue eyes that had an Asian touch. She spoke in a clear but soft voice that sang across the forest like birdsong. "Are you an elf?" she asked curiously.

Vanessa nodded cautiously. "I am. Most call me Princess Vanessa," she answered. She expected some reaction, and she was not disappointed.

The two fairylike beings knelt in the air. "Hail Princess Vanessa! We have awaited your arrival! Excuse my brother's rudeness. We get many unpleasant visitors. My name is Stream. My brother's name is Thorn," said the female creature.

Vanessa nodded and said, "May I see your queen? And may my friends come?"

Thorn looked sheepish. "Um, yes for both questions," he said.

Vanessa looked at Stream. "Forgive my ignorance, for I have not been in Terra long, but what is the name of your kind? I have not yet happened upon such elegant and intriguing creatures," she said this as nicely as possible, not wanting to offend them in her ignorance.

Stream smiled with good humor, amused at Vanessa's politeness. "You speak as if you have lived a long life in Terra. We are sprites. We do not have wings, yet we fly as well as fairies—if not better. There are many things about us that most people do not know. Thorn and I will lead you to our kingdom."

Vanessa nodded and went back to the group to fetch her friends. Thorn zoomed away to tell the sprite city about Vanessa and her friends' arrival. Vanessa started walking toward her campsite. To her astonishment, Stream went along also, claiming that she wanted to protect them from any creatures that may be about. The first one Vanessa found was Rex. She quickly explained what had transpired while they walked to the campsite.

Rex shook his head wonderingly. "Wow, Vanessa, did you know sprites are one of the most dangerous creatures in the forest? That is amazing you befriended them!" he said.

Stream skipped in the air and landed lightly on Rex's nose. "Well! Vanessa is very lucky to have found you! You are *very* good-looking! You seem somehow familiar. How did you two meet?" she asked.

Rex exchanged a glance with Vanessa and turned red. "Um, it's kind of a long story."

Stream giggled. "Oh! How wonderful! Most sprites are less enthusiastic about love, but my mother was a fairy, so I love romance!" she said.

Rex squirmed uncomfortably. "Uh, cool," he said.

Stream realized that he wasn't part fairy and changed the subject to the defenses of the sprite kingdom. This made Rex look very relieved.

They soon came to the campsite and were greeted happily. Vanessa explained her encounter with the sprites and the group agreed to go to the sprite kingdom.

Vanessa was very impressed by the Sprite kingdom. At first, Vanessa could not see anything but trees. Then Stream had sprinkled a light blue dust on them that made Vanessa sneeze. Everything seemed to grow bigger around the group until Vanessa realized that they were shrinking. Soon they were sprite size.

"Now I want one of you—how about you, Vanessa—to step up next to me . . . OK, good. Now will yourself to fly."

Vanessa wished with all her might that she could fly and was sent rocketing into the air.

Stream caught Vanessa and saved her from smashing herself into a tree.

"Much more gentle, Princess. May I call you that?" She smiled soothingly. Vanessa nodded and sent herself gently to the ground.

Neal grinned. "OK, so we don't do what Ms. Rocket here just did?" he asked. Stream giggled at the ridiculous nickname. "At least her landing was perfect," she answered.

Vanessa stuck her tongue out at Neal. Soon enough, the whole group was sailing up toward the branches. Vanessa caught her breath as she beheld the tiny city. It was wonderful. Little houses had been built into the trees decorated with moss to make it look camouflaged.

Stream led them through the treetops and came to a densely forested piece of land. It was surrounded with a forest of fern and mushrooms. They landed in a bare patch of dirt, and Stream called out a code to the silence,

Ferns and bracken,
Make good snackin'.
But put it to a test,
And I like mushroom best!

Suddenly, the woods were full of commotion. Little concealed doors opened from the mushrooms around them, and tiny people with pointy-hooded cloaks of forest color poured out. Vanessa recognized them as gnomes. Sprites spilled from the branches above them, singing little jigs that she had never heard before.

They led the group over a stream and to the front of a large oak tree. The twisted tree had many holes in it and as she gazed at the biggest hole, she noticed it was actually a door. The door opened, and a tall graceful sprite in a silver cobweb dress came out. She was lissome (as her aunt Filix called it) with a brilliant smile upon her curved lips. She had bright green eyes, nice olive skin, and jet-black hair that reminded Vanessa of someone she knew but she could quite place it. The sprite had a fine silver crown inlaid with sapphires that rested upon her head. As the attractive sprite came closer, Vanessa realized that everyone else was kneeling.

She was about to do the same when the beautiful sprite put a delicate hand on her shoulder. "No, my sweet child. A princess does not kneel to another royal. It is not right," she said gently. "My name is Queen Silva. It is a pleasure to . . . Rex? Septimus? Is that you?" she broke off in confusion.

Rex stood, a sheepish smile on his face. "Yes?" he asked.

Queen Silva opened her arms wide, tears of joy in her eyes. Rex ran forward, with Septimus following with surprise. Both boys hugged the queen with all their might as she sang out with happiness. "Oh! Rex! Septimus! I've missed you so much!"

Rex kissed her on the cheek and answered with a laugh, "I've missed you too, Mother!"

CHAPTER 19

THE JEWEL

After recovering from the "mother" surprise, Vanessa realized she was famished. Silva ordered three of her servants to bring out a table. The queen asked several gnomes in colorful pink and green cloaks if they could fetch some food. Vanessa watched as a lily-pink-cloaked gnome with wispy blond hair brought a large tray of mushrooms, berries, assorted leaves, and a hunk of what looked like acorn bread.

Silva took a seat at the front of the table and asked if Vanessa would sit on her right. Vanessa was surprised. "But, Your Majesty, I—" she began.

Silva waved her hand. "Call me Silva. Go on."

And Vanessa continued. "Your Majest—I mean, Silva, don't you want to sit with your sons on either side of you?" she asked.

Silva smiled with understanding. "My sons are happy that I am here. Rex can sit on my left side. Septimus is also happy that I am here, but I am sure that he wants to sit by a special someone other than me," she said and pointed in Septimus's direction.

There, Septimus was talking to a sprite with golden hair. Vanessa noticed that the sprite-girl looked very uncomfortable.

Silva giggled. "Now *all* my children are here," she said. "Go see Calypso. She loves making new friends."

Vanessa obeyed, and walked over to the sprite.

"Hello, my name is Vanessa," she said. Septimus was just talking about some creature in the forest when Vanessa came up. Calypso looked quite relieved to see Vanessa, and she smiled kindly. Vanessa nodded at Septimus, "Hi," she said. He grinned, "Hi. If you'll excuse me, I need to find Rex," he said. Calypso smiled at him as he passed, then her shoulders slumped as he disappeared behind a tree. She seemed to realize Vanessa was there, and she straightened up, "Um, hello. I suppose Queen Silva introduced me already?" she asked. Vanessa nodded, wonder how she knew, "Yes, but—" she got no farther as Calypso grabbed her hand, "How about we go for a flight?" she suggested. Vanessa allowed herself to be pulled into the air as Calypso led her into the tall trees, flying up till the ground below looked tiny.

Once they reached the lush treetops, Calypso sat down on a moss-covered branch that was thick enough to seat twenty-five sprites. Vanessa sat down beside her, not entirely sure how to start a conversation.

"So you are a sprite," she said eventually.

Calypso grinned. "Well, not really. That is something that most sprites and I have in common. We are half sprites. My mother is a sprite. My father ... well, he is something else. What are you? Kapacki?"

Vanessa shook her head, "No, I'm an elf. What is a Kapacki? No one will explain that to me!" she complained.

Calypso nodded. "They probably don't wish to talk about the beasts. The kapacki dislike most creatures, and the feeling is mutual. Kapacki are very dangerous animals, cross between a dragon and a wolf. They are in the same danger category as dragons, tsunami giants, or just giants for that matter, basilisks, and stormkin. They look like wolves, but their bones, claws, and teeth are made of a metal so strong that it can crunch anything from tin to rock to black adamant as if it were lily butter. They can come in any size and color. I believe Truncus has already told you that most kapacki have avatars, like Luna Flask, Aurora Fur, Azure Quall, Gale Woods, Russet Fang, and Nimbus Coat," she said.

Vanessa's eyes widened in astonishment, and she felt a bit of suspicion crawl onto her features. "How did you manage to know about that?" she asked.

Calypso looked a sheepish. "You were close to our forest—I was just curious—I thought that you were intruders, so I spied on you," she explained hastily.

Vanessa smiled reassuringly, but a frown of sadness overtook her. "Then you know that Septimus is a traitor."

Calypso looked away from Vanessa. "I don't want to talk about it now." Vanessa cringed. "Oh! I am so sorry. I didn't mean to offend."

Calypso turned around to look Vanessa in the eyes. "No, I mean I don't want to talk about it here. And I think there is something we need to discuss. Follow me," she said and grabbed Vanessa.

They took off down a steep trail around a few hills. Within a few minutes, they were at a large pond (which to Vanessa, seemed like a sea). In the center, a small island was placed, surrounded by seven other islands, each were smaller than the center one.

Calypso zipped Vanessa to the middle one and landed there herself. "This center island is one of the seven sisters' sacred ground. They represent the seven daughters of Terra," she explained.

Vanessa looked around. "Was Terra a person?" she asked.

Calypso laughed in wonder. "Yes! She was the one who founded this planet. Actually, I suppose that I should not say that in past tense. Terra not only founded it—she *is* it."

And Vanessa gasped. "She is a world? How?" she asked.

Calypso sighed. "Long story. On the shrine, we are protected from the effects of time. How do I begin? OK, so . . . long ago, there was a world far out in space. The world housed peculiar beings. These beings resembled an elf but they were enormous. We call them world giants. They have the ability to turn into worlds when they get into space. The larger the giant, then the larger the world. World giants never stop growing, so even our world is still expanding. Here is a story that might mean something to you. One of the giants was called Ter. He was big, strong, and tough. He fell in love with another giant called Ra, and they soon got married and had three children.

"Ra was graceful, gentle, and beautiful. She was like a she-elf. When Ra gave birth to the three children, an alien race came in and destroyed many of the world giants—but Ra's three children. There were two girls and one boy—who we now know as Luna, Sol, and Terra. The ones who invaded are known as the malus," Calypso explained.

Vanessa could only blink. "Wow. OK, now I know about the giant invasion, but who are the seven sisters?" she asked.

Calypso nodded. "First, I want to ask if you can see the names of Ter and Ra in their daughter?"

Vanessa thought for a moment. "Ter, Ra. Oh I know! Terra! And that happens to mean earth in Latin," she comprehended.

Calypso smiled. "Good, now . . . Terra met another world giant that was named Mons. They married and had eight children; seven were sisters and one was a boy. He was lost to us."

Vanessa raised her eyebrows. "That is a lot of children. My mom can't even handle two!" she muttered.

Calypso giggled and continued. "Each sister had powers that controlled aspects of this world: Aqua was water; Nebula was mist and clouds; Anima for life, growth (like plants), and animals; Lux for light; Tenebra for darkness and stone; Pax for peace; and Freya for love," she said.

Vanessa frowned, deep in thought. "The name *Freya* isn't love in Elvish. It isn't even Elvish at all," she noted.

Calypso agreed readily. "No, Freya's name is actually world giant language. So is yours. In fact, Neal, Abigail, and my name are world giant words. Calypso means jewel. Neal means sword. Abigail means healer. Vanessa means warrior," she said.

Vanessa thought for a moment. "So what would your name be in Latin?" she asked.

Calypso sighed. "My name would be—or is—*Gemma*."

Vanessa gasped in utter shock. "Wait a minute! Gemma is the name of Rex's and Septimus's sister... daughter of the queen!" she said.

Calypso nodded with reluctance. "That's right. I am she. Or more properly said, I am Gemma Lyra Noctis, sister to Rex and Septimus. And as you probably already know, I am the one that should be dead."

Abigail awoke from a dreamless sleep. This was very unusual for Abigail as her vivid dreams were usually filled with flowers, bunnies, snowflakes, and soft things that were cuddly and cute. Then Abigail remembered what had happened: Rex gone, Mom kicking door open, Dark Lord's spells, then darkness. Abigail's eyes flew open, and she was surprised to find that she wasn't in a dark dungeon like she had expected to be. Instead, she was lying on a soft, silky, king-sized bed in a cream-colored room. Half of it was a balcony, which had no doors, letting in sunshine and birdsong.

Abigail groaned in resistance. "Let me guess, I am either dreaming, finally, or I died and now I am in heaven," she said aloud.

A feminine laugh came from the bedside. "Oh, Abigail, you have your mother's humor. You are not in heaven yet, but had Tonitrus not saved you, you would be on your way there."

Abigail sat up straight. "Who are you?" she asked, glancing around the bedside. There sat a beautiful woman with shimmering black hair, who looked like she was in her thirties, a little like Regina. She smiled through curved pink lips.

"You really don't know? Well, my name is Aurora, queen of the elves, wife of King Tonitrus, and mother of Filix and Regina," she answered.

Abigail gasped with utter shock. "Regina? That is my mother's name! Would that mean she would be a princess? No, she would be a queen, since she is too old to be a princess. Filix was also your daughter? Does that mean that I have an aunt? Awesome! If Regina is a queen, that means Vanessa and I are princesses! Awesome! I have met a queen! Awesome!" she said.

Aurora shook her head in amusement. "I think you need to find a new word! Anyway, yes, you are right about all that, except that Filix and Regina are not queens. Long ago, they revoked that title, leaving that responsibility to you and your sister Vanessa. Now I want you to rest. You will need all the rest you can get for the war," she said.

Abigail frowned. "What war? Against the Dark Lord? And by the way, I want to explore. Please let me! I love to explore! she exclaimed.

Aurora's smile darkened, and she became very serious. "Young lady, you will never go anywhere. You are going to be locked up for time and all eternity," she said gravely.

Abigail's eyes widened, and she was about to say something when Aurora cracked a smile. "Just kidding. You and I are going to explore the whole of the Citra Isles," she said cheerfully.

Abigail smiled. "Awesome. What are the Citra Isles?" she asked.

Aurora nodded. "The Citra Isles are seventeen isles or islands located in the Elven Ocean. They surround one big island called Celestis Island. Right now, you are on the eighth isle called Efil, which is next to the more popular Elisium.

"The name Elisium in Draconic means paradise. Each of the seventeen isles has a popular language, like Elvish, Dwarvish, Impish, Wolfish, Felinian, Silvan, Giantish, Terrian, and so on.

"Terrian is the language that we speak now. It is a mix of Elvish and Giantish. To understand it all, it is best that you go to the many libraries. You will also need to go get dressed," she said, pointing to a beautiful light green and blue dress. It had a billowy bottom part, chest, and sleeves, with a snug waist.

Abigail arose out of the cushy bed and wriggled out of the light pink nightgown. After dressing, she went with the queen to breakfast at the roof top garden on the mansion-like building.

After breakfast, Aurora led Abigail out what Abigail realized was a small castle and into a seemingly endless forest of beeches, birches, maples, oaks, and other trees she didn't recognize. They followed a small dirt path, watching the wildlife. Abigail discovered Aurora loved animals and nature just as much as she did.

"Do you like white-tail fox-deer?" the queen asked.

Abigail nodded enthusiastically, even though she had no idea what a fox-deer was. Aurora smiled and sang a song in Elvish. Abigail only caught the ending part, which said something about a stag and a she-elf. Suddenly, two deer bounded out of the trees, leaping around Abigail.

Aurora swung onto a large stag, whose name was Bracken-hoof. After Abigail mounted a graceful doe, they started at a lope around the forest. Abigail tried to make herself lighter, fearing that the young doe would fall down from her weight. Aurora smiled, feeling sympathetic.

"Do not worry about our weight, we are no heavier than feathers. And to add to that, these deer can carry oxen," she said to Abigail.

Bracken-hoof shook his antlered head. "I could carry *two* oxen," he bragged playfully.

Abigail nearly fell off the deer when her own mount talked too. "Don't listen to Bracken-hoof. He is just a big show-off! He nearly collapsed trying to carry a calf," she quipped.

Abigail snorted with slight derision. "OK. Do you have a name?" she asked.

The doe shook her head sadly. "No, my mother ran off when I was a faun. Elves took care of me and prepared me for you. Will you name me?" she asked.

Abigail brightened. "Sure! How about Viola?" she asked.

The doe gave Abigail an uncertain look, as if thinking that Abigail was teasing her, but wisely realized that the young she-elf was not. "No, actually, it has to be a name like Bracken-hoof's . . . like . . . two words . . .," she said.

Abigail thought for a moment longer, searching and prodding her memory furiously. A sudden wind blew around her, stirring a cherry tree in bloom. A storm of petals rained on Abigail, popping a name into her head.

"Oooh! I know! How about the name Petal-storm?" she asked.

The doe skipped in happiness. "Perfect!" she brayed.

CHAPTER 20

THE PURPLE TRUTH

Vanessa strolled around her room, waiting for Silva. Gemma—or Calypso—had told Vanessa that Queen Silva already knew about her little secret, and they were going to have a meeting. Gemma was in the room with her, but she kept quiet. Suddenly, the door of the mushroom house burst open, and the queen came through. "Hello, Vanessa, Gemma. I have bad news."

Gemma frowned. "What is it?" she inquired.

Silva took out a roll of paper from her dress pocket and unrolled it. To Vanessa's surprise, it was a modern-day calendar that was set on June.

"This is the problem," Silva began. Vanessa frowned but was cut off by Silva. "Septimus's sixteenth birthday," she said.

Vanessa gasped with understanding. "Oh! That was when the Dark Lord said Septimus could kill Luna Flask!" she said.

Silva nodded. "Yes. What Septimus doesn't know is that Luna Flask actually *saved* Gemma. Luna is very important to me, so I would rather she were not killed. She is also very important in your prophecy, Vanessa. You will need her to save the world. Today, it is the fourteenth of June. Septimus's birthday is on the seventeenth," she said.

Vanessa frowned. "Can't we just strap Septimus down until June 17 passes?" she asked.

Silva sighed. "Don't I wish. However, Septimus has his means of escaping. He is powerful. Besides, I'm not sure we could catch him!" she said. Gemma raised a hand, "What if we go ahead and warn Luna?"

Silva frowned, "It might work. Let's hope Luna would trust us. That just might do it." She said thoughtfully.

A sudden knocking at the door surprised them all. "Come in," said Silva.

Rex poured through the small opening, gasping for air as if he had run a long way. He looked very distressed.

"What's wrong, Rex?" Silva asked anxiously.

Rex looked up at her. "Septimus is gone!"

Silva helped Rex into a chair and took one look at the two girls. "Vanessa, take Calypso and try to find him!" she exclaimed..

Gemma (now Calypso) frowned. "He has three days till his birthday! We know that he is going to kill Luna, so shouldn't we head straight toward her?" she asked.

"No, you don't know what she looks like," Silva said, shaking her head.

"Vanessa, why don't you—wait a minute! *You* have seen Luna Flask before! I see the white glow around you!" she said suddenly.

Vanessa scanned herself for a "white glow" but could not see one. She just saw the brown interior of the mushroom house.

Silva continued with a sparkle of hope. "You have met her before! You might not have recognized her, but you have seen her before! No Kapacki can change their appearance, besides changing into their natural state, so you would recognize her," she said excited.

Vanessa was very confused, but the queen just continued. "Did anyone seem to look . . . inhuman to you? Perhaps at the grocery store, the park, or at your school?" she asked.

Vanessa thought of the people she had met while on earth. She started on the people she had seen at the grocery store. Nothing.

Silva stared thoughtfully at her. "Did you see anyone with white hair? Dark blue eyes? Pointed ears?" she probed.

Vanessa thought longer, maybe a teacher at her school. Then she remembered—Ms. Carafe.

Vanessa jumped. "Yes! I remember! My teacher Ms. Carafe!" she said.

Silva nodded with wonder. "Carafe means flask, of course!" she said. "Now you need something to ride on to get there."

Vanessa was thinking about how Rex had taught her how to light a fire. The queen's words brought a name to Vanessa's head. "Ventus!" she said.

The queen and her daughter looked at Vanessa with confusion. "What?" they asked in unison.

Vanessa smiled, quite proud that she remembered. "Ventus," she repeated. "It is the name of the mare that I rode to get to Terra."

Silva's eyes widened, "Ventus? That is the name of an elven horse… she is one of the last. If you are sure she can take you, than there is no better ride for you to take. If you rode her, you can call her. You should try." She urged.

Vanessa nodded. "OK. But first, we need to get into normal shape," she said excited, taking Gemma by hand.

Together, the girls flew out of the mushroom house and swooped over to the same spot where they had become sprite-like. Gemma took a handful of blue dust and blew it on Vanessa. Instantly, she began to grow. Gemma needed no dust. She just closed her eyes and began to grow with Vanessa.

Once in normal size, Vanessa willed all her strength to gather. She focused her mind and strength in to one word. "VENTUS!" she said. Suddenly, the sound of a horse's hooves filled the air. A flash of black swirled around her, and a voice like lightning spoke. "Rider, Vanessa, you called me, how shall I be of service?" spoke Ventus.

Vanessa smiled. "How about a little ride? We need to save the world. Oh, and don't call me 'Rider,' please."

Ventus snorted with playfulness. "My pleasure," she whinnied.

Vanessa scrambled onto Ventus and grabbed Gemma. With effort, Gemma swung up behind Vanessa and nodded. Together, they rode to the nearest portal to earth, Vanessa urging the fast Ventus to gallop.

Suddenly, a roar rumbled behind them. Vanessa whipped her head around to see what had thundered such a sound. She gasped as she beheld a thirty-foot malus hurtling toward them.

Ventus had noticed it too. The horse pushed all of her strength into going her fastest. Vanessa could barely stay on as the horse rocketed forward, sending up dust in her wake. The malus was soon behind them. After a long thirty minutes of riding hard, Vanessa sensed a slowing of Ventus. No horse could run forever. Vanessa knew enough about horses that if they pushed themselves too hard for too long, they would get injured. Vanessa told Ventus to stop, and the horse reluctantly halted at a pond. Gemma slid off, rubbing her back painfully. Vanessa hopped off stiffly as well. Looking around the pond, she noticed a large waterfall further ahead. Interested, she walked toward it, stopped, and stared at it. It looked like the perfect lair of some magical creature. Vanessa froze, about to run as she heard an odd sound come from the waterfall. It was like hard scales scraping against rock. Too late. A long purple snakelike tail shot out of the darkness and curled itself around Vanessa's waist. Vanessa tried to scream, but the breath was knocked out of her as the tail pulled her into the cave.

Vanessa yelped as she was dragged onto a slimy wet rock. She looked around her saw only darkness. Sitting up, she tried to make out her surroundings. A purple light flared and the cave was illuminated. Two glowing eyes, intensely violet in color, fixed on her. They were the size of small tables, and they made Vanessa freeze in fear. Not so much from her being mesmerized, but more like I'm-going-to-eat-you fear. Vanessa gulped, "Uh, hello," she said. The eyes flared brighter, and Vanessa made out a huge body. Purple scales coated an immense body where two giant wings were folded on its back. As the scaly tale flicked back and forth, Vanessa realized with a shiver of fear she was facing a dragon.

Suddenly, a rich female voice sounded around Vanessa. "It has been a long time since I have treated an elf to my . . . er . . . *hospitality*," said the purple statue. The terribly weird thing about the dragon was she didn't open her mouth to say what was said. She just spoke them like how she might normally growl.

Vanessa gulped in fright. "Who are you? I am guessing that this beautiful animal in front of me is a dragon," she said as nicely as she could.

The dragon seemed to smile. "Of course. My name is Syringa."

Vanessa figured that dragons were susceptible to flattering.

The dragon lifted her magnificent head. "We must be on our way if we are to stop that mangy traitor. Do you agree, Vanessa?" she inquired.

Vanessa blinked in surprise. "WE?" she repeated. "Wait... I thought you wanted to eat me! And how did you know my name?" she said.

Syringa growled a sound that sounded like a laugh. "Why would I eat my cousin? Though you *would* make a delicious meal . . . well, I will refrain from having you over for dinner, or just *you for dinner*, since my mother would be angry if I swallowed kin. Do they fill young elves' heads with clouds these days?" She snickered.

The sight was strange, seeing a serpentine creature laugh like that, but Vanessa had seen so many strange things that this did not register in her confused brain. Vanessa felt faintly indignant that Syringa had said her brain was of fog, but then she thought back to what the dragon had said and that matter seemed more important, "COUSIN? How? You're a—you know . . .," she yelped.

Syringa frowned. "You really don't know?" she asked.

Vanessa growled with frustration. "Would you people stop saying that? OF COURSE, I DON'T KNOW! Why would I ask? No one tells me anything!" she screamed.

Syringa looked startled. "Well, fit the clues in! If I am your cousin, then that means my mother is your father's sister! That means that he is what she is!" she said.

Vanessa shook her head with anger. The dragoness continued as if talking with a foggy-headed child—which to Syringa, she pretty much was.

The dragoness growled with frustration and spoke in a hurry. "What is embroidered on his flag? What has he tried to tell you for as long as he has known you? Why does he love silver shirts with scales imprinted on them? What are all the books he has given you about? What does his very name *mean*?" she asked seriously. The tense silence was deafening.

Suddenly, Vanessa felt realization hit her like a ton of bricks. "H-he's a dragon!" she cried.

CHAPTER 21

THE SIXTEENTH BIRTHDAY

Vanessa and Syringa flew out of the cave and alighted on a rocky outcropping of land just above Ventus and Gemma. On top of Syringa, Vanessa felt powerful. She felt like she was invincible. Syringa landed gracefully, scaring Ventus and Gemma out of their skins. She was smaller for a dragon but still huge. Syringa's slender body was the size of a school bus with a fifteen-foot tail. She fixed Gemma with a magnificent purple gaze, freezing the beautiful girl mid-run.

"Tsk, tsk. Someone needs to learn manners! You wouldn't deprive a guest of your cordiality, now would you?" purred Syringa.

Gemma struggled against the dragon's paralyzing grip. "Y-you m-must let me g-go!" she forced out.

Vanessa put a hand against Syringa's side. "Let her go, Syringa. She is… a friend," murmured Vanessa.

The dragoness sighed. "Just when I was having fun," she muttered, releasing Gemma.

Gemma fell to the ground and looked up at Vanessa with awe. "How did you do that? You just spoke Draconic!" she whispered.

Vanessa frowned deeply with a hint of confusion. "I did?" she asked.

Syringa nodded. "Yes, you did," she affirmed, purple tail swishing around and leveling a few trees and bushes.

Gemma looked at Syringa apprehensively, "So. You are her charming cousin," she said. If dragons could raise eyebrows, Syringa certainly pulled it off, "And?" she asked. Gemma shook her head,

"Nothing! Just… charming!" she answered quickly, changing the subject abruptly.

"We need to get going. The malus we left behind won't have sat idle. If we want to catch Septimus, then we must leave now." She said. Vanessa nodded,

"Syringa will fly us to Luna Flask. Hopefully we will get to her first. Meanwhile, Ventus will go for reinforcements," she said. The horse nodded, and galloped off. Syringa nodded, "Okay, climb on!" Gemma glanced doubtfully at the dragon's back,

"Um, isn't your back a bit… spiny?" she asked. Syringa looked at the spines along her back, seeming to realize them for the first time, "Oh, that's nothing. Watch this." She said. Suddenly the spines where they would sit sank into her skin, leaving a space for them to ride. Vanessa wasted no time on climbing onto Syringa. She was eager to ride a dragon, even though a bit of her shrank at the idea of the dangerous creature. *Just because it calls you its cousin and talks normally, what makes you think its good? What's to stop it from eating you up and going back to sleep in its cave?* But she ignored those thoughts. Gemma followed her up onto Syringa, and seated herself behind Vanessa. Vanessa grabbed a spine in front of her to hold on, and Gemma wrapped her arms tightly around Vanessa's waist,

"I'm afraid of heights," Gemma whimpered to Vanessa. Vanessa smiled sympathetically, "Sorry," she said.

An instant before they took off, Vanessa could feel Syringa's muscles bunch, and then they were airborne. Vanessa screamed with joy as they rocketed toward the sky. Of course, she had flown before but never like this. Again, the feeling like she owned the sky coursed through her body. *I could live like this!* she thought with relish.

Gemma, however, wasn't enjoying the flight. "AHHH!" she hollered. "I want to take Ventus! I WANT TO TAKE VENTUS!"

A small chuckle rose from the soaring Syringa. "You know I am being gentle? Most dragons would rip your breath away . . . though not for you, Vanessa. You have a very special power. You could be floating in space, and you would breathe as if in a nice meadow, enjoying a fresh breeze."

Gemma groaned, "Can you speak Terrian, please? You seem quite mouthy!"

But Syringa ignored her. Syringa communicated through Vanessa's and Gemma's minds, almost reading their mess of thoughts.

With a sweep of her strong wings, Syringa soared higher. Vanessa grasped tighter the spine in front as they jetted through the cloudless sky.

Vanessa didn't remember falling asleep. All she remembered were the magnificent skies, oddly shaped clouds, and the violet-colored head of her cousin. Suddenly, she found herself being shaken awake by Gemma. Vanessa was lying on soft grass under a maple tree. She sat up and realized that she was in the park next to her school in Monterey, California. Syringa was resting her head on a swing, and Gemma was sitting on a seesaw. The sight was so strange and so funny that Vanessa had to suppress a quick, much needed giggle.

"Um, hi. Why are there no humans here?" she asked with amusement.

Syringa sighed with unrestrained frustration. "Well, duh! They are all in the classes! Are we going or earthbound?"

Vanessa nodded. "OK, let's go!" she said happily.

Gemma nodded, a twinkle of joyfulness in her blue eyes. "Of course. But first, Syringa needs to become a little human!" she said.

Vanessa didn't understand, but she just kept quiet. Syringa sat up, shook out her dusty scales, and transformed into a woman. The sight was so startling that Vanessa nearly fell over. Syringa now had on a purple shirt that had a pattern that looked like scales and boot-cut blue jeans. Her skin was slightly pale with an olive touch, and her hair was tied up into a ponytail and was so black that it seemed to have a purple sheen. Her eyes were like violet stars.

Together, the group walked into the school. Vanessa guided Syringa and Gemma to her old classroom. Just as they were going to open the door, a voice called to them. "Hello? Do you need something?" It was the principal Mrs. Johnson.

Vanessa cringed. "Uh, yeah," she said turning. "We need to speak to Ms. Carafe," she told the overweight principal.

Mrs. Johnson shook her gray-haired head. "Sorry. Ms. Carafe just left. She said that it was urgent. Should I leave a message?" she asked.

Vanessa frowned. *This is not good!* she thought. "That's OK. Do you know, by chance, where she went?" she asked.

Mrs. Johnson nodded. "In fact, I do! She told me that if I saw a dark-haired girl around the age of fifteen asking for her, I should tell her that Ms. Carafe went west by the old parking lot. She said one of you would know where that was," the old woman griped. Vanessa nodded and thanked her.

Syringa took both girls by the hand and raced out of the door at superhuman speed. As they ran out into the open, purple dragon's wings sprouted from Syringa's shoulders, and she flapped several times to get into the air. She soared the two girls to the abandoned parking lot. The window of a nearby building exploded, and out jumped Ms. Carafe. She tumbled out of the building and into a parking lot sign.

Vanessa gasped as the sign crumpled into a lump of metal. Luna Flask dove beside a tree and rolled away into the open. She had two sleek swords in her hands, and her pearly white hair was tied up into a braid. Another figure jumped off the building and ran toward Luna Flask. Vanessa realized that it was Septimus. She also realized he had a gash above his eyes and a large bruise forming on his arm.

Gemma took one look at her brother and sighed sadly. "Wob, emoc!" she said forcefully.

Instantly, an impressive slender ivory bow entwined with purple gems appeared in her hand. In the string, a long slender arrow with three white feathers was placed. Before Vanessa or Syringa could stop her, Gemma drew back the string and solemnly fired at her eldest brother.

CHAPTER 22

A TRICK OF THE EYE

The smooth arrow suddenly bounced off a purple snakelike tail. Syringa had changed back into a dragon and now was blocking Gemma's range.

"What are you doing?" hissed Syringa. "Why are you firing at *him*?"

Gemma hissed back angrily back. "Killing the traitor! What did you think?" she snarled.

Syringa looked confused. "But Septimus is not the traitor—*she* is!" she said, pointing with her tail to the *third* person.

This one had arrived on a black motorcycle, and was dressed in an all-black twinset despite the hot day. Vanessa could not see who it was because there was a black mask covering the figure's face. She was definitely a girl, for the black suit was form-fitting, and the woman let her hair flow out behind her. The strange woman held up a ball of flame and threw it at Luna Flask.

Septimus drew his shield and sword from nowhere and deflected the ball of fire. Luna Flask looked as startled as Vanessa felt. Though she tried to run away from Septimus and the woman, she was blocked by another ball of fire. The woman in black drew a spear from thin air and aimed it at Luna Flask. Syringa slammed into the evil lady and blew a torrent of purple flame at her.

Syringa tried to slash at the woman, but the black-dressed girl rolled away. Gemma attempted to shoot at the girl, but the arrow missed. Vanessa shape-changed into a leopard and tried to swipe at the woman but only got in a shallow gash in the stomach.

The woman hesitated for a second, looking at Vanessa sadly through the oddly shaped mask. Vanessa realized that the mask was in the shape of an animal—a bird. The girl dashed toward Luna Flask, spear in hand, until she was only twenty feet away from the Kapacki.

Suddenly, the woman in black threw the spear. Just before it hit Luna's chest, Septimus jumped in its way, allowing the long spear to pierce his own stomach instead of Luna's. As he fell to the ground, he managed to feebly knock the woman's mask off, revealing her beautiful features.

Vanessa gasped as she beheld the face. The woman that was trying to kill Luna Flask, who had just wounded Septimus, was Regina Nox.

CHAPTER 23

MOON-FLAGON

Vanessa suddenly let out a sob as she looked at her mother. "Mom!" she yelled as Gemma and Syringa charged toward Septimus. Regina turned toward her, but Vanessa was surprised to find that Regina's eyes were green, instead of the usual blue.

"I am not your mother, Vanessa. Haven't you figured *that* out? I suppose your mother never told you she had a twin sister. I was sent here from the Dark Lord to stop the prophecy. That means killing you unfortunately," she said, drawing another spear from thin air.

Just as she was about to throw it, a force knocked her down to the ground. Vanessa found herself staring at one of her favorite people in the world.

"Oh no, you don't. You can't just spear my brother, try to kill my girlfriend, and get away with it!" said Rex.

Vanessa's sob turned into a happy yelp. "Rex! You are seriously the best person in the world!" she shrieked and hugged him.

Rex laughed also. "You didn't already know that?" he asked.

Then from behind her, another familiar voice spoke. "Rex, you never said *anything* about you being my daughter's boyfriend!" said Drake sternly.

"Did I say girlfriend? I meant... er... um... friend-girl... like a friend... but it's a girl.... Um, yeah," Rex stuttered to a halt.

Vanessa turned to her father and hugged him too. "Please tell me that *you* don't have a twin too?" she asked.

Drake laughed. "Nope. But I have an elder sister that looks nothing like me!," he pointed out.

Rex nodded and turned toward Septimus. Vanessa realized that Queen Silva had come too. Now she was healing Septimus and calming Luna Flask. Once Silva mended Septimus's wound, she stood up and brushed the dirt off her pants and shirt.

"Well," said Vanessa, "Luna Flask, now that this trio of kids saved your life, I suppose you owe them. How about telling them your real name?" she suggested.

Luna Flask sighed. "Thank you, Vanessa, Gemma, and also you, Syringa. Oh, and also to you, Septimus. Without you, I would be dead. I suppose now that I am being hunted, I might as well tell you my real name. Vanessa, remember the prophecy? There is a name in there that will tell you plenty," she hinted.

Vanessa thought back to it. "I don't remember any person named Luna Flask," she said.

Luna Flask's lips curved into a smile, "My name now is only a kind of 'translation.' Carafe meant flask, so what does flask mean?" probed Luna.

Vanessa thought for a moment. "Bottle? Jug?" she tried.

Luna shook her head.

"Hipflask? Container? Vessel?" she asked.

Luna shook her head. "Neither of those. Try again," she responded.

Vanessa thought back to the prophecy. *The dark king's blood shall fill M OON-FLAGON.*

Vanessa gasped. "Moon-flagon! Your name is Moon-flagon!" she yelped.

Luna, now Moon-flagon, nodded. "Yes, that is my name. In the prophecy, I am supposed to drink a dark king's blood," she answered.

Vanessa made a disgusted face. "Drink someone's blood? Gross! I thought you were a Kapacki, not a vampire!"

Luna Flask rolled her dark blue eyes with annoyance. "I don't actually *drink* blood. I *eat* them and make their blood into a drink, usually. *Then* I drink their blood. But that is another story. Umbra is the Dark Lord, the one described in the prophecy, so that means that his blood is of shadow. Do know how tasteless shadow is? Have you ever tried to drink darkness?" she complained. Vanessa didn't really want to know how shadow blood tasted.

Septimus stood and walked over to them, a frown on his tired face. "Gemma," he muttered.

Gemma looked at him with sadness in her eyes. "Septimus, I'm so sorry I tricked you into thinking I was gone," she whispered.

Rex looked up. "GEMMA?" he gasped.

Gemma wouldn't meet his eyes. "Yes," she began but was cut off when Rex gave her a hug.

"I missed you so much! Where have you been?" he asked happily.

Gemma seemed surprised by his enthusiasm. "With Silva. Moon-flagon actually saved me," she said.

Septimus's frown deepened. "Why did you hide from us?" the hurt evident in his voice. Gemma looked as if she was going to cry. "I know. But if I hadn't, then maybe I would have caused even more trouble. As I told you—"

She was interrupted. "Can we pause the drama saga? I can smell Malus on their way to finish us off," Syringa begged. Everyone agreed.

"I suppose I will have to turn into Nogard," Drake sighed.

Vanessa frowned. "What's a Nagaurd?"

Drake chuckled. "*Nogard*—in Draconic or Giant, it's a name given to me when in dragon form. It means dragon. It is backward as you can see. Anyway, everyone, back up!" he barked.

Syringa was already in dragon form, so she backed off. When everyone was a good ways away, Drake started to transform. One instant, he had been her regular good-looking dad. The next, he was a silver dragon the size of three school buses with a tail that could wrap around him twice. His eyes were a piercing dark blue, and he had a row of sharp spines along his back just like Syringa. He looked at Vanessa and spoke to her mind in the language that was most natural to them both.

"Your turn," he growled.

Vanessa was about to protest when an understanding hit her like a brick. Stepping away from him, Vanessa thought about her strength and an anger deep inside that had been there since she could remember. Then suddenly, she transformed into a dragon too. She was about the size of Syringa but silver like her father. The sunlight glinted off her dark scales, making them sparkle magnificently. From her radar senses, she could feel pride sparking from Drake, now Nogard, in intense flashes. Syringa was happy too but more surprised than anything. Rex's eyes widened in astonishment, and he backed up next to Gemma.

His fear made Vanessa feel a little hurt deep inside, but it was pushed to the back of her mind as Syringa murmured next to her "Try to breath fire" in Draconic. Vanessa threw back her head and opened her mouth, letting a torrent of blue flame burst out of her. She was exhilarated. She turned to the group.

"OK, who wants to ride on me?" she asked with a grin.

Rex backed away. "I think Gemma and I will go on Nogard," he said.

Nogard frowned. "Vanessa, I think you should carry only one person. It may be too much for your first time to carry several people, especially passing through the portal."

Vanessa nodded. "Sure. What about you, Septimus? Could I be honored enough to tote you around?" she asked with a wink.

Septimus bowed in mock respect. "As you wish, Princess," he said in formal tones then jumped onto her scaly back. Vanessa stretched her wings as everyone got situated. It was time for takeoff.

Syringa followed Drake, and then the very excited Vanessa sprang into the air, flying by what must have been instinct. They soared above

the clouds, Silva put a protective shield around those who could not
breathe well in the thin air. Fortunately, Septimus could. He lifted one
hand in the air, feeling the wind rush through his fingers.

Drake was in the lead, flying them higher. Up ahead, Vanessa could
see a gold mist in the air. It was in the shape of a circle, just big enough
for Drake and Syringa to fly through. Since Vanessa was smaller, she
would have no trouble. Drake flapped again, then dove through the
gold mist, disappearing. Syringa flew through, and finally Vanessa dove
in as well. The feeling like stepping into a hot bath enveloped her. The
smell of spices was around her for a second, then as she passed through
the mist, all of the sensations evaporated. Vanessa stretched her wings,
a new warm breeze filling them, making her fly higher. She knew she
was in Terra. She was beginning to tell the difference. Everything felt
sharper in Terra. The smells were stronger, and on the breeze you could
almost feel the touch of trees against your skin just by the pine scent.
Septimus smiled, his arms in the air. He then remembered the drop
below, and decided to hold on tighter, grasping a spine on Vanessa's
back.

Vanessa smiled inwardly. "Do you want to have *real* fun?" she asked
him. Septimus looked at her in surprise. "More than this?" he asked
with a hint of fear. "Can you handle that?" he added.

Vanessa smiled. "Hold on tight!" she said, just before she soared
above the others. She swirled in circles for a minute, then looped over a
cloud. Septimus yelled, having fun with the agility of Vanessa's flight.
As she flew higher, the stars in the sky became brighter and more visible.
She and Septimus were too absorbed in the twinkling lights above that
they missed the shriek of protest as they hit something.

Vanessa whipped her head around to stare at the person with which
she had just collided. Hovering in midair was a nymph with platinum
hair, glaring at them through midnight blue eyes. Vanessa winced.

"I'm so sorry!" she exclaimed.

The nymph rolled her eyes and dusted off her glimmering gossamer
dress. Vanessa stared in surprise as the nymph muttered, "Can't you
ground lovers leave the sky and us alone? What does a star have to do to

get a little peace around here?" she said angrily with a hint of a Scottish accent. She started brushing off her shimmering dress, checking for rips or dirt.

Vanessa felt a bit embarrassed at flying into the girl, but she was more angry the brat hadn't gotten out of the way sooner.

Septimus gasped. "You are a star!" he said in amazement.

The nymph rolled her eyes again. "Oh, I wonder!" she said with a thick layer of sarcasm. "How did you figure that one out? Was it because she was glowing? Oh, I know! It was that she was just standing here in in the sky at around evening!" she griped.

Vanessa marveled at the radiant nymph. "You are the elven evening star! You are sometimes seen on earth, but usually, your presence is mistaken as a planet," she said.

The girl sniffed. "Humans—they mistake me for a volcanic piece of rock!" she said unhappily, drifting closer to the two.

Septimus smiled. "I know your name! It is Candentia! Sometimes, like you said, people call you Venus."

Candentia frowned. "Venus is my twin sister!"

Vanessa groaned. "Not more twins!"

Candentia smiled slyly, serving to make her features a bit mysterious. "Yes, I saw your little skirmish. You will have an even bigger one later," she said. Septimus raised an eyebrow,

"I suppose you stars will just sit around and watch this time," he sighed. Candentia looked indignant,

"Of course not! I will help. I am not going to just sit around here and shine all night. I mean, come on! How boring! The most interesting thing around here is singing. And last time I did a million stars fell because they were sung to sleep. Luna got soooo mad at me. I was grounded from shining for like, a week! Do you know how awful it is to just sit around here and have a staring contest with the moon?" she asked. Vanessa was surprised by the tirade. She was starting to get a bit sleepy from all the running around. She wondered about Candentia. Who was she?

Sensing Vanessa's curiosity of her, Candentia sighed. "I suppose I should introduce myself. I am Candentia Lyra Lux, daughter of Luna and Sol... obviously." Vanessa started, realizing Candentia was looking at her waiting for an introduction.

"My name is Vanessa Nox, princess of the elves, daughter of Regina and Drake Nox. Your turn," she said to Septimus.

Septimus nodded, hesitating a bit before saying his lineage. "Mine is Septimus Noctis, son Silva and Umbra Noctis."

Vanessa looked at him. "What did you just say?" she asked.

The wind seemed to stop, and the night grew darker before the tall elf answered.

Septimus nodded with more of his previous hesitation. "I am the son of Silva and Umbra Noctis." He shivered and winced on the inside, picturing her disgust of him as she discovered the truth. *But it might be even worse for Rex!* Rex needed a friend his age. Not much he could do about it now. He looked uncertainly at her, thinking about what he should tell her. She would find out sooner or later.

"That is why I, at first, tried to join him, but now I am fighting him. My father is the Dark Lord."

CHAPTER 24

THE SHAPE-SHIFTER INSIGNIA

Overcome by shock, Vanessa forgot to fly. Unfortunately, she was far above the clouds. Luckily, as a dragon, she could breathe at such heights. Then as if time started again, she and Septimus plummeted. She heard a sickening snap as Septimus's arm smashed against her wing. Candentia seemed surprised by their sudden disappearance and looked startled that Vanessa's flight had frozen. Vanessa tried to slow her descent but her skills at flying were still new, and with her enormous weight, nothing was slowing her and Septimus.

At the last minute, she turned into a huge falcon and pulled out of the dive, gently setting Septimus to the grassy ground, next to an oak tree.

They sat there in a forest of oaks, neither wanting to make any eye contact. He was sure that she was going to hate him, maybe not Gemma or even the very innocent Rex but surely him. He was always the outcast…. always the blamed one. He sighed, "It's okay if you're mad at me for being Umbra's son. I'm used to it."

Vanessa, however, didn't. She held his hand and said softly, "It's OK. I am not mad at you. You are nothing like your father. If anything, I am mad at Rex." She calmed. Septimus looked up. "Why?" he responded at last.

Vanessa shrugged. "When I turned into the dragon, he acted as if I was a monster. I'm not, am I?" she asked.

Septimus stared at her with surprise. "Of course not! I was proud of you when you turned into the silver dragon. They are very rare," he argued.

Vanessa nodded. "Yes, but I am not talking about you."

Septimus frowned. It was his turn to comfort her, "Rex will calm down," he said. "The prophecy said that 'the young man will find his jewel.' He has."

Vanessa frowned. "Yeah. That doesn't help me any," she said unhappily. Septimus had figured out most of the prophecy, and he shook his head, "Maybe," he said.

Before Vanessa could answer, a shining figure floated down from the skies. The graceful Candentia had arrived, and she had done so with a flare of light.

She sat down by Septimus and caressed his arm. "You're hurt," she murmured.

Septimus remembered his arm cracking when he fell. How come he felt no pain? It was a mystery to even him. Vanessa suddenly realized it too and climbed up from her stump on which she sat. "I know an herb that will help," she said as she ran off in search of it.

Vanessa quickly found the verdant leaves of the bone plant. She was very glad Filix had taught her about herbs. She collected the bright green leaves, making sure to leave some still on the plant. She put the leaves in her pocket and transformed into a deer. Loping along, Vanessa giggled as she came to the spot where Septimus and Candentia were. They were holding hands while talking in soft but serious voices. They saw Vanessa but didn't recognize her until she changed back into an elf. When they saw her transform back, they quickly let go of each other's hands, looking sheepish. Vanessa laughed. "It's fine, you guys. You make a cute couple."

Septimus turned red and was about to argue but saw that Candentia just smiled.

Septimus nodded, "Yeah, it's too bad that you and my brother don't get along all the time." Feeling the awkward silence that followed, he added, "Shall we be going?"

Vanessa nodded and began the transformation to the dragon, while Candentia put the ossis leaves on Septimus's wounds. The leaves healed his arm instantly. They both climbed onto her back, with Septimus in front. Vanessa took off with a powerful leap, clearing the ground and shooting into the darkening sky. The darkness was no hinderence for them now with Candentia was glowing brightly on her back. Vanessa was sure Candentia was glowing from joy.

Candentia actually did love it. "Now I know what it's like to be a shooting star," she said. They were silent for a while, drinking in the night air.

Vanessa spotted a campfire and angled over there, using her tail to turn. With her super senses, she zoomed in on the campfire. It was Drake and the others.

She made a quiet landing on a large tree and let Septimus and Candentia dismount. Then she changed back into a girl again. Candentia extinguished her glowing and grabbed Septimus in one hand and Vanessa in the other. She leaped out of the tree and floated toward the campfire. When they reached the camp, they landed, and Candentia brightened up. All the heads in the camp turned toward them.

Drake was the first to speak. "Well, I sure didn't expect *that* to be the next spark of entertainment." And everyone laughed. Vanessa smiled, but her good mood quickly vanished as Rex frowned in her direction. Then she realized that she was holding Septimus's hand, and she quickly withdrew it. Septimus realized it too and understood why. Drake lightened the mood with a hearty welcome, and they quickly got settled.

Vanessa knew she had to settle the "Rex Problem" first. She stalked over to him and asked Gemma if she could have him for a little while. She smiled. "Of course!" Gemma said with an evil smile in Rex's direction. Rex grumbled as Vanessa took him and walked to the woods.

Once they were out of earshot, Vanessa gave him a look. "What is your deal?" she asked.

Rex shrugged. "What's yours? You suddenly turn into a dragon, rescue my brother, and your sister and I are forgotten in it!" he said angrily.

Vanessa looked at him in the eyes, remembering that he was just anxious to learn whether or not she had learned about his father.

"Rex, don't be so sensitive! You are still my best friend!" she argued softly.

Rex stared back at her, realizing the ignorance in his words. "I know. It's only that if you knew—forget it," he said hastily, covering up his words.

Vanessa laughed. "If I knew what? That your father is the Dark Lord?" she asked.

"Septimus told you, didn't he?" he moaned.

Vanessa nodded. "But that isn't the point! I don't care who or what your parents are. It only matters that you are a good person."

Rex sighed. "Sorry. It's just that when I learned that my very own father was trying to kill you, well, I was heartbroken. He was disappointed in me that I was friends with you. I know it shouldn't matter, but he is my father."

Vanessa understood. "Yes, I can't imagine how hard it would be. But maybe we can change his mind. There is always a bit of light somewhere… right? Maybe the first thing we should do is decide where we are going."

Rex drew a map from his small pocket on his coat. Vanessa put her hand in the air and murmured a sentence that Rex had taught her a while before, "Lux," and a bright blue light flared in her hand. Rex pointed to where they were on the map. Vanessa recognized the campfire, and she could almost make out tiny figures of their group.

Near the group was a great forest of huge trees larger than redwoods, which Rex would later explain were world trees or *yggdrasils*. Yggdrasils were more than twice as tall as the largest of the redwoods and much fatter than the fattest of the sequoia trees.

Near it, a vast expanse of ocean was spread out. Rex showed her a large island surrounded by seventeen isles. The map showed the Citra Isles and the big island as Celestis Island. He smiled, laying the map out on the ground. He blew on the map, and suddenly, it seemed to come to life. The place where they were had a tiny light that, when Rex zoomed in, she recognized was their campfire. Vanessa asked if she could see where the rest of her family was. Rex nodded, whispered a name into the map's corners, and it zoomed in on another location. The map showed a ship rocking in the waves of the sea. The boat was obviously an elven ship by the smooth workmanship. Rex zoomed in even closer, and Vanessa could make out the tiny details such as the neatly embroidered sails. Vanessa strained to see it so Rex continued to expand the map.

The embroidery was a mix of animals that Rex explained was the shape-shifter insignia. In the center of the ship was a thin black-haired elf woman, wearing a silver crown, stood with a sword in one hand, a bow in the other. To her left was a tiger, and on her right was a stag. On the outside, surrounding the three creatures, was a dragon on the tiger's side and a weird sea creature on the stag's side. It was like a dragon but with gills.

Vanessa focused on a small figure sitting on the large dragon figurehead at the front. She gasped in surprise as she finally realized who the small person was that was trying so hard to get to the small group of Terrian people.

Then Rex recognized the figure too, and he eyes widening in astonishment. It was Abigail.

CHAPTER 25

A TAFFY-TIED GREETING

Abigail felt jubilant. Here was her chance to find Vanessa and Rex. As she stood on the large blue and green dragonhead at the front of the ship, her mother Regina came to stand beside her.

"I am afraid they might have already met my sister Alauda. Her name in Elvish means lark."

Abigail looked at her in surprise. "You have a sister?" she asked.

Regina smiled sheepishly. "Actually, I have six. I am the eldest by two minutes," she answered.

Abigail's eyes stretched even wider. "You have a twin! Please tell me the names of the rest of your sisters!" she cried.

Regina smiled wryly. "Going from eldest to youngest, I suppose, after me, Filix, Aqua, Nebula, Herba, Prati, and . . . Well, the youngest . . . ran away, but her name is Avis. As far as we know, she is dead," she muttered.

Abigail nodded. "Avis . . . What a pretty name," she thought aloud. Regina nodded too but stayed silent. A fog surrounded the boat suddenly, but Abigail thought that was normal and ignored it. Abigail was shocked to see a flicker of a grin cross her mother's face.

"You are all smiles," Abigail noted.

Regina smiled even wider. "Oh well, I suppose I am just happy to be on my way toward Vanessa," she said with a giggle.

"Yes, that pug puppy is really cute, but I wouldn't mind someone else to take care of him for awhile." Abigail caught the eyebrow raise from her mother and rephrased her brisk sentence. "I mean, I miss her witty words. She could brighten me up instantly." Suddenly, a male voice spoke loudly from behind her.

"Huh, brighten you up, you say? Well she is sneaking up on you now. You might want to turn around."

Abigail whirled around just in time to see her sister Vanessa, looking a little older than she had last remembered, shove a laughing Rex away irritably. Abigail charged toward her sister and squeezed Vanessa's waist so hard that Vanessa managed to choke out only two words: "Can't. Breathe." And Abigail finally let go.

"I missed you so much! I have a billion questions! Can you answer them? How are you? How did you escape? How did Rex get to you? How did you get on the boat? Did you and Rex become friends? Like *really* good friends?" she asked.

Vanessa laughed and blushed at the same time. "One at a time! I am good. Rex came and asked me to go with him so we could come back to you. I flew onto the boat. And yes, Rex and I are really good friends," she answered.

Abigail's mouth dropped open. "You *flew*?" she said in awe. Vanessa explained about how she could turn into a dragon.

When she was done, Regina came up from behind Vanessa. "I had a feeling that would happen," she grumbled.

Rex grinned. "You have an evil twin! Hahahahahahaha!" he bellowed. Regina grimaced. "Careful. Your impudence will bring your destruction sooner than you may think, Rex."

Rex snickered. "Yes, O Queen," he taunted, not paying any attention to the threat.

Regina looked as if she wanted to fry him, but just then, a deep voice came from behind the reunited family. "Welcome to the *Cetus*! My name is Astrum. I am the ship's captain."

Vanessa and Abigail whirled around to face a strapping elf in fitted black armor. His hair was long enough to fit into a short ponytail.

Vanessa frowned, trying to remember who was in the scene that popped in her head. "Have we met before?" she asked. There was something about the longish black hair and bright eyes.

This elf was beefier than any other elf Vanessa had seen, but there was some resemblance with how he spoke.

Astrum smiled. "Sorry, Your Highness, I would remember a meeting with such a pretty face as yours. I do have a brother though. Have you met a Neal Lux?" he asked.

Vanessa nodded frantically. "Yes! Neal is my uncle! His wife is my aunt." Astrum frowned. "He never told me that he got married!

Regina smirked with a knowing glint in her eyes. "Well, just so you know, it was my sister he married."

The captain's eyes got as round as saucers. "WHAT? Which one?" he asked. Regina raised her eyebrows. "The only one who hasn't become an Amazon or a servant of Terra: Filix!" she added.

Astrum nodded. "I guess that would make sense . . . Have you heard anything from Avis?"

Regina shook her head. "Nothing, not after she was bani—I mean, not after she ran away."

Rex suddenly became serious. "You can't keep that secret from the people of Terra for much longer!" he whispered in Regina's ear.

Regina dismissed him with a wave of her hand. "Go take the girls to their rooms," she ordered sharply.

Rex frowned but did as she asked. He led them into a hallway carved with ancient script with a language Vanessa thought was Terrian.

"Wow. Look at what it says!"

The Bird shall be found,
Warrior will be crowned.

When a King's sword falls,
At Healer's dying calls,
The Elves are freed by a sly fox
Even the queen, Warrior Nox.

Rex stopped dead in his tracks. "WARRIOR NOX?" he almost shouted, "Vanessa! Your name in world giant means warrior!" he yelped.

Vanessa stomped the rough wood of the floor. "Your name in Elvish means king!"

Rex nodded. "Yes, but I don't have a sword," he said.

But Vanessa could see a glimmer of doubt in his green eyes. He sighed, "Maybe I get a sword or something," he said. Vanessa smiled, "Or I do and you just take it," she suggested. Rex looked indignant, "I wouldn't take your sword. Now if you gave it to me…" Rex didn't notice Abigail, who was stealthily creeping up on him. When she was within reach of him, she pulled out a piece of colorful candy that she had received from Queen Aurora and placed it in Rex's pocket. Rex, who wasn't paying any attention, failed to notice the sticky taffy that was slipped into his *pera*. When Vanessa and Rex settled the argument, they gathered the sly Abigail and kept walking.

Abigail looked curious. "Rex? Do you like sweets?" she asked out of the blue.

Rex gave her an incredulous look, "DO I? Of course, I do!" he exclaimed passionately.

Vanessa winked at Abigail. "I think Abigail and I will go to our rooms. Maybe you should go to yours and get some rest," she suggested as they passed an intricate carving.

Rex nodded. "Yeah. But first, I think I am going to see what I packed in my *pera* to hold me over till dinner. I'm starving!," he said, walking off opposite of where the two girls were going.

Abigail took Vanessa to an elegant looking room, which had no furniture besides a cushy hammock. Vanessa plopped down on it and closed her eyes.

Abigail frowned. "Are you tired?" she asked.

Vanessa opened one eye and stared at Abigail. "Kind of, I haven't slept since . . . Well, I can't remember. But that isn't what I am trying to do. I am trying to contact Filix through my dreams."

Abigail shrugged and took off her shoes, snuggling up next to Vanessa and wrapping her arms around her big sister. Eventually, Abigail fell asleep.

Vanessa shook Abigail awake. "Sis! Your little trick with Rex worked!" she told her.

Abigail scrambled up, yelping with joy, "Did you get any sleep?" she asked. Vanessa raised an eyebrow. "Yes. Nightmares though. You?" and Abigail shrugged, "Dreamless really," she responded. Vanessa smiled, "What did Rex do to you to deserve the candy?" she asked.

Abigail rolled her eyes. "When you found and took Peregrin from the forest, I told Rex that I was hungry. He smiled slyly at me and gave me this green gummy worm thingy and called it the gummy-tummy: the green-queen species. Of course, I gladly accepted the little 'treat.'"

Vanessa grinned. "What happened next?" she inquired.

Abigail snorted. "I started to feel a little woozy. Then my whole body turned green! It lasted for thirty minutes, and eventually, it wore off."

Vanessa nodded with realization. "When I found you, you seemed to look a bit green. Now I know why!" she said.

The two sisters got up and walked out of the room, only to find Rex staring at them with his arms crossed, looking very mad. His lips were sealed together.

Abigail stared at him with pure innocence. "Are you OK? You seem kind of quiet," she said sweetly. Vanessa surprised at the malicious look in Abigail's eyes. She had never seen *that* before. Rex tried to open his mouth, but his lips were glued together by some kind of neon pink substance. All they could make out was an angry groaning sound.

Vanessa laughed hard, then murmured gently, "Visco Curo."

And Rex opened his mouth. "HOW COULD YOU DO THAT TO ME? I TRUSTED YOU. YOU TRICKED ME!" he screamed in outrage.

Vanessa giggled. "Ha! You so deserved it!" she told him.

Rex gave her a look, realizing she was right. "Well... um... I guess... but that still doesn't make it right!" he protested. Abigail raised an eyebrow, "But it was fun," he said. Rex decided to change the subject, "Right. Anyway, I think we should go greet our new guests. I think the rest will be arriving at any moment."

Hurriedly, the trio ran upstairs to the deck to see if their friends were there. They were in such a hurry to climb the stairs they didn't notice the large figure descending them and collided in a heap at his feet.

Abigail screamed with fear, but Vanessa laughed. "Now, now, Neal. You must not have heard the words 'Make way for the princess' before,'" she said happily. Neal sighed, bowing, "Making way for the princess! Making way for the princess!" Vanessa and Abigail stepped to his right. Vanessa introduced Neal to Abigail. Candentia, Septimus, and Syringa also stepped forward

Abigail smiled as she hugged her father and mother. "We should call this band of magical people something . . . Don't you think?" she asked.

Drake nodded. "I agree. Go on," he told her.

Abigail thought for a moment. "What about the Elven Heroes?" she asked.

Neal and Filix, who had been talking with Astrum a little ways off, walked up, smiling. They agreed on the name as did the rest.

Vanessa glanced at Candentia and marveled for a second, wondering how someone could make a person so beautiful. Only a truly artistic creator could have ever dreamed up such elegance. While Vanessa couldn't be certain where Sptimus's loyalties were, she knew Candentia would always stand on their side.

Abigail repeated the question to Vanessa who gave Abigail a long pensive look and said, "I really like that, Abigail. From now on, we are called the Elven Heroes."

CHAPTER 26

THE FIRSTBORN

Vanessa stumbled ashore, soaking wet. She had jumped off the ship, changing into a fish at the last moment but had momentarily forgotten to get out of the fast-moving ship's way. She had been a barracuda. It was the only sea animal that she could think of as she plummeted out of the boat into the murky water. And that thought had come from a fear of being eaten by one.

When she resurfaced, she found herself staring at a striking woman with jet-black hair and crystal blue eyes in on a loose dress in one of Vanessa's favorite colors: silver.

The woman frowned and said glumly, "I thought my granddaughter would arrive in a more orderly fashion. I suppose Rex will come in the same way." Suddenly, a familiar-looking man appeared at her side. He had on a black shirt, dark gray pants, and black boots. His hair was the same color as the woman next to him, but his irises were the color of his pants. To Vanessa, he seemed to be made of shadow. Each seemed to be about thirty years old.

The man spoke in a deep, soothing voice. "Be patient, my queen! When we showed up at Celestis Island, I could have sworn that I was a walking ball of mud! You weren't much different either."

The woman sighed ruefully. "I suppose so. Vanessa, I am Lux Aurora Vesper-Nox. Normally, I go by Aurora. I am the queen of the elves."

Vanessa nodded. "It is an honor to meet you, Queen Aurora. Who are you?" she asked the shadowy man.

He laughed. "I am Tonitrus Nox. I am her husband, so that makes me king. My name is kind of a mouthful, so call me Cool King Toniti," he joked.

Clearly, Aurora didn't think it was all that funny. "No! Just call him Tonitrus," she told Vanessa.

Vanessa smiled and looked at her surroundings. Tropical beaches, glittering waters, and a huge jungle were bathed in the fading moonlight. She crouched down to feel the white sand and picked up a pretty shell.

Vanessa smiled. "The sand looks like it is from Florida."

Tonitrus smiled and put an arm around her. "Yep. I have been to Florida once before . . . I believe in the 1840s," he whispered softly.

Vanessa smiled and laughed at the oddness of it all. "Did this sand come from Florida?" she asked in awe.

Tonitrus grinned even wider. "No, my silly girl! This is the most beautiful beach in the Citra Isles."

Aurora rolled her eyes, a hint of humor shining in her eyes. "Not even close! He just likes it because it's named after him. This is Tono Beach. There are many beautiful beaches here in the Isles," she said with a smirk.

Then out of the waves came Rex, making a hang loose sign. "Oh yeah! Toni rules!" he yelled, interrupting the peaceful silence.

Tonitrus grinned. "You finally caught on. Now come over here and let me hug my nephew!" he cried back.

Vanessa suddenly felt sick. "Nephew? That means I am related!" she said to Aurora.

The queen smiled. "Not exactly. The truth is rather complicated but I will try to keep it simple. Tonitrus and Umbra are not related by blood. Umbra is an elf, while Tonitrus is . . . different. Tonitrus was adopted."

Vanessa could not help uttering a sigh of relief, and she instantly regretted it because of the look on the queen's face.

Aurora smiled knowingly. "Rex is a good person. He would be a good future king."

Vanessa yelped in shock. "What? NOOO!" she cried, causing the exotic birds that had been resting in the trees to flutter up in annoyance.

Rex glanced over his shoulder curiously then whispered something in Tonitrus's ear which made the king smile.

Vanessa sighed but kept quiet. Within a few minutes, a large shape came into view. The *Cetus* had arrived.

Aurora sighed then touched a fist to the ground. A stone dock arose from the sand, stretching to the ship.

Aurora smiled. "It has been a long time since I have manipulated the earth, and it is not my favorite. However, it can be satisfying sometimes. My sister is better at it."

Vanessa was confused. "You have a sister?" she asked.

Aurora smiled. "I have six."

In the dim light of the fading moon, Vanessa thought that she could see a memory flash across the queen's face—a book. The book was dark leather with a silver title. *The Book of Prophecies*—Vanessa suddenly remembered a prophecy in there that she had almost forgotten.

> *The sun will give his first light,*
> *for the rightful heirs of day and night . . .*

Vanessa remembered the names on the page. *Tonitrus Nox . . . Lux Aurora Vesper. . .* Vanessa looked over at the queen. Vanessa was slowly piecing together the pieces of the puzzle. Lux—where had Vanessa heard that name before? Then Vanessa remembered a night before all this craziness. Gemma had been talking to her on an obscure island, and "the seven sisters" had been what they had talked about. Vanessa strained to remember what their names had been: Aqua, Freya, Anima, Nebula, Pax, and Lux.

Lux was for light, and light was given at dawn (*aurora*), evening (*vesper*), and night (*nox*), when the stars and moon were out. Then Vanessa realized that Aurora (or Lux) was the firstborn. Regina was the firstborn *too*. Vanessa gasped as she remembered that *she* was a firstborn as well.

Aurora smiled. "So you have it all figured out. *I am* the first daughter of Terra. Regina *is* my first child. And *you are* the firstborn of her children. That means that you are to be queen. Many other talents will be given to you for being first born," she told Vanessa.

Vanessa frowned, not wanting to leave her sister out of this. "What about Abigail?" she asked.

Aurora's look saddened. "The healer has a different path," she answered before striding away from Vanessa.

The Elven Heroes greeted Vanessa. They all bowed to Aurora and Tonitrus.

"Mother! Father! You wouldn't believe the adventures we have been through!" Filix said happily, making Regina giggle like a little girl. Tonitrus smiled warmly, but Aurora seemed a little troubled. Vanessa could only wonder why.

CHAPTER 27

JUST THE USUAL MIDNIGHT DISTURBANCE

Alauda crouched like a cat on the roof of her next victim. A rich Dwarven governor that went by the name of Erik was whom she meant to kill. The Dark Lord was unhappy with Erik, for the dwarf had angered him at the last visit and had threatened to reveal the whereabouts of the Dark Army. Umbra had given specific orders to her to kill him in his sleep, making it look as if he died of natural causes, and not raise an early alarm.

Alauda almost felt sorry for Erik. He had shown great bravery, and she respected that. But orders were orders. Alauda knew that if she didn't obey them, not only would her life be in danger but those she loved. There were few people Alauda loved, and those she did were precious. Umbra knew just how to bribe her. That was how he had gotten her to betray her sisters and deny the throne of the elven kingdom. Just as the elf was about to swing down into the window of Erik's quarters, Alauda heard something behind her. As she turned around to see the source fo the noise, a long shape whistled through the air and hit her in the back.

Alauda was knocked off the roof of the building and thrown unto the roof of a nearby tavern. She slid off the slippery tiles and landed in a bale of hay. She grimaced as the golden straw covered her sleek black clothes. She glanced to her left and gasped to see that the object that had hit her was a long black staff. At the bottom of the staff was a carving of a bird.

Alauda was about to get up when, out of the dark, a figure stepped. The shape was of a slender elf, but it was too dark to see its face. The figure dropped to a crouch next to Alauda and said in a familiar voice, "I thought that we had stopped playing these little games, Alauda,"

A silken cloth was shoved under Alauda's nose by the figure, allowing a sharp smell to waft into her senses. Alauda blinked once, a mist seeming to cling to her vision, and she slipped into a drugged sleep.

The old tavern keeper and his wife awoke to a loud clanging noise. Irritably and armed with a club, the wife went outside to check the place. When she glanced to the hay bales on the side of the building, nothing was there.

The tavern keeper greeted his wife in the kitchen by asking, "What was it, Agnes?" He spoke a gruff tone, with a Scottish accent.

The woman waved a dismissive hand. "Just the usual midnight disturbance, my love."

CHAPTER 28

A FLYING STEED

Vanessa awoke to the sound of birdsong. She dreamily lifted her head, glancing out of the marble window at the lush forest. All she could remember was that she had been walking through the jungle with the Elven Heroes when suddenly overcome with weakness, she had fallen into her mother's arms. Now she was lying on satiny sheets with cloudlike pillows. She wondered when she had last slept that deeply, probably when they had visited the sprite kingdom. She stretched then got up, groaning with pain at the slightest movement of her body.

Walking over to a table at the corner of the large room, Vanessa found a set of silky clothes laid out for her. She put them on and realized they were a pair of black yoga-like pants and a loose white shirt. The clothes were very quite comfortable. Once changed, she gazed through the window taking in the smells and sights of the tropical surroundings.

A sudden knocking at the door made Vanessa jump. Rex poked his black-haired head into the room and smiled. "You decent?" he asked.

Vanessa rolled her eyes, "Defeats the point of asking, really. Come in," she sighed.

Rex strutted in, grinning like it was his birthday. He sat on the bed, and Vanessa plopped down beside him. "Are we on Celestis Island?" she asked.

Rex shook his shaggy-haired head. "Nope. We are on Elisium. And I am telling you, Vanessa, there is a good reason it is called paradise!" he said passionately. Vanessa smiled. "Really?" she asked.

Rex nodded. "Oh yeah! Maybe we can go for a spin, and I can take you to see a few old haunts!" he offered.

Vanessa laughed. "And how old am I exactly? Last I checked, I was thirteen!" she told him.

Rex stared thoughtfully at her. "Well, you were five when they took you away from Terra, but they used a simple spell to make you seem younger until you came back . . . So add thirteen plus five, and I think you are old enough. Besides, what harm could I do to a shape-shifting dragon girl?" he asked.

Vanessa laughed even harder. "More than you could understand! But I suppose my being eighteen is good enough. That sounds so strange! I think you will have to persuade my dad!" she said.

Rex grinned. "Your dad and I are really close. Growing up, he would act as Dad in Umbra's place. It's your mother I am worried about."

Vanessa stood up and opened the door. "OK. I say yes. Let's go for a spin! But first, I am starving! Becoming a dragon is hard work. Let's go see what's for breakfast."

They both left the room. Vanessa caught her breath. Tall spiraling marble buttresses rose, holding the elaborately carved ceiling high above their heads. A marble staircase led to a dinning hall. At a long table sat Abigail. Her strawberry blond hair was tied back into a cute bun, and her little sister wore a pretty summer dress of pink and pale yellow. Vanessa's stomach noticed the food on the table. Huge wooden bowls carrying exotic fruit and thick loaves of dark bread. Vanessa's mouth watered. After greeting her sister, Vanessa took a plate woven out of palm tree leaves and started loading it with the most delicious looking food. Rex seemed to be trying the most exotic offerings, but Vanessa squirmed inside thinking of the weird tastes. As she sat down, Vanessa

feasted as Abigail recounted her adventures. Finally, with Abigail done
with her story, and her hunger satisfied, Vanessa could talk.

"Why was I so hungry?" she asked.

Rex shrugged. "For a lot of reasons but mostly becayse you haven't
eaten in a while, and you have been doing a lot of magic.

Vanessa blinked and smiled. "Sooo, Abigail? Will you tell my mom
that Rex and I are going for a trip?" she asked.

Abigail smiled too. "Sure!"

Before Rex could thank her, Vanessa pulled him by hand and ran
out of the door. She paused. "So do you want me to turn into a—" she
began but was cut off at the sound of thundering hooves.

Rex smiled. "Aurum and Ventus will save our energy."

Out of the clouds, two whirling shapes appeared then swirled to the
ground. The first to touch the earth was the mare Ventus. The second
was a majestic stallion with a jet-black mane and pure golden pelt.

He muzzled Rex and whinnied aloud, "So this is the girl you talked
about." Ventus nodded, black hair spilling into her face, almost covering
her pearly white star. "She is with him often."

Vanessa clapped a hand over Ventus's muzzle and grinned sheepishly
at Rex. He was smiling. "Why do you look so bashful?"

Vanessa then realized that she was the only one who could
understand both horses. Vanessa didn't answer Rex, but got an idea.

She jumped onto Ventus and yelled playfully as she started to gallop
off, "Race you to the beach!"

Rex looked surprised, and sprang onto Aurum to race after her.
Vanessa glanced behind and saw how easily he was catching up. She
whispered into Ventus's ear, "Do you want him to catch up? Let's win
this little race!" Instantly, Vanessa felt Ventus's muscles bunch together,
and she zipped at lightning speed to the beach.

Just before they disappeared out of sight, Vanessa heard Rex yell,
"HEY! NO FA—" But he was cut off, and he vanished into the undergrowth.

Vanessa laughed and threw her hands into the air. She didn't need
to hold on, she was stuck to Ventus until she wanted off.

Suddenly, the jungle disappeared and was replaced by glittering white sand and crystal clear waters. Ventus's hoof clunked into a shell as she slowed. Vanessa hopped off Ventus and picked up the perfect shell. She recognized the pinkish shell as a conch.

Out of the peaceful jungle hurtled Rex and Aurum. Aurum stopped suddenly in front of Vanessa, and Rex flew through the air, landing at Vanessa's feet.

"I thought that you were attached to the horse!" she giggled as Rex wiped off the sand from his clothes.

He spat sand out of his mouth, "I forgot to hold on!" He said. Vanessa noticed she had dropped the shell during the commotion. She picked it up again, held it to her ear, and tried to listen for sounds of the sea. Instead she heard something completely different. A small voice sang:

> *The beautiful sea,*
> *Oh, if I could watch,*
> *The Warrior free,*
> *Me and Layatch!*

Vanessa jumped back with surprise. Rex looked at her in shock. "What?" he asked.

Vanessa gave the conch to Rex. His eyes widened in alarm. "Nymphs only say that when someone is in trouble! Let's see if there is more," he said, giving the conch to Vanessa. She listened intently.

> *Find me at backward Lraep Retaw.*
> *Dodge the gold dragon's maw.*
> *While singing this song,*
> *Don't go wrong.*
> *For if you lie,*
> *Your friends will die.*

Vanessa gasped, and Rex looked worried. Slowly, he grabbed the shell and spoke into it. "We will be there."

Together, Vanessa and Rex mounted their horses. As they rode along the beach Vanessa tried to piece together what was going on.

"Find me at backward Lraep Retaw. Well, that is pretty self-explanatory. Where is Pearl Water?" she asked.

Rex frowned. "It is at the very tip of the eighteenth isle, Artana. We would need to fly. Aurum and Ventus will take care of that." he said. Vanessa cocked her head, "How?" she demanded.

Aurum whinnied, "Lady Vanessa, did you know that elf horses fly?" Vanessa shook her head.

Ventus stomped. "Yes. Magic is woven into us. We can do many things. Flying is only one of them. For instance, we don't need wings to fly."

She demonstrated by galloping a few feet before leaping into the air. Vanessa gasped as the horse kept going, flying without wings.

Ventus laughed. "A very long time ago, I had several names: Pegasus; mother of the wind; the shadow horse; and many more. But my father was named Nimbus, not Poseidon as myth would have you believe about the Pegasus. There was never more than one god. Humans confused the elves and monsters that would visit earth with gods. Posido was an elf crossed with naiad and was the one who loved and controlled the water. Zae was a she-elf that loved the skies and mastered magic that bent weather to her will. Haed was a powerful elf crossed with shadow titan. He controlled the stone and killed many. His power over death was great." she said. Vanessa had loved ancient myths and understood them now in a new way. Ventus continued. "Anyway, Aurum was known for his speed. That was laughable, for I am the fastest, but back then, I had not yet been born, so he was the fastest of the day," she explained to Vanessa. Vanessa held her hands in the air as she and the flying horse soared through a cluster of clouds.

Rex suddenly appeared beside her. "You realize that this could be a trick?" he asked her.

Vanessa frowned. "A *trick*?" she repeated.

Rex shrugged, "Who knows. Wouldn't it be fun to find out?" he asked. Vanessa knew where he was going,

"Don't even think about it!" she scolded. Rex made his face go blank, giving her an innocent stare, "What? I wouldn't do anything bad... well, not all *that* bad. A more serious problem is we might be spotted the Dark Lord's friends." He said.

Vanessa nodded and said that they would just disguise themselves. Hours passed with them galloping in the fluffy white clouds, occasionally flying lower to the ground. Vanessa thought it was a dream, except for the unpleasant experience of dodging crows and other poor fowl. Rex whooped as his horse did a fancy dive, then stopped short, grasping at his throat and making a choking sound. Vanessa began to worry until Rex finally swallowed and made a face,

"The bugs in these parts are nasty. Don't open your mouth, Vanessa. I think there is a swarm." With that, flying continued. The sun was setting as Rex and Vanessa looked for a campsite or lodge to stay the night. Soon they came to a small town. Rex had them stop near a cottage that had a large sign which read: CLOTHING AND FOOD FOR TRAVELERS.

Vanessa and Rex nodded at each other then entered the small house. The richy decorated house's interior was a stark difference from the exterior. An old woman greeted them, and by her size, Vanessa guessed that she was a dwarf. Her wrinkled skin gave her a folded in look, and Vanessa felt guilty think how much she reminded her of Peregrin. The plump old woman stared cheerfully at them. Her voice was like sandpaper.

"Hello, younglings! My name is Ursa. Have you any interest in my merchandise? Or do you need some food in your tiny guts? I also sell Chimera tongues for starting quick and easy fires. Ooh! And troll teeth are on sale today." she asked. Vanessa felt repulsed to hear that, and she resisted crinkling her nose at the old woman's breath. The smell of onions and spoiled milk hung in the air with every breath the old woman exhaled.

Rex smiled and produced four silver coins. "Will this pay for two changes of clothes and some food? I think we will pass on the chimera tongue and all."

Ursa nodded. "Of course!"

She showed Rex where his clothes could be found. The dwarf lady then led Vanessa to another room. There, she told Vanessa that she could shop for whatever she liked.

"So the young man is your . . .," she trailed off.

Vanessa smiled. "He is my brother," she lied smoothly.

The old lady nodded, jowls flapping vigorously. "Well, stay away from the western part of the city. Sperno lives there."

Vanessa frowned. "Who is Sperno?"

Ursa shuddered. "He works for the Darkest Knight."

"Do you mean the Dark Lord?" Vanessa asked.

"He goes by a lot of names, but yes, the Dark Lord suffices."

Vanessa shivered. "I see. Anything else we have to look out for?"

The dwarf nodded. "Be careful where you go in the city as not to run into one of the Dark Lord's creatures."

Vanessa cocked her head. "A malus?"

Ursa shook her head and continued. "No. These things are called Prowlers. They seem like shadows, but shadows cannot be touched. These creatures have a strong solid grip. Perfect nightmares in my opinion."

Vanessa thanked her and started shopping. She came upon some dark gray stretchy pants. The shopkeeper explained that they were made of spiderweb. Vanessa tried them on and was surprised that they were perfectly comfortable. She noticed that they were boot-cut, and she liked the way that they accommodated her movements. Stretchy, soft, and durable were qualities that Vanessa loved. Next, she chose a shirt that was the color of a pine forest in winter—dark green.

The old lady smiled. "They look good on you. Your brother is coming."

Vanessa gave Rex a wink and said, "Hello, brother. I love your new clothes!"

Rex caught on. "Thanks, sis," he said.

Ursa grinned and asked, "What are your names?"

Vanessa was the first to answer. "Mine is Fulmen. My brother's name is . . . Claudius." She quickly stepped in front of Rex to disguise his look of outrage, for in Elvish, that meant lame or crippled. The old woman did not notice the byplay, and was focused on arranging the fruit and bread in the basket. Vanessa raised an eyebrow as she spotted some mold on a piece of bread. The old lady simply picked it off and tossed it on the floor, and went on. Rex still looked mad from the 'claudius' thing, and was refusing to look at Vanessa. Vanessa pointed at a slug that was climbing up a pear,

"Um... Ursa? Is that a bug?" she asked. Ursa looked at the pear, squashed the slug, and threw it on the ground as well,

"I don't see no bug! What are you talking about?" she asked. Vanessa decided it was a hopeless cause,

"Oh, I must have been imagining it," she said, taking the food, making sure the woman got her pay, and dragging a seething Rex out of the doorway.

CHAPTER 29

THE SWORD

Vanessa and Rex set off down the hill to Krag. They kept a weary eye out for enemies and tried not to call attention to themselves. Once they were out of earshot, Rex glared at Vanessa. "CLAUDIUS?" he exclaimed indignantly.

Vanessa nearly fell over, laughing. "Sorry! It was the first thing that came to mind!"

Rex snorted in derision, "Fine, but next time, I pick my name."

They headed to the eastern part of the city, Krag, staying in the shadows and making sure that their cowls were pulled up. Vanessa wished she had a weapon. A knife would be nice at a time like this.

Rex seemed to know what she was thinking. "Hang on, I need to check my *pera*."

He pulled out a long dagger from his pocket. It had a gilded silver hilt and a black adamant blade. Vanessa tried to thank him, but Rex shook his head, claiming that he had plenty. Vanessa loved naming objects, so she began thinking of a name for the beautiful blade. Finally, she came up with the perfect name for the elven dagger, *Flumen* or river. Vanessa fashioned a sheath from a strip of leather and a cloth.

She fingered the knife as the two passed a group of unsavory-looking shadow nymphs. Vanessa glanced over shoulder.

"I thought that these Citra Isles were ruled by elves!" she whispered into Rex's ear.

He shook his head. "Not this isle. It's called Silex Isle. It is the eighteenth island. The Citra Isles are only seventeen. This is one of the thirty others. The name is Nymphian, and it means stone." Vanessa nodded.

They sneaked into one of the quieter inns. The sign read OCEANSIDE INN. Opening the door, they were greeted by an older man with wild curly hair and a goatee. Vanessa noticed that his pants were fluffy gray, the same color as his hair.

The man looked surprised. "Great mama goat! I suppose you two elves are wanting to stay the night?"

Rex smiled. "Yes. I am Octavius Pyra, and this is my sister . . .," he trailed off, looking at Vanessa.

She answered promptly, "Reyna Pyra."

The old guy laughed in a way that sounded more like a goat in distress. "So this is your sister? I will give you separate rooms. My name is Haedus Sheepshank," he said as he let them in.

Although the exterior of the building was shabby, it was beautiful on the inside. The wood seemed alive, with sprouted leaves and ferns. As Haedus led Rex up some stairs he let Vanessa that his wife would be along shortly to take her to her room. As the innkeeper tromped upstairs, Vanessa almost shrieked at the sight of his cloven. Vanessa caught on: Sheepshank, Haedus (which meant kid, as in a goat).

She jumped as a voice spoke from behind her. "Hello, Haedus tells me that you go by Reyna Pyra. My name is Lilia Pacini."

Vanessa turned around to see an elegant nymph in a bright green dress that appeared to have moving leaves on it. Vanessa was surprised by Lilia's face. The girl seemed to be only fourteen. Her face was oval and had an ageless look. Her eyes were the color of hot chocolate with swirls of green in them.

Vanessa nodded weakly. "Um, Mrs. Pacini? I am waiting for Haedus's wife. Do you know where she is?" she asked.

Lilia grinned. "Oh sorry, I meant, Lilia Pacini Sheepshank. *I* am his wife. And I know that the young man is not your brother. You'd act differently around him if you were related. You also look nothing alike."

Vanessa stared. "Oh" was the only word she managed to get out.

The nymph walked out from behind her and stopped, looking her dead in the eye. "I also know that your name isn't Reyna Pyra. It is Vanessa Nox."

Vanessa reached for Flumen, but Lilia just laid a hand on her shoulder. "There is nothing to fear. I am on your side. I am an elder nymph. You can trust me."

Vanessa relaxed a little. Lilia smiled kindly and showed Vanessa to her room upstairs. A sudden flurry of limbs leaped from a corner, scaring Vanessa out of her skin. A cute girl who looked about eight years old with a mess of hair sat smiling at them.

Lilia gasped. "Fael! You need to be respectful!" she scolded.

Vanessa grinned. "Is she your child? She is adorable!"

Lilia smiled. "Oh, she is my child, all right!" And she showed Vanessa her room while leading her child by the hand.

Once they left, Vanessa sighed. It was a nice space, with dark mahogany floors and light-colored walls. In front of the window was a medium-sized bed with thick pillows and soft sheets. She crawled inside, shut her eyes, and fell asleep instantly. Dreams welcomed her without warning.

Vanessa found herself in a dark room. She couldn't see anything. Suddenly a light from a struck match lit up the room. The match went to a candle, and the whole room lit up. Instead of being in her cozy bed, she was slumped in a chair. Opening her eyes, Vanessa found herself looking at Filix. The white walled room had no furniture besides the two chairs Vanessa and Filix were sitting on. Filix was staring intently at her,

"Vanessa." She said. Vanessa wanted to hug her, but she found herself unable to move,

"*Filix, where am I?*" *she asked. Filix smiled,* "*You are in my dream. You wanted to know something.*" *She said. Vanessa nodded,*

"*How did you know?*" *she asked. Filix raised her eyebrows,* "*I know you, Vanessa. Better than you know yourself.*" *She answered. Vanessa shifted in her seat, finding she could now move.*

"*I don't know what I want answered first. I have so many questions,*" *she said. Filix leaned forward and touched Vanessa's forehead,* "*I do.*" *And suddenly pain arched through Filix's fingertips and into Vanessa. Vanessa found herself on a bridge. A fire raged on one side, and there was a cool, calm forest on the other. Then the scene changed back to Filix. The she-elf sat back in her rocking chair,*

"*That is what you want to know,*" *Filix said simply. Vanessa was even more confused. Filix sensed this and elaborated,* "*You want to know what to choose. There is always a choice,*" *Filix said. Vanessa didn't understand,* "*What do you mean?*" *she asked. Filix smiled,*

"*You have the choice to run away,*" *she said. Vanessa sat there, shocked. Could it be that simple? True, she sometimes wanted to curl up in a ball and die with the thought of being a ruler. Not only would she have to make choices, but those choices would affect others. Millions could die because of her. But she could imagine joy at being a queen, seeing her kingdom blossom under her rule, and being with those she loved. Now, Filix offered a choice that she hadn't considered before. Leaving. She could just disappear. She could go far, where no one would recognize her. Only Filix would know she had left. And Filix, she knew, would keep that secret. She knew being alone would also be miserable. Vanessa looked into Filix's trusting green eyes. Knowing eyes. At that moment Filix looked so much like...* Abigail. *Filix spoke,*

"*I made my choices. I ran away. I banished myself. Had I stayed, we would not be in this mess,*" *she said. Vanessa knew she had to make a choice.* "*I'll stay, and be queen,*" *she declared. Filix smiled,* "*I knew you were strong enough to say that,*" *she said, then saddened,* "*But beware, Vanessa. We all have faults. Yours could mean our destruction. There are reasons Umbra didn't try harder to kill you,*" *she said. Vanessa was a bit hurt by her words.*

"*Why must we have faults?*" *Vanessa asked. Filix smiled at her question.*

"If there is good, there must be evil as there is opposition in all things. Our job is to learn the difference. As we become aware of our faults and see the evil in them, we work to remove them from our life. Sometimes we do it ourselves and sometimes it is done to us. Like a tree, we must all be pruned from time to time in order to reach our full potential," Filix explained.

Vanessa nodded and asked, "What is my fault?" Filix touched her arm. A wave of anger rolled through Vanessa. She felt like she knew everything. She could do everything better than anyone else. She could best any foe. She would rule a kingdom like none before her. None would stand in her way. Vanessa also felt like she was the most beautiful in the world. She felt like anyone— even Candentia— would never be as beautiful as she was, or as smart, or as brave, or as wise. Then Filix retracted her hand. The feelings instantly died down. Vanessa felt shocked and embarrassed. Did she really feel that way? Filix nodded,

"Your flaw is pride. You must bridle these thoughts. If not, you will find yourself in a pit. A pit of which there is no way out," she said. Vanessa felt overwhelmed. She remembered her snotty outbursts. Just before she left for northern Idaho, she remembered yelling at her mother. Regina had been trying to pack for Vanessa, but Vanessa had told her she could do it herself. It had ended badly. Vanessa now felt so sorry. How could I have been like that? she asked. Suddenly, Filix's eyes turned black. Even the whites were turned dark. The voice that came out was guttural,

"Death... despair.... PRIDE." As suddenly as it had come it left and Filix turned back to normal. The she-elf gasped for air,

"Go! There is an enemy close to you! Run!" she screamed. Her eyes again turned black and she rasped, "Come closer, little princess. Let me feast of your powers." And then Filix's hand closed over Vanessa's, cold as death, and the world turned black.

Rex shook Vanessa awake. She opened her eyes to see his face with a worried expression. He put a figure to his lips and motioned outside in the hall. Vanessa listened intently and caught the faintest sound of slithering footsteps. They padded down the hall, barely making a sound.

Vanessa looked at Rex. "What?" she mouthed.

He looked horrified. "Can't you hear what he is saying?" he mouthed back.

Vanessa shrugged, feeling a little chilled.

Rex shivered then said in the tiniest whisper, "Kill, hunger, thirst, revenge . . . Free me. I think there is a wraith. They whisper such things as they hunt."

Rex's voice betrayed a bit of panic. He looked like he had seen a ghost. *He might have,* Vanessa thought. He motioned for her to listen. A chill ran down her spine as she heard it. A cold quiet, then the chanting began. She could hear a raspy voice saying something, and she had no desire to know what it was. Then, the chanting stopped. Vanessa felt the blood drain from her face as she stared at the door. Slowly, an inky black claw started to leak from underneath the door.

Rex, in quick shallow breathes whispered, "We need to get out of here."

Thinking quickly, she pulled Rex to the window and motioned him to get on her back. He didn't protest as she shape-shifted into a gigantic snowy owl and took off into the night.

Once they had flown a good distance, Rex let out a breath. "Oh man, that was bad. Somehow my dad knows we are here. Oh, and why an owl?" he asked. Vanessa shrugged her feathery shoulders as she glided over the sleeping city. "I don't know. It was the quietest bird I could think of. And how did you get into my room?" she asked back.

Rex smiled. "You never locked it. By the way, I think I know what a Prowler is. It is cross between a wraith and a— well, maybe I shouldn't say. Do you know what wraiths do to you?" he asked. Vanessa shivered, "I don't want to know," she said. Rex would not be stopped,

"First they grab you in their icy cold claws, then they—" but Vanessa would hear none of it,

"Rex Noctis, I swear I will drop you if you say anything more about that," she threatened. Rex was about to make some not-so-witty retort when Vanessa whispered, "SSHH!" and pointed with her beak at a spot down below.

Rex gasped. On a deserted lane below, ran a dark creature. It had the shape of a human but seemed to be made of shadow. It strode noiselessly, following the two elves' path. Vanessa wanted to curl up into a ball and cry. She had never liked scary movies, especially ones that had supernatural beings in it. Rex shuffled in his *pera.*

"Vanessa, the only thing that can kill a wraith or a shadow titan is black adamant. Your blade, *Flumen,* is going to be very useful. I wish I had my sword!" he said.

Vanessa frowned. "So you *do* have a sword! Liar. Don't you have a necklace with a tiny sword on it?" she asked.

Rex jumped. "Yes! I do! Thanks!"

From his neck, he brought out the charm. He tore off the sword from the chain and tapped the blade. Instantly, a black-bladed sword sprang to life. The hilt bore an intricate design adorned with diamonds and gold.

He smiled grimly. "OK, let me down. Prowlers don't tire, so he'll chase us until we land out of exhaustion. And then we are in no condition to fight. Better to get it over with now."

Vanessa swooped down, transforming into an elf at the last minute. She pulled Flumen from its sheath, brandishing it in the way Rex had taught her. The Prowler stopped, staring at them through hollow pits where eyes should have been. It held up its hand, and a silver-hilted sword appeared. It was the most fearsome weapon Vanessa had ever seen, with a jet-black blade and a blue sapphire imbedded in the silver hilt. Vanessa found her strength seemed to double at the sight of the long blade.

Without warning, the sinewy figure jumped gracefully over her and landed on Rex. Rex, not expecting this move, fell down and rolled to the side. The Prowler's sword missed Rex's head by inches. He yelped, scrambling away from the hideous creature.

The dark being raised the dreadful weapon, preparing to strike. Vanessa saw her chance and leaped up, piercing the Prowler's back with her dagger. As soon as Flumen touched the wraithlike being, a searing light appeared, and the Prowler vanished, leaving the slender sword behind.

Rex had his eyes closed, not realizing that the danger had passed.

Vanessa ran over to him and touched his arm. "It's fine. I killed it."

Rex opened his eyes wide. "WHAT? Nobody just *kills* those things!" he exclaimed.

Vanessa smiled. "I just did. Didn't you see it trying to kill you?"

Rex got to his feet. He dusted himself off and pointed to the silver sword lying on the ground. "Then that's yours. Spoil of war you keep," he said.

Vanessa, lost for words and fearing to touch it, stared at it. Finally, she picked up the blade. As her soft flesh touched it, the sword flashed a brilliant blue light and seemed to hum in her hands. It was surprisingly light, and Vanessa twirled it around, liking that her hands fit perfectly with the sword. She studied the hilt and realized that there was a carving of a dragon blowing fire. The figure of the dragon made her smile as she remembered what real dragons looked like. She thought of her father and family. The memory was a short-lived one, for her eyes moved on. The slender blade was a perfect weapon for her. She felt the name of the sword pop into her mind, and she realized that the sword was trying to tell her its name. Vanessa listened then said the name aloud. "The name of this sword is *Ensis*, the sword of wisdom and lightning."

CHAPTER 30

THE DARK FIGURE

Filix sighed as she watched the stars. She sat by Neal and held his hand. "It is nice to be home."

They were in the backyard of their small castle, enjoying the night. The evening air was tainted with the sweet but fresh smell of Plumeria blossoms. Neal was spread out on the soft grass, a smile on his face.

"You are right," he agreed.

Filix closed her eyes and felt a wet tongue rasp over her face. She opened her eyes to see both of Neal's elf hounds—Juno and Venus—staring back at her. They rambled off, curly tails wagging in delight.

Filix looked over at her husband, wondering how she should present this. She had an idea. "Neal? You know, it sometimes gets lonely at our home."

Neal glanced at her in surprise. "Really? How so?"

Filix shrugged. "I don't know… it can get cold sometimes…" she said, trailing off.

Neal frowned, "Sometimes. But then then I light a fire and it gets warm again." He said, not sure where she was going.

Filix sighed, "I heard more bodies make more heat," she said.

160

Neal looked at her, "If you are suggesting getting a puppy, then you'll make Venus and Juno mad. They like being the only two dogs," he said.

"Not a puppy! Something more…. Elf-like," she said with a smile. Now she had lost her husband. He stared at her blankly. Filix decided to finish it, "What if there were three of us?"

Her husband shrugged, and then realizing what she meant by that, leapt in the air. "ARE YOU PREGNANT?" he asked in astonishment.

Filix giggled. "I am!" she answered.

Neal sprang into the air whooping with joy. "I'll be a father!" he cried.

Filix laughed and got up to hug him. Neal kissed her and started to the door of their castle. "I'll get something for you to drink! How about Blacka fruit juice?" he asked.

Filix nodded. "Sure!" He disappeared into the building, and Filix sat down, happier than she had been in a very long time.

Startled by a rustle of branches came behind her, Filix turned, staring into the darkness of her shadowy orchard. A black figure appeared, slinking toward her. Filix stood, frozen in shock, and tried to summon a spell. Unfortunately, her surprise and fear made it hard for her to follow through with the charm, and the alarmed Filix found herself quickly backing away from the tall figure.

The being spoke. "Filix, you must come with me. I must protect you and the rest," it said softly. Filix recognized that voice, and she gasped, "You should be dead!" she whispered. The person nodded, "Come. We must make haste."

She grasped the the outstretched hand and allowed herself to be pulled away. Together they vanished into the darkness.

CHAPTER 31

PEARL WATER

Vanessa called the horses to her. Rex had suggested that they walk a little further before they rode, but Vanessa had disagreed. What if they ran into another Prowler? Vanessa mounted Ventus, and the mare leaped up into the air. It was better that they left no footprints. Once they were airborne, Rex steered them south.

While flying, Vanessa figured out a simple spell that would allow her to shape the clouds. She need only wave her hand and the cloud bits would follow her movement. She entertained herself by shaping wafts of cloud into an orb the size of a tennis ball then throwing them at Rex. IRex would catch the balls of cool moist air and playfully throw them back. After their ensuing cloud fight, Vanessa listened as Rex gave the name of every elven cloud. This led to a conversation on birds, and eventually to Regina's sister Avis.

Vanessa wanted to hear about the missing princess. "So what do you know about Avis?" she asked.

Rex blinked then responded shortly, "Well, she ran away. We heard rumors that she had been killed, probably by a malus or something. I did see her once, and all I have to say is 'Wow.' She looked a little older than you. She had silvery crystal blue eyes and jet-black hair. She must have been the one of the prettiest of Aurora's children."

Vanessa tried to picture this in her mind, but all that came up was a very confused version of her dead aunt. She decided to focus on what was ahead, realizing they were above the sea. This part of the ocean was quite shallow, and Vanessa could make out the shapes of large fish when she focused. Vanessa looked ahead, trying to spot land. Then she saw it: there, on the faint horizon, was a spot of land. The horses flew quickly, darting closer to the beach. Rex told her that the beach ahead was Pearl Water.

As she got closer, Vanessa realized why it was called that. When the morning sun shone on the water, it looked as if it was the inside of an oyster. She inhaled the salty tang of the strong breeze that flowed around her. The elven horses landed gracefully on the sandy earth. Ventus and Aurum began to graze on the sparse grass further away from the beach.

Vanessa and Rex studied the ground and confirmed that their footprints were the only ones. She had expected to see something different. What exactly, she didn't know. It was almost disappointing that there was no sign of anyone. "Maybe the message was just an accident," Rex suggested.

Vanessa ran though the riddle in her mind. "Who is Layatch?" she asked.

Rex started, "That's right! Layatch means evening in bird language! We are supposed to wait here till evening!" he said.

Vanessa checked the sun. "It is still early afternoon. What do you suggest? Should we wait here till evening? We could swim, collect food, and relax until then?" she suggested.

Rex nodded. "Yeah, that sounds pretty good. Right now, we should collect food," he said.

Vanessa paused, thinking about her family. "Rex, is there some way to send my mom a message? I'm sure they are worried about us." Rex winked, pulling a mirror out of his Pera, "I have just the thing."

They headed into the jungle that ran along the beach. After searching for a while, Rex called Vanessa over and showed her a tall tree. She would have missed it normally, but with Rex's focused attention and sharp eyes, they had found dinner. Large clear fruit with pinkish hues sat up at the top of the tree. Rex suggested Vanessa use shape shifting.

Vanessa shape-shifted into a macaw and flew up to the top of the tree. Once she landed there, she carefully nipped the stems, letting the fruit fall. Rex gently caught them and placed them in a pile. She bit off one with her beak, and aimed it, letting it fall. Rex yelped as the fruit hit its target. He glared up at her, wiping the pink juice out of his eyes,

"Very funny. Come down here and I'll have roasted bird for dinner. That was a foul trick."

"A *fowl* trick? Rex! That was an awful pun," she squawked with mirth. After a short flight down to land on Rex's shoulder, she shape-shifted back to an elf, making Rex grunt at her weight. She slipped off his shoulder and onto the ground.

Rex showed her where a common Australis nut bush grew. As they harvested the large hard nuts, Vanessa was surprised at their size, nearly as large as her fist. Having collected enough food, Rex led her back to the beach, where they sat down to feast on the odd assortment. The nuts tasted a little Brazilian nuts, and the fruit was like nothing she had ever had before. Maybe like star fruit? The clear melon fruits were the size of her head, and they were a delicacy to Vanessa.

Vanessa looked out to sea, feeling sticky with all of the fruit juice on her hands and mouth. She took off her shoes, "Time for a dip!" she told Rex. He grinned, "Race you!" and he took off. Vanessa, caught by surprise, followed. Rex reached the water before Vanessa, and started to wade in. Vanessa dove in, splashing Rex with saltwater. Once the water came up to her chest, she submerged, turning into a Mako shark. Rex plunged his head in, and started to swim strongly after Vanessa as she explored.

They explored many little nooks of coral, and Rex collected some shells. Vanessa swam over to a seemingly bottomless hole and motioned for Rex. He was about to swim to her when a shape came out of the hole and darted closer to Vanessa. It was a boy. Startled, she swam away as quickly as she could with Rex close behind. Once they were in shallower water, they resurfaced, and Vanessa shape-shifted into a girl again.

The boy resurfaced too. Vanessa noticed that he looked a bit like her dad but had the nose of her mom. His impish smile, complexion, and messy black hair was very familiar.

"Um, well, hi!" she stuttered, forcing a smile. The strange boy grinned, "Were you Chama diving like me?" he asked. Vanessa shook her head, not even wanting to know what a Chama was. "No. We were just exploring. I'm Vanessa. This is Rex," she introduced. The boy froze at Vanessa's name, "What's your last name?" he demanded. Vanessa felt a bit uncomfortable giving out her last name, but the boy seemed so young she doubted he would cause them harm, "Nox," she said. The boy seemed taken aback, then he grinned broadly, hugging Vanessa with great enthusiasm. Vanessa didn't know what to do as he stepped back, still smiling excitedly. The boy saw Vanessa's look of confusion. "I suppose you don't remember me?" he asked, his smile fading.

Vanessa felt exasperated. "Would you people stop asking me this? I DON'T REMEMBER ANYTHING!" she exclaimed.

The boy looked hurt. "I am Nero!" he offered.

The name sent a vibration through Vanessa, but she couldn't place why. Rex suddenly seemed to remember. "We thought you were dead!" he said.

Nero nodded. "You thought Avis was." Then he turned to Vanessa and said, "Vanessa, I am Nero Nox . . . your younger brother."

CHAPTER 32

THE SECRET TRUTH

Regina Nox sat on her bed at one of her mother's many palaces. She had just received a letter of which told her that her sister Filix had disappeared. She sat immersed in worry, thinking of her lost sisters. She was also a worried about Vanessa. It had been now 2 days since she had left. Were they captured?

"Mom?" a voice said, startling Regina so much she jumped,

"What? Who said that?" she asked, looking around. It was Vanessa's voice, "Mom, look at the mirror," and Regina turned to the long mirror in the corner of the room. Vanessa's face appeared, around her looked to be beaches. Regina gasped,

"Vanessa! How are you doing that?" she asked. Vanessa smiled, "Rex gave me a mirror and whispered Regina into it. He said it was best in elvish real-time communications. Something like that." Regina nodded,

"Rex got it from his mother. Umbra uses one as well. Where are you?" she asked.

"Rex and I are at Pearl Water. It's a long story." Vanessa replied. Regina sighed, "You've been gone for days! I won't ask what you are doing at Pearl Water. Rex has his reasons I'm sure. How much longer will you be gone?" she asked. Vanessa shrugged,

"Not sure," she said honestly. Regina frowned, "Tell Rex that if he gets you in trouble, there is no power on Terra or Earth that will stop my claws from shredding him. Be careful, Filia. I wouldn't use the mirrors again. Others can listen in if they have the power," Regina said. Vanessa blew a kiss,

"Bye mom," and her face disappeared. Regina sat back down in the bed, thinking about her children.

The door opened, and Neal poked his head in. "Regina? May I come in?"

Regina nodded her assent. The handsome elf walked in, her husband Drake following him with a hint of reluctance.

Great, the old group, thought Regina.

Neal sat beside her. "Regina, I received a note delivered by falcon that gave news of the disappearances of your sisters Alauda, Nebula, and Prati. I am starting to see a pattern."

Regina looked startled. "PRATI? Who could possibly take the leader of the Amazons and get away with it!" she exclaimed.

Drake nodded. "Yes, but it still happened. There was no evidence of footprints. It's as if a shadow came in and took them."

Neal nodded. "Or something swooped down from the sky."

The three of them were quiet for a while. Finally, when no one could stand the silence, Regina spoke up. "Do you really think . . . ?" she asked.

Drake nodded. "It would make sense."

Neal sighed "We need to rescue the rest of your sisters," he declared.

Regina stood up. "Very well. I will summon Herba and Aqua. Then we can think more about this problem."

Once Neal left them, Drake and Regina sat down on the lawn outside. Drake leaned over to Regina and held her trembling hand. The lawn outside the large white building overlooked a garden full of colorful plants. Beyond the garden, the city of Pardus stretched forth, bright and cheery. The garden was Regina's, and the elf had gone to great lengths to make it beautiful. Sunflowers the size of wagon wheels, roses ranging from white to pink to blue to deep red, and delicious-smelling lilies decorated one half of the garden. The other half was devoted to vegetables and fruit trees of an exotic sort. Normally the gardens were a sanctuary for Regina, but now she could only feel a cold, dark feeling creep over her. She shivered and pulled Drake closer staring beyond the garden at the town of Pardus.

Drake glanced at Regina. "You do realize that a new danger has come to the elves. You can see it when . . ." but he was cut off but a horrifying sight.

As he looked out past Pardus, a dark cloud had appeared, thickening as it moved toward the elven town. Looking closer at it, Regina saw that the cloud contained winged animals—gargoyles. Drake rose, helping Regina up. They had to reach the city before the gargoyles. The foul stone beings must have come from Umbra. Regina and Drake started to run forward, propelled by a desire to protect their people. Regina's heart stopped at a chilling sound. The cry of a small child as the first wave of the stone demons reached the city.

CHAPTER 33

EVENING TIME

Vanessa and Nero had a lot to talk about. He told her that he was a master of Draconic and could light a fire a mile away.

Vanessa was impressed that Nero had such a mastery of magic at so young an age. He looked around twelve, but of course with elves, one could never tell.

Nero sat on a piece of driftwood. "You know, I could teach you some more Draconic," he offered.

Vanessa liked that idea, and she nodded with enthusiasm. "Of course! I would love to learn!" she agreed. A small part of her felt a little resentful that one younger than her would teach her, but she realized that was part of her flaw. Pride. She shook it off. *No time for flaws*, she told herself.

Nero rose from the piece of driftwood and showed her how to strike the log with lightning. When he said the word "Fulmen," a small lightning bolt appeared out of thin air and smashed down on the log, which became a smoking pile of coal.

Vanessa focused her energy into her words, "Fulmen!" she said. Nothing happened. She tried again, and felt the hairs on her arms stand up. She dove out of the way as a thin strand of lightning came out of nowhere, striking the spot she had last been. She decided not to play around with that anymore, and asked Nero to teach her about other things.

She listened intently and made some mental notes while asking meaningful questions.

Her brother smiled as Rex came over and sat by Vanessa. "So, Nero, you look an awful lot like this shape-shifting girl." That was true. Nero had the same black hair and greenish blue eyes.

Her brother seemed to take that as a complement. "Why, thank you. But I wish I looked a little more manly than a shape-shifting girl," he joked.

Vanessa elbowed him in the ribs. "Shush! You look plenty manly. I think he was teasing. *Weren't you, Rex?*" she asked in a tone that told him not to disagree.

Rex paled considerably. "Uh, sure. You are plenty manly . . .," he said quickly, and Nero laughed until he snorted. Then they all laughed.

Vanessa rolled her eyes and looked at them. "No one is girly. Well, Abigail maybe. I mean, can you think that the Nox children are girly? Can you imagine me girly?" she asked.

Rex coughed and Vanessa scowled at him.

They talked for a while and then started skipping rocks along the smooth sea. Nero muttered a word, and a perfectly flat rock skipped across the water. The stone skipped countless times before finally sinking into the waves. Vanessa cheered, but Rex told Nero it was cheating. While Nero was teaching Vanessa about Elvish and Draconic, Rex lit a blazing fire and started to forage for things that they could eat. He came up with some vegetables of which they roasted then ate. It was almost getting dark, and the three sat on the beach and waited.

Vanessa was getting slightly sleepy. She propped her head in her hands and stared at the forest absently. Her eyes focused on a shadow, and she jumped as it moved. The shadow came closer, and she pointed it out to Rex and Nero with growing alarm. They sprang to their feet and readied their weapons. Nero held his hand out, and a flame hovered just above his hand. Rex unsheathed his sword.

Vanessa realized that she had stored her sword in her *pera*, and she brought it out, cursing herself for not being better prepared. Nero's eyes widened at the sight of the Prowler's beautiful blade, but he stayed quiet. As they watched, the shadowy being came out into the open, and defined in the light of the rising moon— it was the shape of a woman.

The shadowy woman stopped once she saw they had noticed her. Vanessa was startled by she repulsive face of the woman as the hag drew nearer. The woman seemed to be counting. "Regina was the one who was supposed to get that message! She was the one supposed to be here! Not these weaklings! Well, I suppose I will finish off these trespassers," she thought aloud in a cackling voice that sounded like the call of a crow.

Vanessa shivered, and Nero snarled in hatred. The shadowy female drew a stick with the carving of a bird on it and a curved dagger. Then she charged the three young elves.

CHAPTER 34

THE ATTACK OF THE GARGOYLES

Abigail ran outside and summoned a protective shield around her. For the last two days, she had been taking classes on Elvish and Draconic. As she ran to where her mother and father were standing she saw on the horizon a cloud of stone creatures. They had wings, and their faces had long pointy noses or beaks. Abigail remembered when she had traveled to a castle once; there had been statues near the windows and gates that had looked similar. Now she realized what these beastly beings were—gargoyles.

A stream of the horrible stone creatures flew toward them. Her father started running to them and jumped up, turning into a dragon at the last minute. He was huge, and the gargoyles shrieked their grinding calls as he tore them apart. The dragon swooped into the air and set off to help the elven town. Once he was out of reach, a dozen more gargoyles loomed toward them.

Abigail knew that her calling was to be a healer, but she realized that she would be helping her people more if she fought. She summoned a tornado as she had been taught by the Kapacki, Luna. The tempest brought down six of the twelve gargoyles, and she smiled as they crumbled to dust. The other six charged her mother, and Abigail shrieked, for she saw another cloud of gargoyles coming toward them.

However, her mother was more than capable of handling it herself. Regina jumped up at an incredible height, as one of the foul stone creatures dove for her. It was unable to stop in time, and it smashed into the hard ground. Abigail was impressed, for her mother had easily sprung five feet into the air. Regina threw a seed on to the ground, and it sprouted instantly, growing into a wild grape bush. She controlled the vines to strangle two of the gargoyles and jumped away. *Three more to go*, she thought. Two of the three dove to meet her, and Regina dodged them with ease. She summoned raw energy into her hand and melted one of the gargoyles. The other she punched so hard it shattered.

The last gargoyle hovered in midair, glaring at her through hollow pits for eyes. This gargoyle was larger than the rest, and Regina guessed that this was the captain of the army sent here. He towered over her, while the others had been half of her height. He snarled and dove at her. She rolled to the side, and the gargoyle pulled out of his swoop just before he hit the ground. She was just about to melt it with energy when it suddenly exploded. As the creature crumbled, Regina saw that behind the broken monster stood Abigail. She was coated from head to toe in dust and chunks of rock wearing a scowl on her face.

Regina smiled, and nodded at Abigail. Abigail nodded back, dusting herself off. Behind her, several mounds of rock stood where gargoyles had been before. Regina tossed Abigail a spear that was lying on the ground, "No need to use magic all the time." Abigail grinned, "Elvish is not the only way to victory," she repeated, looking at the spear. Regina smiled, "I *really* love you!"

CHAPTER 35

A BIRD TO THE RESCUE

Vanessa shrieked as the dark woman lunged directly at her, slicing Vanessa's cheek as she went. The odd figure summoned a spell that made two pale wispy versions of her appear which charged at the boys. As the woman went for her, Vanessa raised her sword and met the attacker with a powerful blow. However, the woman raised a club to fend off the slash. Vanessa grinned. She had this fight she thought. Her confidence was replaced by pain. The woman had thrown the rest of the club, smacking Vanessa on the forehead. Vanessa fell as darkness crept over her mind. She landed hard on the beach, fighting the black. How could she have been so stupid? Vanessa saw Rex glance over at her desperately, narrowly missing the wispy creature's blade.

Nero tried to come to her aid, but was almost decapitated. Vanessa was on her own. As the woman walked towards her, Vanessa found a bit of strength and sat up. She needed to win this. Not just for her. Vanessa feinted, catching the woman by surprise. The woman threw up her staff, leaving her left side open. Vanessa was quick with the blade, but not quick enough. The woman would have stabbed her if Vanessa hadn't

174

tripped, still dizzy from the blow to her head. Regaining her balance, Vanessa lunged with her sword, but the woman parried it away.

Vanessa tried to stab at the dark figure, but the evil shadow evaded the stab and swung at her legs with the club. She must have miscalculated, for the heavy weapon smashed into Vanessa's waist, knocking the breath out of her.

Just as the woman was about to hit Vanessa's head, a sound like a song bird's whistle interrupted her. The dark figure froze, hissing. "What? NO! NO!" she cried as a shape seemed to shoot down from the sky.

Two other shapes that looked like large falcons dove in behind her. The two birds that followed flew off to help the boys, while the first figure landed gracefully on the strange woman. The dark figure crumpled under the weight of the falcon-like creature drew a spear and sank it into the woman's leg.

A bright flash appeared as the woman disappeared, taking the wispy figures who had been fighting Rex and Nero with her. The girl helped Vanessa up and healed her wound with a word. Rex and her brother sat down hard and tried to regulate their breathing. The young woman smiled kindly, her crystal blue eyes twinkling. Rex stumbled over, looking exhausted.

"Who is our rescuer?" he asked, not even looking up.

The girl with crystal blue eyes and black hair smiled again. "I am not much of a rescuer, but I couldn't let you be killed by Gracula Crow. Of all people, Rex, you should know me well."

Rex jerked his head up and grinned like a lunatic. "YOU?" he asked.

The girl grinned back. "Remember when you were ten and you wouldn't stop giving me love notes. You were a 'not-so secret admirer,'" she teased.

Rex looked sheepish.

The girl nodded and turned toward Vanessa. "Hello. I am very pleased to meet you. I am known by many names: Avis Vesper, the bird, the dead princess, or, more truthfully, the banished warrior."

CHAPTER 36

THE KAPACKI FOREST

"Avis?" Vanessa shrieked, breaking the silence. "We all thought you were dead! How on Terra?" she cried.

Rex shrugged. "Well, that isn't exactly how it went."

Vanessa was about to say more when Avis spoke up. "I will explain everything later. Right now, we are in great danger. A spy from the Dark Lord is heading this way. My scouts have already located him, and they tell me that it is a being we are not prepared for."

Vanessa frowned. "OK, but how do we escape?" she asked.

Avis smiled and hugged Vanessa. "Oh, you will love it," she said then let out a whistle that sounded more like a warbler. An instant later, three shapes flew through the air at amazing speeds. They landed on the sandy earth, feathers glinting in the moonlight.

Avis grinned. "Ever heard of hippogriffs?"

Vanessa smiled widely. "Yes! I have! I have read several books that told of them," she answered with glee. Avis looked at the graceful creatures, and they bowed to her.

Vanessa cocked her head. "I thought that you had to bow first."

Avis nodded. "If you are human, then yes. However, elves are highly respected by hippogriffs, so they bow first. Let's go."

Vanessa chose the silver hippogriff, while Rex had a white one. Nero picked a black one and rode at the back of the group. Once they had settled down on the bare backs of the flying animals, the hippogriffs leaped into the air, spreading their beautiful wings and taking flight. Vanessa held on to the thick front feathers of her steed's neck to keep her balance.

The creature turned its head to stare at her, while flying perfectly straight. "You know, you don't have to hold on so hard. I won't let you go." Vanessa didn't feel surprised due to the fact that everything she had come across could talk.

"What is your name, hippogriff?" she asked politely but in a firm voice that assured the flying being that she was a worthy companion.

The hippogriff, obviously a male, made a noise that sounded half between a horse and a bird. "My foes call me Crow-bane. My friends call me Thunder-wing. Unless you act otherwise, I will consider you a friend," he said curtly.

Vanessa smiled. "And I will act as your friend. My foes call me stupid. My friends call me Less-so," she joked.

Thunder-wing's mood seemed to lighten. "As you say, Less-so," he jested back.

Avis was in front of the group and glanced back at Vanessa from her bluish hippogriff. "Vanessa, you have an extraordinary talent. For five years, I have tried to get Thunder to not frown. Within five minutes, you have gotten him to jest with you!"

Vanessa laughed, but the sound was carried away, and the hippogriffs rose above a huge cloud and were lost to sight of anyone who might have been watching from below. Unfortunately, someone was watching from above.

Avis was the first to spot the huge roc. She sounded the alarm and steered her hippogriff away, leading the others further from the giant birdlike monster.

Nero muttered a word, and a fireball shot from his hand. The flaming object scorched a few feathers but only served to make the bird angrier. Vanessa pointed a finger at the bird and yelled a word, and lightning flashed in the almost clear sky, hitting the roc in the head. The giant bird screeched in pain as the bolts crashed down on it. Vanessa paused, staring in panic as she realized just how big the beast was. It was twice the volume of Syringa and had a beak the size of a limo. Avis raised her hand and a wave of silver crashed into the roc, making it plunge beneath the white clouds below them.

Avis told her hippogriff to speed home, and they began to fly quickly to Avis's hideout. Just as they were escaping, an earth-shattering caw came from the clouds beneath them. Vanessa cringed as yet another shriller shriek came from the clouds above her. She yelled a quick warning to Avis and the boys just as a large brown shape hurtled out of the skies.

The second roc was the half the size of the first one, and while the bigger one was gray, this one was rubicund brown. Vanessa shut her eyes as the smaller roc opened its beak, about to snap it down on her. With a violent screech the roc began to descend, a long silver arrow lodged in its eye. Avis grinned and looked up. Far above them circled strange horse creatures.

They looked like horses, anyway, but on their slender backs were birdlike wings. The wings were the color of the horses, and Vanessa noticed that the horses' tails were made from long feathers. She realized that these majestic horses were Pegasi. One Pegasus dove toward them, and the closer it got, the more detail Vanessa could see. She now realized that on each of the Pegasi was a warrior. The first to approach them not only had choppy golden hair, but one eye was green and the other blue. She flew her horse to them and seemed to land on a cloud.

"Avis, it's a pleasure to have you return as always. I wonder if you will ever come back without a story to tell. For now, I suppose that we might be of assistance to your friends?"

Vanessa guessed that the woman had met Avis before and was relieved by her friendliness. She decided to introduce herself. "Hello, my name is Vanessa Nox, and these are my traveling companions, Rex and Nero. Nero is my brother, and Rex is our friend."

The blond woman smiled. "It is a pleasure to know you, Princess Vanessa. I have also heard a lot about your friend Sir Rex. However, I have not heard much about your brother Prince Nero," noted the nymph-like woman.

Nero nodded, obviously relieved. "That is how I've wanted it. I don't handle fame well," he confessed.

The woman nodded. "Well, thank you all for leading the two rocs here. It has been a very long time since I have had such a great challenge. My name is Auri Tempestas. I also go by Gold-storm."

Vanessa recognized the way that the name was presented. "It is a pleasure to meet another Kapacki. I already know one."

Gold-storm froze. "Really? Did you happen to meet Moon-flagon?" she asked gently.

Vanessa nodded. "Yes! She is my friend!" she beamed.

Gold-storm smiled. "She is my sister!" she replied.

Now Vanessa was beginning to see the resemblance—the same angled face, same eye shape, the same nose too.

Vanessa grinned. "She is really fun!"

Suddenly, Gold-storm frowned. "What? She was the most quiet and reserved Kapacki I knew."

Avis intervened, "Goldi, why are you and the huntresses flying *here*?"

Gold-storm sighed sadly. "You have never stopped giving everyone nicknames. The Dark Lord's minions have destroyed your hideout. We are trying to track down these monsters. Obviously, he is trying to dispose of Vanessa and her friends as well. But I don't think he knows about the palace. Going there would only attract his attention and place everyone there in greater danger. I would suggest something with a little more . . . safety," suggested the Kapacki.

Avis nodded in grim determination. "I suppose so. I would normally go to the Northern Stronghold, but your kingdom is closer."

Gold-storm agreed. "My people would gladly accept you. Bring them this if they doubt you." She held out a golden necklace with a gold whirlwind molded on to it. Avis gratefully accepted it and thanked her. The Kapacki waved their thanks away with a hand. Avis flew the group to the north and they all silently departed.

After two hours of straight fast flying, the gray clouds cleared and Vanessa found herself staring at beautiful cliffs and peaked mountains. Vanessa thought that this mountain range looked a little like an Asian painting of mountains. They glided over the valley and came to a large forest of dark green. The woods spread across several mountains and rivers. A large lake lay in the center of the woods, and Vanessa knew that this was their destination. She flew up to Avis and smiled. "I guess we land here?" she asked.

Avis nodded. "We do. This is the Kapacki Forest. It is far more dangerous than the Silva Woods, *far* more dangerous."

They descended into a small clearing, and Vanessa and Avis dismounted easily. However, Rex and Nero groaned with every little movement. The girls snickered as they watched the two boys fall on to the ground with aching cries.

Avis's smile turned to a determined frown. "Get up! Kapacki do not favor weakness. Just because Gold-storm gave us her necklace doesn't mean that we are safe! There are many rogues in these woods, and they would jump at the chance for a tasty meal. Even though humans are much more delectable, if a Kapacki is hungry enough, it will surely eat you," said the bird woman.

Rex helped Nero up and nodded at Avis. Avis told her hippogriffs to relocate to a safe place until she needed them. They obeyed and took off into the sky, leaving the elves alone in the dark forest.

They set off north, keeping themselves aware of their surroundings. Vanessa fingered her sword in its sheath. The blade gave her a sense of confidence she didn't have before.

Avis led them, while Rex stayed at the back. When they had walked through the woods for an hour, a light emerged through the leaves and branches. Suddenly, a howl sounded from somewhere behind them.

Avis froze. "That was a hunting howl," she said in a frightened voice. They hurried away from the trail and dove beneath some good-smelling wildflower bushes. Avis had turned a pale color. "I can hear them over that ridge," she whispered. Rex and Nero nodded.

But Vanessa was confused. She glanced at Avis. "You can?" she asked.

The woman stared at her in shock. "You can't? I thought that a princess would have the most sensitive hearing of us all!" she exclaimed.

Vanessa shrugged. "I have great hearing for a human!" she said defensively.

Avis frowned. "But not for an elf."

Vanessa stared at her feet, but Avis put a hand on her shoulder. "I am guessing that my sister Filix removed the curse of your age and looks. But she didn't release your senses. No matter. I will awaken you."

Vanessa looked up to see Avis put a finger to Vanessa's heart then the other hand to her forehead. The touch was gentle, but to Vanessa, Avis's fingers seemed to be made of ice.

Avis looked her dead in the eye. "I, Avis, daughter of Queen Lux and King Tonitrus and first guardian of the Northern Stronghold, awaken the buried senses of this maiden and support her as the first born of three.

"Vanessa Nox, for so long, you have believed that you were human. You have been deceived, and I renew the prophecy of every hero that has ever lived. *The time will come when you will stand alone.* But remember, you will always be watched. There will always be another with you. To stand alone, you will not be utterly alone. You will just feel alone. You *will* have *someone* to help you. Now rise! Vanessa Regina Nox, future queen of all good creatures in Terra," commanded Avis.

Instantly, Vanessa felt like she had pulled muted headphones from her ears and she began to hear with new found clarity. She heard another howl, this one sounding much closer, and she widened her eyes.

As soon as the hearing came, smell followed with it: the wildflowers around them became so intoxicating that she had to step out of the bush.

After that came sight. She had always had amazing eyesight for a human, but this was like nothing she had ever experienced. The trees were distinguished so clearly that they nearly gave her a headache.

Next, feeling like never before prickled her skin. Through her feet, she could feel a large body charging though the undergrowth, creating vibrations.

Then taste. She opened her mouth and nearly screamed as she tasted the scent of a big piglike creature. She opened her mouth to warn the others, but Avis already had her bow and arrows out. The boys had their weapons out too and poised for attack. Vanessa whipped out Ensis and pointed it in the direction of the monster.

All of a sudden, out of the thick woods, came a giant boar. It was the size of a truck, and it smashed the large trees with no apparent effort. Vanessa and the others dashed aside as it charged toward them. It could not turn in time, and it rammed into a huge boulder. Its tusk missed Avis by five inches and sliced a thick tree in half. Rex stabbed his sword at the creature's flank, and it bounced harmlessly off the wiry hairs, which served to get the massive boar even madder. It turned its beady eyes to Vanessa and whipped its body around to face her. She cried out as it barreled toward her.

Time seemed to slow down. She felt her reflexes sharpen their hold on her, and she jumped out of the way a second before the boar rammed into the tree behind her. Her mind told her that if she listened, she could hear the boar's thoughts. She listened intently and was surprised to discover that her mind was correct. A whirling mess of thoughts was first thing that met her. She sensed that the creature was about to gore her with one of its tusks, and she nimbly danced away, drawing her sword Ensis.

At the sight of the fast-moving blade, the boar squealed and turned aside. Vanessa swung Ensis at the boar, accidently cleaving a tree as she went. To her surprise, the blade went right through, cutting it in half. She stabbed it at the boar as Rex had done, expecting the same result he had had. But instead of harmlessly bouncing off, it cut deep into the boar's side. The boar, in frenzy, ran into Nero, trampling him. He covered his head just in time and made a shield over himself. Unfortunately, Avis fired her arrow then, and it hit the animal in the side, making it stumble toward Rex.

Vanessa was closest to Rex, and dashed toward him. Just as the huge pig was about to make contact Vanessa, smashed into Rex, and pushed him out of the way. The boar drove itself into a tree and fell still.

Rex slouched on the ground, a large gash on his forehead. Beside him, Vanessa lay on her side. She looked at him, and he stared back, grimacing in pain. "Vanessa? Thank you," he whispered hoarsely.

She grasped his hand tightly. "You're welcome. Are you OK?" she asked.

Rex frowned. "I think I have a . . . What is it called again? A concussion. The boar smacked me in the head with a hoof. I think I remember him slashing my side too." Although Vanessa had saved him from getting gored, he had been whisked away a little too late.

Vanessa winced. "Sorry. I—"

But Rex put a hand on hers. "No, Vanessa. You saved my life. Thank you. Wait who . . .," he said, head leaning to hers.

She smiled. "OK. You're welcome. Wait a minute. It got your side?" she asked, turning Rex over with her hand.

On his left was a large puddle of blood. She shrieked as she noticed the gash in his side.

He yelped, "Wait, who are you? What are you doing? Ouch, that hurts!"

Vanessa rolled her eyes. "Oh stop, Rex!" she said.

Rex seemed perfectly serious. "I'm sorry. I don't remember you. I wouldn't forget *your* face, that's for sure."

Avis appeared at Vanessa's side, brow furrowed in worry. "His head injury is bad. *Really* bad. I can stop the bleeding and heal the injury on his side but he has been poisoned by the hoof of the boar. That I cannot do. He will need a skilled healer and if we don't find one soon, he will die," she explained.

Rex's eyes widened. "Who will die? I don't know what is going on!" he said in frustration mixed with fear.

Avis calmed him by pressing her hand to his head, but it only lasted for a few minutes. At least the bleeding was stopped and the gash on his torso was healing.

Vanessa felt inhuman strength touch her muscles, and she leaned over and picked up Rex. She was shocked, but later, she would realize that being part dragon made her stronger.

Rex frowned. "What's happening?" he asked.

Vanessa just smiled. "I am taking my friend to get much needed help," she answered.

Rex cocked his head, not understanding, then realization dawned on his face, allowing her to take him to safety.

Just as Avis was about to call on the hippogriffs, a rustle came from behind them, and they spotted the boar getting up. Avis cursed in a language that sounded like a bird chirping and drew her bow. Just as the boar recovered, another howl sounded behind them, and seven huge shapes leaped over the bushes behind them.

At first, Vanessa thought they were wolves, but later, she realized that they were too slender and large. They all were the size of large elk, except one. That one was the size of a giant moose. Muscles rippled along its back as it pounced on the boar and killed it with one bite to the throat. The five other wolflike beings circled the area while one trotted toward them. Vanessa set Rex down and put herself between him and the wolf-like creature, raising her sword.

The sleek animal seemed to let out a bark that sounded like a chuckle. "I respect bravery. I am our pack's healer, Frost-leaf. I will not hurt you," she said soothingly.

Vanessa grimaced. "How can I know?" she asked.

Avis put a hand on her shoulder. "Because she is my friend. Frost-leaf, meet Vanessa Nox. She is my niece."

Suddenly, the wolflike being changed into a young woman. "Here, let me heal the young man," she offered.

Vanessa stepped aside but kept close to Rex. The lady put a hand to Rex's forehead and immediately drew back, "He touched the boar's hoof, yes? One of the most deadly poisons which exists comes from the touch of the Pravis Boar. It is called bloodbane. Rex will not live a day more if I do not get him to our healers."

"What? No!" Vanessa yelped, worry clutching her heart.

The healer looked at Vanessa. "And he would not have lasted another minute had you not rescued him. Do not worry, I will get him to our pack in less time than either of those," she assured Vanessa with a wink.

The healer made a howling sound, and the other wolf beings drew nearer.

"Storm-coat, we need a messenger to go to Forestpack. The other healers must know," she said to the biggest creature.

He nodded and ordered one of the smaller wolves, "Yes, Frost-leaf. Red-dawn, you must let our healers know about this patient. Tell them he has bloodbane in him."

"As you say, Storm-coat," the small wolf with a coat of a dark shade of red said reverently and dashed off in haste.

Storm-coat offered to carry Rex and instructed Vanessa to hold on to Rex as they sped. Vanessa mounted the big wolf being, holding the now unconscious Rex. Vanessa was surprised by the smoothness of Storm-coat's gait. Covering Rex, she closed her eyes as they passed through brambles. One such bramble caught Rex's shirt pocket, ripping a sizable hole. Vanessa noticed a small piece of paper about to fly away and caught it.. The message read

TO: BRECON BELLUM
FROM: REX NOCTIS

Vanessa froze and stared at Rex then at the letter. Who was Brecon Bellum? She shivered at the thought and shoved the letter into her pocket.

Rex moaned as his head bumped her waist. She held it up and stared further into the woods. With her new sight, she could almost see through the trees. Suddenly, they were out in the open, staring out from a high cliff. The cliff overlooked a valley, and on the other side of the valley was a pristine-looking kingdom.

Vanessa had been expecting a camp or something but was completely shocked to discover that the odd creatures were so elegant. The ground was a far way down, and Vanessa shuddered at the thought of falling. Just then, the creature beneath her did just that.

It jumped.

Vanessa help back a scream. She just held on to Rex and the wolf as they plummeted. Although the wolf was prepared to land alive, Vanessa was not, and when she realized that they were about to hit the ground, she tried to relax all but what she needed to in order to hold Rex and Storm-coat. As they landed with a thump. Storm-coat's legs absorbed the shock wave which rippled through them.

The wolf creature glanced at her. "Perfect. Is your friend OK?" he asked casually.

Dazed by the frightening height and the would-be suicide jump, Vanessa nodded, and the being continued to run at a fast pace. They reached the kingdom within five minutes, and Vanessa gasped as she beheld the magnificent halls and castles built there.

Vanessa frowned. "Pack? This is your *pack*?" she asked.

They were met by a bunch of others. These were dressed in white colors and were gentle-looking, though each was unique as far as skin and hair colors went. Moreover, they were in human form.

Vanessa set Rex down on the ground, and the white robed healers carried him off. Only one of them stayed behind to help Vanessa follow them. This was a strapping young man in yoga-like clothing and ebony hair who reminded Vanessa of Rex. He helped her follow up large flights of stairs and into a big chamber. She sat down on a rocking chair, the only piece of furniture in the immense room.

"Umm . . . My name is Vanessa, what is yours?" she asked.

The man glanced at her. "My name is Black-tail."

Vanessa felt dazed and failed to connect everything she had just learned. "Black-tail, I do not want to be rude, but what are you?" she asked. Vanessa was always careful to not mention too many impolite things when she was in the presence of dangerous beings.

She glanced at the person in front on her and was surprised by the canine teeth he showed when he looked at her to answer her question. The young man smiled a wolfish grin and said, "You haven't already guessed? We are Kapacki, the warriors of Terra or most commonly called dragon bane."

Chapter 37

Falling Stars and Cures

Vanessa woke up from her deep sleep. She looked at the moon and guessed that it was around midnight. She crept from her bed and opened her door. For a week now, she had been doing this. She glided to the healer's room and crept to where Rex slept. Only now was he starting to remember his own name. Vanessa held his hand and knelt by his bed. Rex hardly stirred, and Vanessa once again felt tears threaten to overwhelm her. She tried to fight them, but eventually, she let them out. Her friend was helpless and weak. Vanessa had never seen Rex like this before.

She sobbed silently, so incredibly sad that Rex didn't even *remember* her. He was *dying*, and he didn't remember his best friend. Only yesterday a healer had said that they could do no more for him and that they could not find a cure. They were unsure if the Kapacki treatment would work on an elf.

She was so absorbed in her crying that she didn't realize that one of her tears had slipped on to Rex's face. He woke up and stared at her. She jumped as a hand reached her shoulder. She looked up and said, "You are supposed to be sleeping."

Rex nodded. "Yes, but how can I when a beautiful maiden is weeping over me?" he asked in a daze.

Vanessa hated this and rolled her eyes. "Oh shush! I wasn't crying! I . . . I had just yawned and. . ., and I—Oh, Rex!" she exclaimed as she looked at his face.

The tear that had landed on his cheek glowed a silvery blue then spread across his face over his entire body. In a bright flash, the room was lit up. When the light died down, Vanessa, still seeing spots, looked at Rex.

"Hey, Vanessa. Where am I?" he asked.

Vanessa broke down again and hugged him. He looked surprised and hugged her back. Suddenly, the door was opened, and Avis and Frost-leaf charged in. They stopped dead in their tracks, staring at the two.

Rex looked at both of the women. "What? Avis? Wha- what's going on?" he asked, completely oblivious to the fact that he had been severely wounded and worried over for days.

They dropped their jaws while Vanessa explained what had happened. "You've saved the boy, Vanessa! He no longer has the dose of bloodbane in him! That was the cure we needed!" the Kapacki breathed.

Avis shot Frost-leaf a glance. "Vanessa has the blood of a healer in her."

Vanessa finally stopped strangling Rex in her bear hug and wiped tears from her eyes. "Rex! You lost your memory and were mostly unconscious for nearly a week!" she explained quickly.

Rex blushed. "I . . . I . . . I don't remember a thing!" he said. Rex laughed. "Actually, I do remember something."

Vanessa froze, remembering the nights she had said words she would have never said to him in person if he were in a conscious state. She had told him things about her old life, before Terra, things she felt surely he would tease her about.

"Uh, what?" she asked nervously.

Rex laughed, dispelling her fears. "I'm hungry!"

Vanessa breathed a sigh of relief and relaxed. "OK. I'll get you something."

But the healer put a hand on her shoulder and said, "No, I will. Avis wishes to speak with you."

Vanessa nodded and followed Avis through several hallways into one of the courtyards. Avis offered a seat on a bench and looked up at the stars. Vanessa sat and stared at the constellations like her aunt.

Avis sighed. "I remember when I used to do this as a little kid. I had a friend with me at the time. He was my best friend."

Vanessa glanced at her then back at the stars. "Who?"

Avis sighed. "His name was Astrum Lux."

Vanessa jumped. "He was our ship's captain when we sailed to Elisium."

Avis looked at her. "Yes. I liked him because he never got angry with me, and he was quick to defend me when I got in trouble."

Vanessa frowned. "He seemed very sad when he mentioned you but threatened to obliterate what ever killed you."

Avis chuckled. "Really? That doesn't sound like the Astrum I know! He used to be so . . . mild."

Vanessa was about to reply when a yelp of surprise came from above them and a bright light hurtled down fast. Vanessa gasped as she heard complaints from the falling object.

"Ouch! That's my hair!" said a feminine voice.

A response came from the light as well. "Well, if you move over, I wouldn't—hey, we're falling!" said a male voice.

Another angry response followed quite swiftly. "Imagine that! That's what happens when you knock the glass locator from my hands and poke me in the eye while you're at it!"

It didn't take long for Vanessa to recognize the voice. Just before the shining ball hit the ground, it slowed then landed. The brightness of the light was dazzling, and Vanessa was temporarily blinded. When it stopped moving, the shining ceased, and two shapes became visible. Septimus had his hand wrapped around Candentia's hair, and she was pushing him away, her hand in his mouth. The other covered her eye.

Vanessa snorted. "Wow, guys. Really elegant landing!"

Septimus bowed, and Candentia rolled her eyes (a movement repeated many times that night) and stomped over to her, ripping her hair away with a vicious tug.

She hugged Vanessa and looked her deep in her eyes. "It is *his* fault! Drake gave us a locator, and just as we were in the middle of the ocean, he *knocked it from my grasp*! WE WERE IN THE MIDDLE OF NOWHERE, AND HE THROWS IT INTO THE SEA! DO YOU HAVE ANY IDEA HOW RARE AND EXPENSIVE THOSE THINGS ARE?" she screamed in outrage.

Septimus shrugged in defense. "Hey, it was *you* with the idea of flying in the first place! I wanted to take a horse!" he responded smugly. They glared at each other for a while then started arguing again.

Avis glanced at Vanessa. "Are they always like this?" she asked.

Vanessa could barely contain herself, and when Avis asked that, she let her inward laughter surface and exploded into giggles.

Septimus and Candentia looked confused. "What's so funny?" they asked in unison.

Vanessa gasped for air as she fell to the ground. "Hardly eight days ago, you were telling *me* how to behave with Rex! Now you are bickering like jackdaws!"

Septimus looked at Candentia, and she stared back. "Oh," they both said at the same time. They looked a bit chagrined, and their frustrated demeanor turned to embarrassment.

Vanessa grinned and asked, "So why are you guys here? Is something wrong, or are you here to say hi?" They shared an uneasy glance, and Candentia frowned.

Septimus coughed as he spoke first. "Well, that is the problem. We need Rex to be here when we tell you."

Just then the problem was solved. Rex sprang out of the open doors and dashed to Septimus. He barreled into his brother and gave him a bear hug.

"What are you peeps doing here?" he asked, repeating the same question that Vanessa had asked in variation.

Candentia was the one to answer, her blond hair swishing over her oval face. "Drake sent us here. We are to meet at Shadow Island as soon as possible. The time of the battle for Terra has come."

CHAPTER 38

REUNION

Abigail closed her eyes. She was lying on a hammock in the *Cetus*. The ship was sailing her and her family to a remote island called Shadow Island. Regina had told her that Vanessa and Rex would meet her there. Abigail hadn't been told why they were going there, but she felt she knew the reason. They were going for the battle: the battle for Terra.

Once they arrived at the island, they would await their friends. Abigail listened to the waves splashing against the wood. Suddenly, the boat lurched and she knew they had reached sand. She hopped off her hammock and ran out onto the deck.

They had reached a forested island. It was smaller than she had expected. Abigail felt relieved when Astrum put a hand on her shoulder and said, "This isn't Shadow Island. This is an obscure little isle called Margarita. We are just stopping to pick up food. There is a village of friendly dwarves here that will be willing to give us supplies."

As Abigail watched, five short figures waddled out of the undergrowth. One strode to the ship. "Majack triki layraf!" bellowed the squat person. Abigail was repulsed at the gruesome sight of his face. His complexion was scrunched up and his nose shot straight out. Abigail was sure it was pointy enough to spear a peach.

Astrum grinned and whispered into Abigail's ear, "He said that he welcomes all visitors that do not mean them harm. The reason I know this is because I've had to master of every language in the Citra Isles. Dwarven happens to be one of them."

Then to the dwarf, he yelled back, "Twa Comee. Leya veane mack teo Terrian."

The dwarf nodded and came close enough that he did not have to yell so loudly. "Welcome, elves! We have supplies for you, and we are willing to share."

Astrum nodded and replied. "And we are willing to pay for it!"

The dwarf smiled. "That would be appreciated," he responded.

Astrum led Abigail, Drake, and Luna Flask to the isle. The Kapacki had insisted on coming, for she was stronger now. When the dwarves caught sight of Luna, they all bowed. She smiled as the tiny children came up with shouts of glee.

Abigail raised her eyebrows. "They seem to like you a lot!" she noted.

Luna nodded. "Yes. I once saved them from a rabid malus. It was nothing."

The dwarf leader (who had been walking beside them) turned around with eyes wide with shock. "What? NOTHING? You saved our entire village!" he said.

Luna Flask shook her head but stayed completely silent. Astrum purchased several large bags of bread, nuts, and fruit. Abigail and Drake walked around for a little while, looking at the sights and other buildings. They had been sent to gather tonight's food, and Drake had bought two large lumps of cheese. Abigail got some fresh fruit in weird shapes. Drake identified them as red melons and other names Abigail had never heard before. Astrum greeted them heartily. "Guess what Regina found? Birch beer!" he said.

Abigail cocked her head. "Am I allowed to have it?" she asked.

Drake smiled. "Of course! It's like root beer but better! It tastes a little more like wintergreen."

Abigail felt her mouth watering already, and she followed her father to the mess hall aboard the ship. Regina, Neal, and Gemma met Abigail and her father at the mess hall. Syringa lounged on the couch in human form, ignoring the group. Abigail loved Syringa, and noticing that she was reading a small letter, Abigail grinned. Neal noticed Abigail and shook his head violently, seeing what she was going to do. Abigail smiled at him and did it anyway. She plopped down on Syringa's lap and started reading the letter too. Syringa snatched away the paper and shoved it under her.

Abigail smiled at her innocently. "What? All I got to read was 'Dear Syringa,' and that was it," she announced.

Syringa frowned. "Well, I have got news for you, miss! You are *not* going to snoop over *my* letters!" she stated.

Abigail smiled even wider. "Who was it from?" she asked playfully.

Syringa looked away. "No one."

Abigail put a hand to her heart. "Oh, I think I know! Is it from a secret admirer?" she asked.

Syringa went purple—literally—and rolled her eyes. "In your dreams!" she responded hotly.

Abigail made cooing noises. "Oooh! Is it from Astrum?" she asked just as Astrum himself walked in the room.

Syringa swatted Abigail in the arm. "No, you silly thing! Go make yourself useful!" she griped, blushing more.

Abigail skipped away from Syringa. "Pleeeeaaassseee tell me?" she asked nicely.

Syringa sighed. "The letter is from Thorn. Happy?" she asked.

Abigail shook her head and reached out with her hand.

Syringa sighed and said "Whatever" before handing Abigail the letter.

Abigail thanked her and skipped away to read it in the corner. She smiled even wider as she read it.

DEAR SYRINGA,

MY LAST LETTER WAS ABOUT MY SISTER STREAM. YOU MAY WANT TO KNOW THAT SHE IS WELL AGAIN AND THAT I AM NOW THE COMMANDER OF THE SPRITE AND WOODLAND ARMY. I KNOW THAT THE BATTLE FOR TERRA IS NOW HERE. DO NOT TELL THE OTHERS IN CASE THERE IS A SPY, BUT I WILL ARRIVE WITH AN ARMY OF MY SPRITES AND OTHER WOODLAND CREATURES IN TIME. UNTIL THEN, I HOPE YOU ARE WELL.

SINCERELY YOURS,
THORN

Abigail finished the letter. "Oh," she muttered, slightly disappointed that it wasn't a secret admirer.

Syringa had been talking to Regina and glanced at her when Abigail said that. She mouthed, "Told you so!"

As she stalked out of the room, Abigail caught her stare and mouthed two words, "Lips sealed!" Syringa smiled and nodded.

Abigail went back to the mess hall and noticed that a table had been set out with food pile high. She selected a plate and got some cheese, bread, and slices of red melon. Then she spotted a jug of birch beer. She got a cup then poured herself a glass. As she was sitting down at a table, Syringa appeared and sat beside her.

The dragon looked at her. "I will explain why Thorn is mailing me. When I went to the sprite kingdom once, Stream would love to explore. We were great friends. Thorn is her brother, and he was jealous of us. One day, we were exploring a dark cave, and Thorn wanted to come. He secretly followed us into the cave and got lost in a tunnel.

"With my senses, I found out that a griffin lived there. It stayed away from us, and went for Thorn. I turned into a dragon and found him. When I did, the griffin had nearly killed him, but I saved his life. As for the griffin, well, they are tasteless, shall we say. After that, Stream and I took him along whenever we would go exploring. Now he and I are friends, not friends like you might want to think but friends like

Stream and I are. I am known throughout Terra as the dragon maiden. I quite like the title, and intend to keep it," she added.

Abigail nodded and bit into her red melon. It tasted sweeter and stronger than watermelon, and Abigail loved it. But her favorite of the three was the birch beer. Abigail quickly drained her cup and went for another. She savored the sharp cheese while feasting on the fruit and drink.

Syringa chuckled. "Wow. The only time I have seen food put away like that was when I was visiting an eastern group of dwarves. They had this plump pig in their barnyard that ate much the same," joked the dragon.

Her uncle Neal Lux was on Abigail's other side, and hearing their playful quarrel, he laughed quite hard. "You guys are like two hog goblins fighting over a turkey." Abigail looked confused and glanced at him. He shook his head. "It's another way of saying that you two bicker a whole lot! Actually, scratch that. You two are worse than that," he corrected seriously.

Abigail bit into a blue tomato-like fruit. She was surprised to find that it tasted more like a papaya. She started thinking about Vanessa and saddened a bit. Finishing her food, she made her way to the upper deck of the ship to practice with Luna Flask.

The Kapacki was waiting in a crouched position. "Lapis!" she shouted, and Abigail rolled to the side as a stone whistled through the air and landed in the spot that Abigail had just been standing in.

She raised her hand and yelled, "Ignis!" And out of Abigail's hand, a ball of fire was thrown at the Kapacki.

Luna Flask made a fist in the air. "Scutum!" she returned. The ball of flame bounced off the shield that appeared and landed in the sea. Luna smiled and stood.

Abigail relaxed as she gave the signal for a pause.

"Great job! But in a fight with a shadow titan, you'd be a puddle of melted stone," said Luna

Abigail hung her head. "I tried really hard!" she complained.

Luna Flask nodded. "And you did great. Next time, give a following spell with that fireball, maybe a wave of water or something very powerful like that. I know lightning is too hard, so why don't we focus on something that won't take up all our energy so that we can fire multiple times?" she urged helpfully.

Neal brought up a wooden dummy so that she could practice on it. To make it more interesting, Luna Flask sat on a chair next to the dummy and made it seem to be moving. Abigail spoke a word, and with her mind, she made small long shoots of water come up from the sea and turn to ice as they pierced the wood.

Luna nodded in approval and made the wooden object spin around. "Good. Now try to hit its heart. You have three tries," she challenged.

Abigail took a deep breath and bent a sleek stream of water, turning it into ice. With a measured stare, Abigail aimed at the dummy and fired the ice spear. It smashed into the dummy's chest, but it missed the heart. Abigail readied another ice spear and fired it too, but she had aimed too far down, and it hit the stomach. Frustrated, Abigail summoned a tidal wave of the water. It crashed down on the area opposite Abigail, and she froze it with a word.

Unfortunately, Luna Flask was caught in the middle of it. Abigail watched as the Kapacki breathed out and made a little warm air bubble around herself. Once her arm was warmed up, she made a fist, and it was engulfed in flame. Luna Flask made her way out of the ice and laughed once she was free.

"That was perfect! You threw little ones, making yourself seem weak, then you pounded them. Great. Now we will fight. I will protect you with a simple spell. I will need no such things. I am already almost invincible," she said, placing a protection spell on Abigail.

Once they were ready, Luna Flask allowed Abigail to start first. As she thrust her hand at Luna Flask a huge rock appeared and sailed toward her. Then as a follow up, she kicked her foot out, and fire blasted from it. Luna dodged the boulder and was surprised by the blast of fire. It washed over her, and Luna fell to the ground, groaning with pain.

Abigail shrieked and ran over to her, afraid that she had hurt her mentor. She knelt by the Kapacki and checked for injuries. Suddenly, Luna Flask sprang into the air and breathed a torrent of flame at her.

Abigail yelped and threw her hand into the air and spat out a spell the Kapacki had used on her. "Scutum!" she cried. As she did that, she made a wave of water come up to extinguish the flame while dousing Luna Flask. The Kapacki rolled to the side and wrapped her arm around Abigail. She hefted her into the air without strain and easily caught her. She repeated it a few times, each throw going higher and higher.

Abigail shrieked, "Stop! Stop!" And Luna Flask set her down. Abigail rolled on to her side. "Ugh. I am Kapacki sick," she muttered.

Luna laughed and helped her up. Staring over the deck and gazing at the horizon. Luna smiled as her gaze encountered a dolphin-like creature leaping into the air.

Abigail studied it. "What is that?" she asked, expecting anything.

Luna smiled. "A cetus or, in other words, an Elvish dolphin. It is a bit larger than your normal porpoise, but it is about the same shape. The name of our ship comes from that creature."

The ship drew nearer, and the dolphin swam right next to it. The dolphin waved a tail at her then splashed off to join his pod. As Abigail stood staring at the clear water, she beheld that the water seemed to be moving oddly. As she stared harder, she realized that a translucent woman was swimming beside the ship. She waved and more joined the glasslike woman.

Luna Flask smiled and rolled her eyes. "These water spirits are called Nereid women."

Abigail waved back to the lady and turned her head to ask Luna, "Why are they here?"

Luna Flask seemed to realize that something was wrong. "Yes, good question. There is usually only one, and even that is rare. Unless . . . Oh no! We must stop the ship!" she shrieked.

Abigail sensed that it was important, and she refrained from asking the burning questions. Instead, she frowned hard, concentrating. "Why don't we just make the water stop pulling us? If we made a barrier, then we would be just fine," she suggested. Luna Flask agreed and made a pulling motion with her hands. The water suddenly seemed to be slowly stopping the ship.

Abigail gasped. "That is so cool!" she said.

Luna ground her teeth in concentration and pulled even harder. "This is more difficult than you might think! Do you mind helping? It'd be a bit easier if you would!" she said.

Abigail guessed that "more difficult than you might think" was a big understatement. She nodded and started pulling her hands in the same way that the Kapacki was. Suddenly, she felt like she was pulling a boulder. The ship stopped, and Neal and Astrum bounded up to the deck.

Astrum was vivid with fury. "What are you two doing? Have you no idea that we are on a—" he began, but he stopped as he beheld the many gathering Nereids. He gasped and ran to the helm to turn the ship around.

Syringa, Drake, and others came onto the deck to see why they had stopped. Syringa jumped off the railing, turned into a dragon, swooped into the air, and pulled the ship back with her tail.

Drake jumped onto the front of the large ship and opened his mouth. Out jetted a torrent of hot white flame. With the momentum of the jet of flame, the ship moved backward. But even with all that, the waters pulled them closer.

Drake stopped blowing his fire and dashed down to help Astrum. Abigail and Luna stopped their pulling, and Abigail ran to the front of the ship to see what was the matter. She gasped as she beheld the terrifying sight. A large whirlpool swirled directly in front of them. She yelped and turned to the deck to stare at the Nereid that had first arrived.

A smooth voice greeted her. "Hello, milady. You and the others now know you are in great trouble. We can help if you say so," she murmured in a voice that penetrated deep into Abigail's soul.

"Please do!" she responded.

With a flick of her hand, the Nereid summoned her sisters and dove to the front of the ship. Once they started pushing, the whole ship lurched, turned slowly and began moving quickly away from the swirling waters. After they were in a safe spot, Abigail leaned over the railing to thank the Nereids, but they were gone.

Luna Flask didn't seem too surprised by that. "They are normally very shy beings, but they love elves and other creatures of light."

Neal and Astrum came back to the deck and patted Abigail on the back. "That was good thinking asking the Nereid. She is a friend to all of us, and she held our life in her hands. Nereid women are very secretive beings but have great power and strength over the seas and other large bodies of water, actually any water for that matter. We owe them our lives," said Astrum.

Neal smiled. "It has been a long time since I have come close to the whirlpool. She is a feisty being. It has been an even longer time since I faced danger with my brother by my side."

Astrum grinned. "Ha! You have plenty troublesome adventures without me. Though probably more when I am with you," he joked.

Luna Flask nodded. "That is true. Abigail showed a lot of strength in that small battle."

Abigail felt utterly exhausted. The sun was slowly going down, and she could feel her strength draining with it. She retired to her bedroom and closed her eyes. But when sleep overcame her, it was not what she expected.

Abigail's vision was fuzzy, but she seemed to be in the middle of an all-out war. A large malus towered over her. It grinned, showing razor-sharp teeth, and it raised a club and brought it down on her. She screamed as darkness enveloped her, and she could barely hear her sister Vanessa cry out from somewhere to her right, "ABIGAIL, NO!" and the dream ended.

She sat up, skin damp with sweat. She looked over to her left, and then to her right. On her right sat a dark figure cloaked in a black robe. He shoved his hood back, and Abigail was startled to see that it was a very

SOPHIE EVANS

handsome man. His irises were pure black, and he stared at her with a pleasant smile on his face.

"Hello, Abigail. How is your little cruise going?" he asked.

Abigail sprang up. "Who are you? Why are you here?" she screamed.

The man waved a hand. "I am simply visiting. My name is Umbra."

Abigail cried out and scooted away. She remembered how much Silva had looked like Rex and Septimus and was very shocked to see their father had no similarities besides the shape of his face. The Dark Lord had paler skin and flaxen hair. Abigail guessed that his eyes might have been blue.

The Dark Lord chuckled. "It's fine. I won't hurt you! Why are you frightened?"

Abigail frowned. "You're evil. You tried to kill Luna Flask. You are threatening the elves."

Umbra's smile turned into a thoughtful scowl. "It seems that you have been misinformed. For your sake, it seems, I must tell you the truth. Luna Flask killed one of my children—not Gemma but Olea. She was the youngest, you see, always getting into trouble. She loved me very much, and when I went away on a trip, she tried to follow me. I was passing through the Mars Valley not realizing that my daughter had followed me on the ground riding her horse Blossom. She accidently crossed into Luna Flask's territory. The Kapacki mercilessly killed her—the end."

Abigail widened her eyes and wanted to yelp, but she was frozen in shock. "What? Impossible!" she said.

Umbra nodded. "It is true. By the way, you seemed a little sad when Neal compared you with Vanessa. I didn't realize you were so . . . unappreciated?" he asked with a look of concern.

Abigail frowned, surprised that he would be so understanding. "Yes, I actually was. Well, Vanessa does deserve it, right?" she said.

Umbra nodded his head. "Of course, but you do too," he insisted.

Abigail felt confused. "Why?" she asked.

The Dark Lord looked astonished. "You just single-handedly saved the ship! You have healing powers that can best any doctor on that realm you call earth! You deserve to have a palace in your honor! You deserve anything a queen would have."

Abigail shrugged, feeling embarrassed. "Uh, well . . . I don't know. I didn't exactly do—" She began but was cut off as the Dark Lord stood up and waved a hand.

"And has anyone given you praise? Has anyone even thanked *you?" he asked.*

Abigail felt uncomfortable, but deep inside, she felt a twinge of resentment. She shook her head.

Umbra looked disappointed. "I didn't think so."

Abigail didn't like making him feel disappointed. She wanted to please him badly. Abigail tilted her head back to look at him. He did *have a point.*

"Oh, I must go. I have important business to . . . finish. I'll see you on the battlefield. Just make sure you know which side you're on—the one who appreciates you or the one who does not. I give my word that you can trust me. Now you just need to wake up and decide where your loyalties lie," he said.

Abigail shrieked as the world started to spin, and she woke up with a start.

The ship lurched to shore, and Abigail came out of her room. She had been dressing in the clothes that had been laid out. She opened the door and stepped out into the open.

She found herself facing Gemma, who folded her arms. "I can sense my father's presence. He visited you, didn't he?" she asked.

Abigail nodded sheepishly. "Uh well . . . " she began but was silenced as Gemma frowned. "I know. I woke up when you began that dream. I overheard your conversation."

Abigail winced. "I—" she tried but failed to speak more as Gemma's scowl deepened.

"Abigail, there is something that I have learned about my father. He could give you his word, but that is like handing out a piece of paper. His word means nothing. He is not the person that he orchestrated in your dream. He—"

But it was Abigail who interrupted. "Did Luna Flask actually kill Olea?" she asked, remembering what the Dark Lord had said. He seemed really believable.

Gemma's eyes filled with sorrow. "It was an accident. Olea fell into a hole that was inhabited by a basilisk. The large snake didn't pay her attention, but Olea's screams drew the attention of Luna Flask. The Kapacki was in wolf stage, and she did not recognize Olea. She pounced on the basilisk and accidently slammed Olea against the wall, killing her instantly. Luna Flask apologized relentlessly, but Father simply ignored her apologies and tried to kill her. Silva was the one who stopped him," she explained.

"Doesn't seem like a 'merciless attack,'" added Gemma.

Abigail slumped beside her and sighed.

Gemma gently wrapped her arms around the young girl. After several moments Gemma asked, "Want to go get some fresh air?"

Abigail frowned as the sunlight hit her eyes, squinting at the island they had arrived on. It was full of hills and small bits of forest here and there. She enjoyed a fresh breeze that carried the scent of lavender plants and sea salt. She and Gemma basked in the sun for a while, the early morning air seeping into their lungs.

Astrum strode toward them, armor clinking as he strode towards them. "It's nice that you two are awake. Now if you can help us unload, that would be splendid," he said curtly.

Gemma rolled her eyes as he turned away, making a face of disgust. "No wonder he's single. Bossy! Bossy!" she whispered to Abigail. Abigail giggled and slapped a hand over her mouth to stop the noise.

Regina was closest to them, and she glared at the two young girls. "How dare you make fun of him! He has had a very rough life. He does not enjoy being a bachelor," she chided.

They stopped their humor and went to help unload some supplies. Gemma smiled slyly at Abigail and lifted a barrel with a word of Elvish. She told Abigail the word, and Abigail was able to help with the lifting. Neal sat down next to them afterward, cooling down in the shade of a nearby maple tree. Abigail felt tired. Even though Elvish was the simplest type of magic, she knew that she was too young to do much. Only a few elves could maintain Draconic as it was stronger magic and required even more energy. She scanned the skies, trying to glimpse any of her friends flying in but could not spot any of them. She waited awhile, fading in and out of sleep. Suddenly, a spot of light appeared in the clear skies.

Abigail jumped up, yelping in excitement, "It's them! It's Candentia and Septimus! They have Rex and Vanessa!" she cried.

The slender shining light landed gracefully, and Candentia stopped her glow. She and the others seemed to appear out of the light.

Vanessa was massaging her head, and Rex and Septimus were spinning in circles looking dizzy. Abigail hugged Vanessa, and they both smiled as Gemma gave a group hug.

Candentia knelt on the sandy ground and grimaced. "Ugh. I hate traveling with so many boys. Flying with girls is no problem, but boys smell. Bad. And when I say bad, I mean *bad*," she griped, and the girls laughed. Rex and Septimus glared at them, and Abigail caught Rex trying to smell himself.

Abigail studied Candentia. The star was prettier than most of the women in the group and seemed to remarkably clean. Candentia noticed Abigail watching and smiled. "I can get filthy when I want to. Stars are just naturally like this. Though most of my sisters claim that I am the prettiest, I do not care," she said, answering Abigail's silent questions.

Candentia had a different dress on then when she had departed with Septimus. It was a silver dress that hung just below her knees. It was sleeveless with a turtleneck. Abigail wondered where Candentia got these extravagant dresses but quickly dismissed the thought, worried that Candentia would, once again, read her mind.

Septimus fell to the ground next to Rex, and Vanessa frowned. "OK, Nero. Come out," she ordered. Abigail felt confused but yelped as a young boy appeared in front of her. He had shaggy black hair and blue-green eyes. He smiled sheepishly, and Abigail realized he looked familiar. He and Vanessa looked very much alike.

She felt surprised as Vanessa answered her questioning thoughts. "Everyone? Meet my little brother. His name is Nero."

Regina hopped off the boat and regarded Nero with suspicious eyes. "You aren't supposed to be alive. You let me believe you were dead." she said with a glimmer of fright in her eyes.

Nero looked ashamed. "I am sorry I led you to believe that, Mother. But I needed to disappear. I thought that Vanessa was dead."

Vanessa obviously had been told this story, but Abigail had not. She walked up to them. "What? You thought he was dead!" she exclaimed in pure shock.

Regina winced. "Before you were born, Drake, Vanessa, Nero, and I lived in Terra. When neither I nor any of my sisters would accept the throne, we knew the responsibility would ultimately fall on Vanessa. To save her, we decided to leave Terra and settle in California. The morning of our move, we found his crib smashed in pieces and your brother, Nero, no where to be seen. We searched for him for weeks and could only assume he was killed. Abigail frowned, but understood.

Nero smiled awkwardly, "Hi, sis," he said, and gave her a hug. She numbly hugged back and sat on the sandy ground.

Candentia took in the awkward reunion and most of the discouraged faces. Leaping into the air, she got everyone's attention. She raised her voice to be heard. "Hey, guys! I hate to interrupt but we are about to fight an evil lord. You may have been separated once but you are together now. I have seen many wars, but never have I seen one army with a better chance of winning! Now who wants to kick some Dark Lord butt?" she asked with a beautiful smile.

The whole group, now named the Elven Heroes, broke out in cheering. Candentia slowly drifted down, and Septimus met her with a bear hug.

Abigail, though initially elated, began to feel a worm of doubt. What if these people were misguided? How were they sure that they were on the right side?. Candentia had somehow managed to squeeze away from Septimus and was gliding over to her, feet barely an inch off the ground.

She came up to Abigail. "I sense fear and doubt. Those two feelings are not going to help us win the war."

Abigail realized that this was a person she could talk to. "Well, yes. I don't know how you managed to raise up the Elven Heroes so easily."

Candentia frowned, marring her ethereal features. "Didn't you feel happy?" she asked, a glimmer of uncertainty in her dark blue eyes.

Abigail realized that she had felt a sense of joy too. "Well, I suppose so," she agreed.

Candentia let out a sigh of relief. "OK, good. I haven't lost my touch."

Vanessa wormed through the crowd. "Avis is here because she is bringing reinforcements."

Abigail gasped. "What?" Regina had told her a lot about Avis, the "dead" princess.

Now Vanessa realized she had to explain. "Avis is alive and more than well. She saved us from an evil crow lady. Then she saved us from a roc and several other nasty beasts. She has been very helpful."

Abigail grimaced. "Did you ask her about Filix, Alauda, Nebula, and Prati?" she asked balefully.

Vanessa frowned. "Why? Is something wrong with them?"

Abigail raised her eyebrows. "Don't you know? They were captured, and Avis was the one that we were told was guilty. Within the week, three of her sisters were reported missing. Neal told Mom, and I overheard."

Vanessa raised only one eyebrow (something that terribly frustrated Abigail because the younger sister had only been able to do both at the same time). Vanessa was starting to see what was wrong. "But Avis would never do something like that. Why would you say—" she began but was cut off as Regina wove her way toward them.

"I heard about Avis, Vanessa. Septimus and Rex told me everything. Nero added the bits and pieces. I get the picture, and I know that Nebula and Prati were *not* captured . . . not by Avis at least. She did, however, *retrieve* Filix and Alauda," she said.

Vanessa wanted to bet that the Dark Lord was responsible for the disappearance of Alauda, Nebula, and Prati. She had seen what the

Dark Lord was capable of, and she knew that they were only alive because he wasn't trying his utmost to kill them. He had the resources to wipe out nations, yet Vanessa didn't fear him. She feared for her friends and family but she did not fear the Dark Lord.

Abigail, however, felt quite differently. She thought they had no chance. The Dark Lord was powerful and capable. Maybe if he ruled the whole of Terra they could have peace. She went inside the ship and looked in a nearby mirror. She stared at her face and remembered she had not been transformed like Vanessa had. She noticed her auburn hair and green eyes. She sighed and was about to move on when a graceful woman appeared in the reflection. Abigail turned around and faced the person in the mirror. Just then, Herba stepped through the mirror.

She had bright green eyes and wore a placid expression. The slender woman's dress was a shimmering evergreen.

"I suggest you stop moping about your appearance. There are more important things than beauty. My name is Herba. I suppose you would call me your aunt, she grumbled.

Abigail stared at her in shock. "Where did you come from? And how did you do it?" she asked,

The slender woman frowned. "Your mirror acts as a communication channel and with the right magic, a portal. Do you young people know anything?"

Abigail wondered why Herba had such an attitude.

Regina suddenly appeared in the doorway. "If I remember right, you are one of the 'young people' in our family.

Herba grimaced. "Whatever you say, sister."

Abigail admired Herba for a while. The she-elf was very striking and so young-looking to be her aunt. Her black hair had a green sheen, and her face was angled.

Regina was about to speak when a yell sounded from outside.

Herba rolled her eyes and frowned. "Great. My other unruly sister has arrived."

Abigail raced outside and gasped at what she saw. A figure dressed in a blue beach dress was surfing on an oval plate of ice, being trailed

by a bunch of cetus. With long hair streaming behind her, the woman
dove into the sea and sprang out of the water, causing a tidal wave to
douse the Elven Heroes. The girl flipped off the ice and landed neatly
on the sand while making a peace sign. Abigail immediately liked her.
The girl had wild black hair that hung in wild waves around her face
framing her tan complexion. The girl had a spray of freckles on her face,
serving to give her a mischievous look, and her sea blue eyes made her
look piercing. She grinned and strode over to Herba and Regina who
had made their way off the ship and onto the beach to greet her. Making
sure to wipe off the water on them, she gave them both a bear hug. She
glanced around and spotted Vanessa and Abigail.

"Wow, I didn't realize my sister had such lovely children! So these
are the poor girls who have had the decision made for them to take the
place of supreme rulers of the elven court of puppets!" she said with a
sly smile. Abigail could tell Vanessa liked her too.

Vanessa and Aqua got along wonderfully. They acted like sisters,
bonding instantly. Vanessa led Aqua away, talking about her adventures
and telling stories about magical creatures. Abigail felt slightly jealous
but did her best to shake that feeling away. Walking back to the ship
she noticed her mother laughing with Vanessa and her own father
brushed past her without stopping to say anything. She felt small. As
she stepped up to a balcony of the ship, she looked over the sea and felt
very forgotten. She wished for a place she could feel loved—*accepted*.
She looked up having made her decision.

CHAPTER 39

A STARRY GHOST

Rex slipped away from the group, his eyes on Herba. He remembered what Septimus had said about the many traitors, and he grimaced as he beheld another.

He shot a look at Vanessa as she glanced at him. He motioned with his head for her to join him, She made her varied excuses to get away. She reached Rex in a pile of underbrush and gave him a wary eye. "What's wrong?" she asked as he pulled her deeper into the undergrowth.

Rex blew out a small sigh. "Herba's a traitor," he said.

Vanessa recoiled. "What? How would you know that?"

Rex frowned. "You don't believe me? There is a good reason she hasn't been captured by the crow lady."

Vanessa looked hurt. "Of course, I believe you, Rex! But what about Aqua and my mother?" she asked.

Rex grimaced again. "They have been under a lot of protection. Remember, your father is a powerful dragon, and few enemies would dare anger him. And Aqua . . . Well, let's just say that she is as invincible as the sea. She can even *turn* into water. None can catch her."

Vanessa looked like she had been punched. Rex felt bad for sharing his suspicions about Herba. Vanessa straightened up and looked Rex in the eye. "I am thankful the traitor is not someone closer to me."

Immediately, he felt defensive, but Vanessa put a hand on his. "I am glad that I can trust you. I don't know what I would do if *you* were a traitor. You are a great friend, Rex," she said and gave him a hug.

Rex felt guilty for thinking she didn't trust him. He knew that she would be right to not trust anyone. He hugged her back. "I am glad that I can trust you too. Oh... by the way, Candentia and Septimus are engaged."

Vanessa recoiled. "WHAT?" she asked, the words taking a while to register in her mind. Suddenly a big grin spread on her face just by the thought.

"They are," Rex affirmed.

She widened her eyes. "But he is only sixteen!" she protested happily.

Rex shook his head. "No, no, you don't get it. He is a hundred and sixteen. We just like to put the 'hundred' behind us as elves. You wouldn't guess how old Tonitrus is. I think it was around eighty hundred. Terra is not a young realm. She has at least a trillion years on her . . . if!"

Vanessa smiled. "Can I be the bridesmaid?" she asked.

Rex chuckled. "You can talk to Candentia about it. I would imagine she couldn't be happier to have you. But you'll be fighting for your place as bridesmaid with a million stars, twelve kapacki, eighty sprites, and countless elves. Candentia will be overwhelmed."

Vanessa frowned. "But we are about to have a war! Will they be waiting till after?" she asked.

Rex nodded. "You should probably get back."

Vanessa agreed. "OK, but what about you?"

Rex cringed for a second but quickly changed his features to appear nonchalant. "Oh, I'll be there in a second. Drake told me to scout around."

Vanessa shrugged and had that look on her face that read *Why would he ask you? Last I noticed, a drunken elephant was quieter than you!* But she just grinned and ran off.

Rex checked that she was really gone and sighed. He looked up at the sky and, shot up, flying so quickly that no one could catch sight of him. After he was high enough, he stopped so that he could look down on the island. A sudden movement out of the corner of his eye caught Rex's attention. A blindingly white horse was galloping to the ship. Rex jumped with curiosity. He flew to the camp and landed out of sight close. He ran to where Drake was and reported what he had seen. Drake took in the information with a grim stare.

Vanessa walked over and asked what was wrong. Rex again related the story, skipping the flying part. Candentia was sitting nearby and heard what they had said. She frowned and came to the conversation. "That sounds like Alba. She is my friend."

Rex nodded. "Let's hope she's a friend. We don't need more enemies," he said ernestly.

Drake scowled thoughtfully, "Alba, you say? And Rex claims it was a horse?"

Rex nodded. "Yes, why?"

Drake suddenly seemed to come to a realization. "Did you see the horse up close with detail, or was it far away?"

Rex didn't understand what his old friend was trying to get at. "It was far away," he answered promptly.

Drake looked at Candentia. "You say your friend was a horse?" he asked her.

She shook her head. "Not at all! She would kill me if I said that! She does not come from that race, though some might claim it! She is a unicorn!"

Drake smiled. "Then that is your answer! We have a unicorn for a guest!" he said just as a pearly figure leaped from the trees and sailed majestically to the ground.

Majestic wasn't the right way to describe the elegant equine. It was nothing like a horse. It had a smoother shape than one. Of course, it had a two-foot horn in the center of its head. Looking closer, Vanessa beheld carvings on it. The carvings were of leafy vines which crawled up the horn. With longer legs and a soft mane of silky hair, the unicorn reared around and faced the group.

Rex's legs felt weak as a voice spoke from the horse. "*Ave!* How are you, Candentia, and who are these scraggly people around you?" she asked.

Candentia giggled. "Oh, I am perfect! These are my friends"

The unicorn whinnied in a sound that was similar to a human laugh. "Well! I haven't seen you in a while! Much less on the ground!"

Candentia began to glow. "Well, two certain elves brought me down," she said as her eyes lingered on Vanessa and Septimus.

The unicorn nodded. "Well, enough of that! I must take you to the queen."

Candentia grew pale. "What? She is much too busy! She could not possibly want to talk with me!" she said panicked.

Alba shook her head, white locks shimmering in the sunlight. "She *wishes* to see you. You may take three companions if you'd like."

Candentia nodded. "Oh yes! Vanessa, Abigail, and Gemma."

Vanessa and Gemma nodded enthusiastically, but Abigail backed away. "Ah no! I don't want to do that. Take someone else."

Candentia nodded, her blue eyes worried. "OK. What about you Luna?" she asked.

Luna Flask nodded. "I would be honored."

Vanessa ran to the ship and packed her *pera* while Rex followed her. "Vanessa, it's too dangerous! I think I know whom she is talking about, and you must be very careful! Remember to keep Ensis handy. Always be alert!"

Vanessa finished packing and rolled her eyes. "OK, OK! Sheesh! You worry more than my mother," she shot back.

Rex shivered suddenly despite the balmy temperatures. "Sorry," he winced. "That is bad, isn't it?"

Vanessa glared at him then laughed. A sudden cry called them from the ship. Candentia was arguing with Septimus. "I have to go! If I don't, everything will fall apart. You don't want my mother getting angry," she said. "I dread the place, and I really don't want to go but there is no other choice."

Vanessa walked up. "Why? Where are we going?"

Candentia grimaced. "I am going to my mother. You people are staying here. I am going alone!" she snapped.

Vanessa was very confused but didn't say anything. Candentia hugged the Elven Heroes and kissed Septimus on the cheek.

Candentia hugged Vanessa last and nodded. "Take care of them."

She turned to Alba and told her that she was ready to leave. Septimus stood there, watching Candentia gracefully climb onto the unicorn and ride off swiftly, silvery hair flying in the wind. Her silver and white dress lightly fluttered in her wake as she urged the majestic horse onward. The beautiful horse's pure white hooves made no sound as she departed, but Septimus seemed to be hollow, as if his spirit had left with her.

Vanessa looked at Rex with a note of some confusion, wondering why everyone was so sad. "What is so wrong about Candentia visiting her mother?" she asked.

Rex shuddered. "Well, if you survive getting to her palace, she usually makes you go on a quest. The problem is no one has ever survived a quest or came back sane. Actually, I take that back. One person survived a quest without going crazy and lived to tell the tale. That was Aurora, and she had a special spell on her that protected her from most harm," he said sadly.

Vanessa felt the air rush out of her as she heard that. Candentia had a husband waiting for her when she got home. But in the dimming light, Vanessa caught sight of the star, and could not help but think that Candentia looked much like a ghost.

CHAPTER 40

A SURPRISING BATTLE

Vanessa grimaced as she awoke from another bad dream. Darkness, a terrified scream, a malus—she had been having those dreams for a while after Candentia had left, and she was convinced that the star had given them some kind of spell for dreams when she was there.

She shuddered as she put on a cloak. Everyone had had a fair amount of tension through the days but tonight they were resting. Though it was a new moon, the starlight cast enough light for Vanessa to see, and she walked to the deck of the dragonhead. She sat and waited, watching the stars.

A floorboard creaked behind her, and Vanessa sighed. "Rex, you are the master of clumsiness! Why—" But she broke off as she turned. A lone dark figure was standing right behind her and it wasn't Rex. The figure looked like he was made of shadow, except he was much taller: a shadow titan.

Vanessa shrieked the alarm and rolled to the side as the shadow titan lunged toward her. She yelped and nearly plummeted into the water. Out of instinct, she held out a hand and snapped her fingers. Ensis appeared out of thin air, and she slashed at the shadow titan, slicing off an arm. This seemed to pain the creature, but it did not slow. With lightning speed, the creature took Vanessa's feet out from under her. She had expected this, and as she jumped to avoid him, she stabbed at the figure's heart. The sword sprang from her hand with unseen force and pierced the shadow titan's heart, killing it with a flash of light.

A pearl was left where the titan had been standing, and curiously, Vanessa picked it up. The pearl was twice the size of a normal one, and Vanessa admired the color. How could something so pure come from something so evil she thought.

She caught sight of a dozen shapes moving in the undergrowth a little way from the ship, and she yelled an alarm. Within seconds, Astrum and Neal sprang from the ship, closely followed by Drake and Rex.

Rex stopped and ran toward Vanessa. "Are you OK? Why did you yell the alarm?" he asked then yelped in shock as he beheld the pearl.

"You *didn't*," he said, eyes wide.

Vanessa shrugged her shoulders uncomfortably. "I killed a shadow titan. But I think we are in a bit more danger than that. And why did the creature leave a *pearl* behind, of all things?"

Rex grinned at Vanessa. "That pearl is a wish. The are a few things you can't wish for such as bringing back the dead."

Vanessa sighed. "I suppose this may be useful in the coming days."

Rex hastily pulled out a leather string and handed it to her. Vanessa fastened the leather around the pearl and tied it on her neck, nodding her thanks to Rex. They went silent as another cry came from the woods. They could hear the clashing of sword against sword, crashing, and the undergrowth snapping. The sounds of battle raged through the forest near the ship, and Vanessa and Rex raced after it. Vanessa's sword felt like it was pulling her toward the fight, and she bounded, leaping off the ship and landing on the sand on her feet. She sprang like a cat into the battle.

Rex was close behind her when they met the first huge malus with their swords. The malus dissolved, and Vanessa smirked with her pleasure. They killed two more of the malus and one wraith. Her father had shape-shifted into a dragon and joined them in the fight, swooping overhead to distract the malus.

Vanessa heard Neal call out in pain and caught sight of him, trapped beneath a fallen tree with a malus looming over him. Blood was welling from a deep cut in his leg, and Vanessa and Rex raced to help him. Astrum got there first and started battling the huge beast. He glanced to Vanessa and Rex and shouted, "Hurry! I will hold it off! Save my brother!" Vanessa and Rex lifted the tree, and Rex quickly carried Neal away in his arms.

They were halfway across the beach when they heard Astrum cry out in agony. Vanessa turned back to see the malus pound Astrum and pin his back to a tree as he aimed a killing blow. She screamed and started running back towards him but would not make it in time.

Suddenly, a figure appeared out of nowhere in front of Astrum. She blasted the malus with a bolt of silver energy and sent the beast rocketing into a boulder where it exploded.

The rest of the malus retreated, confused by the death of their defeated leader. Vanessa looked back at the woman that had appeared and saved Astrum's life. She gasped with recognition and smiled. The woman wiped sweat from her forehead.

"And don't you ever—*ever*—mess with my fiancé!" she yelled after the retreating malus.

Vanessa grinned broadly, while Rex shouted gleefully, "OH YEAH!"

Astrum looked up at Avis. "You never did say 'yes'!" he said happily.

Avis grinned and kissed him on the cheek. "I never said 'no.'" With that, she helped the injured Astrum into the ship.

Regina and Gemma met them on the deck, and Vanessa explained the whole story. They looked even more astonished as they greeted Avis. Rex carried Neal into the ship so his wounds could be dressed, and Rex came back in a few minutes later to Vanessa.

She smiled at him and hugged him. "I'm so glad Avis is back," she whispered.

Rex nodded, "Me too."

Vanessa gave him the evil eye. "And what about those 'secret admirer' notes?"

Rex grinned guiltily. "That was when I was eight! I told you that I was almost too young to remember it! Septimus encouraged it too!" he yelped defensively.

Vanessa rolled her eyes. "Yeah right! Blame it on your brother! I bet Avis knew that it was you!"

Rex opened his mouth but shut it again. Avis passed them and winked at Vanessa. She helped Astrum lie down on a couch and started talking while Luna checked his wounds. Drake came in later and joined the conversation.

After a while, Rex got Avis's attention. "Hey, how did you know to come?" Regina smiled knowingly, expecting the answer before it was said.

Avis grinned slyly. "A little birdie told me."

CHAPTER 41

BRECON BELLUM

Gemma shook Vanessa violently to get up, and Vanessa awoke with a start, groaning with unhappiness. She stood up very quickly, startling Gemma.

"What? What is happening? More malus?" she asked confused.

Gemma shook her head, relaxing and sitting on Vanessa's hammock. "Nope. I can tell you have been dreaming of more nightmares!"

Vanessa nodded. "You guessed right. What's up?" she asked.

Gemma sighed happily. "My friend is coming. She's an Amazon."

Vanessa was even more confused. "Huh? What are Amazons?" she asked groggily.

Gemma laughed at her half asleep frined. "The Amazons are a group of tough warrior women. Their warrior queen, Prati, has just been taken. They are very afraid, and as such, are splitting up. I used to be one of them. Now . . . I am not."

Vanessa cocked her head. "And . . .," she silently asked.

Gemma sighed with weariness. "As a result, we are about to have a visitor. Her name is Brecon Bellum. Most call her Brecon for short.

She is a friend of mine, and Rex has been keeping in touch with her for a while because . . .," she trailed off.

Suddenly, Vanessa felt horrible. "Wait! Does he . . .," she began to ask.

Gemma shook her head. "No, Amazons are not to marry or anything like that. They can depart from the group and get married, but only the queen can have a husband . . . It's complicated," she answered, still smiling with joy that her friend was coming.

Vanessa sighed. "OK. I'll get dressed," she said.

"Brecon has already arrived, so we can go upstairs. You know what, I actually think she is Nero's age! And Nero hasn't even met her yet," she said with a sly grin.

"Are you trying to get my brother a girlfiend?" she asked.

Gemma shook her head. "Nope he just needs humbling."

They both giggled and then went up to the deck. There, Vanessa found that she was looking up to a tall girl with short coppery hair and tan skin.

The girl grinned. "What's up? You're the new girl? Welcome to paradise." She spoke in a Southern accent.

Vanessa felt embarrassed by the confident stare of the girl. She *did* look about Nero's age and had a spray of freckles around her nose. She held a heavy metal spear in one hand as if it weighed nothing and rested the other on her hip. Vanessa was impressed.

"So um, Brecon, you are an elf?" she asked.

Brecon giggled and shook her head. "Nope, try again."

Vanessa frowned. "A nymph? A dragon? A very tall dwarf? A Kapacki?" she asked curiously, but Brecon Bellum shook her head.

"Nope. Do I look like a dwarf? Wait! Don't answer that question!"

Vanessa made many guesses, but Brecon denied them all. Finally, Vanessa gave up and asked for the answer, but the girl grinned. "Nuh, uh! Try something a bit less exotic."

Gemma sat and giggled. "OK, here is a hint: you used to think you were one!"

Vanessa gasped. "Are you . . . *human*?" she asked incredulously. She almost didn't want to believe that this cool girl was not an elf.

However, at that moment the Amazon girl shouted with glee, "Bingo! Wow, that took *ages*! I am from Texas, USA. It's nice to know someone who has heard of the Declaration of Independence or nail polish! Do you have any idea how hard it is to explain those two things to anyone around here? And forget the Cowboys!" She complained grinning.

Vanessa nodded smiling, and her gaze trailed over to the ship door, where Nero and Abigail were coming out to see who had arrived. Gemma winked at Vanessa and introduced the human girl. Abigail seemed happy to meet her, but Nero was a pest. He slapped his leg and snorted his way into laughter.

"You are a *human*? HA! That is hilarious!"

The human girl growled, walked up to him, and punched him in the gut. "Yeah, but not nearly as hilarious as it would be to stab you with my spear! I became second in command in the Amazons for a reason, punk!" she growled.

Nero yelped and stepped back. Gemma and Vanessa snorted with mirth, while Abigail looked confused. Nero and Brecon began to bicker, and Abigail stared at the two.

Vanessa felt a hand on her shoulder and turned around to stare at Rex. He looked shy. "Can I speak with you?" he asked.

Vanessa nodded. "Of course!" she said, curiosity tugging at her.

Rex pulled her onto the dragonhead where they dropped to the sand and began walking. "It's about Herba. I think she is missing. When I ask your mother, she says that Herba was trying to get 'supplies' from somewhere. I think she is reporting what she has seen. Drake already knows. By the way, why was Nero looking so scared when I left? I swear I saw him wet his pants!" he said with a smirk.

Vanessa was glad he changed the subject. "I think Nero has finally met his match," she said.

Rex laughed. "OK, let's go back and watch the play. I'd hate to miss the action. You are right about Brecon. She is beautiful and resourceful—a deadly combination. I know very few girls that can say the same. I am thinking of some right now."

Vanessa laughed. "Oh?" she asked.

As they walked back, Rex smiled. "Yep, *all* the girls here, including the one talking to me."

Vanessa smiled, blushing slightly. "You are very funny. Let's hurry! I don't want to miss a second of this."

Rex grinned. "Want to fetch some popcorn?" he asked, but they had already come upon the arguing kids.

Nero had his hands made into fists. "You know what, missy-prissy-princess, I have a lightening spell up my sleeve currently, and I am thinking of unleashing, or would that mess with your tiny human brain?" he said the last bit as an insult, and Vanessa winced at her brother's stupidity.

Brecon grinned and shoved her metal spear into his hands. "Good! Hold this while you are at it, dumbbell! You might want to stand in a puddle of water too!" she encouraged.

Nero choked on the spell he was saying and yelped as he dropped the spear. "Ack! Get that away, you miserable wretch! What, are you trying to kill me?" he said frantically.

Brecon laughed. "Oh it would only be a little shocker... literally. Come on, you don't want to hold my spear for me? What a gentleman!" she said sarcastically.

Nero fell for it, and bent down to pick it up. "Geez. What a foo-foo Amazon! Can't hold her own spear!" And when he said that, Vanessa winced again, knowing this was not going to go well.

Brecon said a word and the spear wriggled away, momentarily turning into a snake. Nero yelped and jumped back. "That is for calling me foo-foo! And ya want to see 'prissy'?" she challenged.

Nero was red with anger. "Oh yeah! You try to do that again and I'll show you! Wait . . . Did you just say that you were second in command?" he asked.

Brecon punched him in the arm. "Yeah, you stupid imp! I was Prati's deputy! That's how I learned to do this!" she said, jumping in the air and kicking Nero's face—feet first.

He thumped painfully to the ground before making a mad dash back to the safety of the ship. Brecon sprang back up and dusted herself off. She sauntered over to Vanessa and Rex.

"Hey, dude! How have ya' been? You don't have to introduce me to Vanessa as I I met her already. She is awesome. Mind if I steal her away to join the Amazons?" she asked.

Rex smiled. "You'd have to ask her."

Brecon looked at Vanessa. "And . . . ?" she asked.

Vanessa smiled. "Nah, I think I will let another girl have that job. By the way, I thought the Amazons were splitting up."

Brecon grimaced. "Without Prati, things have fallen apart. She was our leader, and our girls are afraid without her. Prati told us that we should stick together, but many girls are taken by fear or pride, and we must not corrupt. The corruption would lead to destruction. I'm afraid this is the end of the Amazons," she said.

At that moment conch horn sounded from a far off in the sea.

Brecon froze. "Vanessa, Rex, go into the ship. And whatever you do, don't come out until dawn tomorrow." Another horn sounded, and she turned to them. "NOW!" she yelled forcefully, and Rex scrambled into the ship, but Vanessa stayed out.

"Wait, why?" she asked.

Brecon grimaced. "I guess you can stay but all males must stay inside," she ordered.

Rex turned pale with his realization. "Ug, not them."

He went to warn Astrum not to let any men leave the ship or go outside. Brecon grabbed Vanessa, and they went to the dragonhead.

Brecon took a deep breath and turned to explain everything to Vanessa. "OK, we have a small problem. Have you heard of sirens?" she asked.

Vanessa nodded. "Yes, but shouldn't we be inside too? Aren't they harmful to both men and women?" she asked.

"No, silly! The Amazons used to absolutely love this story! Sailors only said that because, in those days, almost the only people out fishing and sailing around were men. The sirens only affected men because there was a long drawn-out story of the two queens of the sea, Pacifi and Atlanti, who were once offended by a man, an unruly sailor who did not know his place. After that, only men were affected by the siren song."

Suddenly, a large object rammed into the ship from in the water, and webbed hands grasped the side of the vessel. Vanessa shrieked and stepped back, but Brecon stayed in her place, obviously not impressed by the terrifying sight. Once again, Vanessa could see why Brecon had been chosen as Prati's deputy.

The webbed hands hauled up a woman dressed in seaweed. While Vanessa had expected the woman to be beautiful, she was sorely mistaken. The dripping being was slightly hunched, with scaly skin that resembled fish scales and long greenish hair that was twisted and stringy. Several others followed the woman, and they stopped in front of Brecon. It was the leader of the trio who spoke first.

"Brecon Bellum? What a pleasure to see you! And who is this lovely young woman that you have with you?" asked the siren. Her voice was soft and pleasant, like that of a young woman, and Vanessa was startled to hear it.

Brecon smiled. "Hello, Zephy. How siren life been treating you? Have you been upgraded to general of the seas yet?" she asked.

The siren nodded proudly. "Being a siren is great, my love. I suggest you be one! I have just the right spell. Why yes! I am now a captain! Isn't that perfect?"

Brecon nodded and motioned for Vanessa to approach.

She did so with care. "Hi, my name is Vanessa Nox. Is your name Zephy?"

Zephy laughed in a singsong voice. "No, just as your name is not Nessa. My name is Zephaniah. My name is popular among sea people. Brecon just loves to make nicknames for anyone she comes across. I am surprised to find that you are not called missy-prissy-princess or foo-foo or even smarty-pants!"

Brecon nodded as if she had swallowed a grape whole and struggled to keep her face straight. Vanessa grinned and choked down a laugh. Then Brecon and Vanessa looked at each other, and seeing the other's response to the comment, they both broke out laughing. Vanessa was the first to calm down.

"OK. Why are you here? Not to be rude or anything of course," she asked.

Zephaniah grunted, "You may think it is because we want the men. You are mistaken. We wanted to tell you that we set fire to several enemy ships. We are honored to serve an Amazon." Brecon nodded her thanks as the sirens slinked off.

"While the boys are hiding, can you teach me any new Draconic spells?"

Brecon nodded, and they began practicing. Brecon taught her how to summon birds, manipulate sand, and meld things together. Finally, she began to tire of teaching, even though Vanessa was still ready to learn more.

Brecon smiled. "OK, this last one no one has been able to do it right. Even the masters of Draconic nearly died of this one. And since you have a tireless amount of energy, I'll teach you the words."

Vanessa listened as the ex-Amazon drew in a breath. "The word is *anima*. It means life. Sometimes you can summon spirits with it. Other times, you can raise the dead to life but you need to alter the word. They will receive new bodies. You may try to bring spirits to you, and you can talk to them, but that would make you very tired, even for a born spell-castor like yourself. I was in a coma for a week just trying. And that was when I was at the top of my strength. You may try this but if you attempt to raise the dead, it might kill you."

The night was getting darker, and Brecon felt sapped from all the enery she had used that day. Vanessa, however, felt full of enthusiasm and power and was not the least hungry. She pondered on what person she wished to bring as a spirit. Vanessa nodded to herself at her decision and held her hand in the air as Brecon instructed then pooled in her remaining strength to summon the spirit.

Vanessa's energy was stored for this, and she was ready to utter the word. She looked at Brecon then back at the mist which was forming in front of her.

Brecon paused and asked, "What spirit are you looking for?" but it was too late.

"*Anima*!" Vanessa yelled. The mist became thicker. Brecon shouted something, but Vanessa was suddenly too weak to hear.

The mist gathered color and formed details and then solidified. Vanessa hardly stood. The girl who stood before her had pale skin and honey gold hair. One eye was blue and the other green. The girl was wearing a colorless dress. Brecon turned to Vanessa in confusion. The girl stood weakly and asked in a foreign accent Vanessa couldn't place, "Where am I?"

Brecon recognized the girl and gasped. "Vanessa, what were you thinking?" The amazon barely caught Vanessa before she collapsed.

CHAPTER 42

ERA

Vanessa was in a soft bed looking up at Tonitrus who was smiling at her. "You will be alright, Vanessa, but you must rest. You are a very strong girl but you need to recognize there are consequences to your actions. As you gain more experience with using magic, you will learn your limits." Tonitrus laid his hands on Vanessa and his image faded.

Vanessa woke. She was lying in a velvety bed and staring at the back of Septimus. who was staring out of the window with a mournful expression and a bowed head.

"First, Vanessa dies. Then Candentia does too. What am I going to do now?" he asked softly to himself. His usually clean-cut hair was shaggy like Rex's, and his clothes were soiled.

Vanessa choked. "Candentia is . . ." she gasped.

The startled Septimus whirled to see Vanessa. She smiled and said weakly,"Hey!" as he hugged her.

She pulled back from the embrace and stared at him. "You are growing a beard?" she asked playfully.

He rubbed a bit of stubble on his chin. "No," he replied solemnly.

Vanessa frowned. "You said Candentia is dead."

Tears welled in Septimus's eyes, and he lowered his head. "Yes. A frost dragon killed her.."

She frowned. "Where is the frost dragon?"

He pointed up to the sky. "Dead. His brother killed him and gave us a promise that he would allow Candentia one day to return but on a condition; He wants one of us to pay a debt."

Vanessa sighed and asked, "When? Who?"

Septimus shrugged. "We don't know yet. I have another question for you though. When you fainted, a girl appeared. Brecon whisked her into a room before any of us saw what she looked like. Do you know who she was?"

Vanessa frowned and told him what happened. "Except I summoned a male from the grave, not a female."

Septimus cocked his head. "Who?" he asked.

Vanessa looked at him curiously. "I thought I summoned my grandfather. He popped into my mind, so I asked his spirit to come forth. But a girl appeared instead."

Septimus jumped. "What did the girl look like?" he asked urgently.

Vanessa frowned, trying to remember. "She had honey blond hair and fair skin," she said, thinking hard.

Septimus looked a bit distressed, "Anything else?" he asked.

Vanessa frowned in thought. "One eye was blue and the other was green," she answered.

"What?" Septimus gasped. He scrambled to the door, calling for Vanessa to follow him. She did so in surprise. When they met at the hull of the ship, Vanessa asked, "How long have I been asleep?"

Septimus grimaced. "Two weeks. We all thought you were dead. You didn't even breathe."

Horror settled in Vanessa like fog on a field, and she realized what Abigail and her parents would think. She raced ahead and burst through the door, surprised to find a depressed Rex. He screamed like a little girl and hid in a corner.

"NO! Please don't haunt me! I am so sorry for anything I did wrong to you! The rat in the bed was only a joke!"

"Wait, you did what?"

Rex looked twice as confused. "Wait a second! You... you're alive!" he said happily and ran to hug her.

He felt more solid than she remembered him, and she was surprised that he was so quickly turning into a man. Yes, he still had years to go, but with elves, there was no exact age that you became an adult. She enjoyed the smell of pines mixed with the tang of the sea for a moment longer, and then she stepped back to face Rex with a smile on her face. "Have you been working out?" she asked jokingly in a girly voice.

Rex smiled. "Kind of. I was training harder at the sword so I could beat the heck out of some malus for you," he said, and Vanessa's heart felt warm at the thought.

"Thank you!" she said, grinning back.

They stood for a moment, as if trying to read each other's minds. Finally, Rex broke the silence.

"Well, I think I'm the most glad you're back."

Septimus had been at the corner of the room, watching the encounter, and Vanessa realized with a jolt that he had a video camera in his hand. She instantly recognized it as the one she had taken with her when she had traveled by train to get to North Idaho by the blue tiger stripes she had drawn on it. She stared in surprise, and Septimus hit the stop button.

"There. I'll make sure to keep this for a while." he said with a sly grin. "I'm sure there are plenty of people who would love to see this!"

Vanessa shrieked in outrage and grabbed the video camera out of his hand. "How dare you! Where did you get that?" she cried.

Septimus snatched it back. "Hey, I found it in your pack, and I figured out how to work it, thanks to Abigail!"

Vanessa tried to steal it back, but Septimus laughed and held it above her head. "Wait, we could have so much fun with this! Imagine what we could do to Rex!"

Vanessa paused and thought, *why not? It's not like her friends at school were going to see it!* "You are right!" she said with a smile.

Vanessa and Septimus burst into laughter. Brecon stepped into the room, and Septimus told her about the video of Rex thinking Vanessa was a ghost and hiding in the corner. She broke out in laughter as well. Rex's smile suddenly disappeared as he realized that what they were planning was not going to benefit him in the least. He frowned and stalked off.

Brecon caught up to him and tried to keep a straightface, but it disappeared in her laughter. "Wait, Rex! We are only going to show a really embarrassing thing to a thousand people."

Vanessa and Septimus looked at each other and giggled as they caught up with the red-faced Rex. He spied Vanessa and scowled at her, "Here I was wanting you to come back from the dead, now I'm not so sure," he said crankily.

Vanessa made a pouty face. "Really? Darn it!"

They reached the top of the ship and an armored Astrum came into view. Vanessa halted in surprise, and Septimus frowned. Brecon cocked her head, and Rex almost ran into him.

Astrum seemed not too surprised by Vanessa's arrival and stared at them all. "Battle. We must get to the center of the island. Umbra's people are ready for war. So shall we be. Reinforcements will be arriving soon by Thorn of the sprites."

Vanessa nodded and asked if he wanted her to scout for him. He agreed and told Rex that he should go explore the south corner while Vanessa explored the north. She changed into her dragon form and was surprised to find that it was now white. Avis explained that this was her power was maturing. She told Vanessa that her energy would now be white, which was a fitting color for a princess. Vanessa rather liked the pure color, so she didn't complain.

With her powerful wings, she swooped into the air and took off at an amazing speed, seeming only to be a streak of cloud in the sky. From her fantastic sight, she watched Rex run down a much-used game trail. As she searched for approaching enemies, she kept an eye on the path Rex had chosen and made sure to scent the air for anything unusual. She soared through the skies, wings spread out, and to the usual passers-by seemed to be a fast-moving cloud.

Suddenly, she felt an excruciating pain erupt. As she lost her flight, she caught a glimpse of a red-feathered arrow lodged in her wing. She plummeted to the ground, stunned by the landing. She roared as she hit the stony earth and turned into an elf again.

She groaned and looked up. She found she was staring a red-haired warrior in the face. The warrior laughed, but it came out as a harsh cackle. "You thought that you could steal from me? Ha! Well, I have news for you: Stay out of my way!" she spat.

Vanessa was completely bewildered. "Who are you?" she asked.

The girl rolled her eyes. "Yeah right. You have to remember *me*. I am Era," spat the red-haired girl.

Vanessa raised her eyebrows. "And how exactly did I get in your way? I haven't even met you."

Era scowled, "You have tried to steal the throne—*my* throne."

Vanessa felt confused. "Um, OK. Isn't the throne rightfully mine?"

Era snarled, "How dare you! Your mother Regina has been hiding behind her pet dragon like a coward. And her mother hid behind her husband. And you are now alone, so I—" she began but was cut off by Vanessa.

"I'm sorry, but I haven't hid behind anyone! Most of the time *I* am alone! Aurora and Regina may have had to hide, but I certainly haven't."

Era stopped. "Well, I . . ." she trailed off, bow still ready.

Vanessa knew she had to be careful. "Why do you want the throne?"

Era growled, "It is rightfully mine!"

"WHY?"

Era's mood suddenly changed and she appeared sad. "Well . . . I don't know . . . I have been betrayed so many times that . . . I want something I can have for myself." Tears welled in her eyes, and Era folded her arms, hands retreating into her cloak.

Vanessa felt sorry for the girl. What if she had a life like this? Vanessa walked over to Era and tried to hug her. Suddenly, Era's hands shot out of her cloak, a gleaming black knife in each, and plunged them into Vanessa's side. Vanessa cried out.

Era retracted the knives and let Vanessa fall to the ground. The blackness leached from the knives onto Vanessa, obviously poison. Then she felt everything grow hazy.

Era stood over her, smiled wickedly, and left.

Then she saw Rex. He stood over her, looking panicked. Tears splattered on to her face as he leaned over to look at her. Why was it raining? Or was Rex crying? She tried to smile and tell him she felt fine, but she could not make her face move. She closed her eyes and tried to sleep. A sudden peace swelled within her, and she lay still.

CHAPTER 43

THE OLIVE RETURNS

Vanessa knew something was off. She opened her eyes and found she was floating above Terra. She tried to cry out but found she could not. She turned and looked beside her and was alarmed to find an almost transparent woman next to her. The woman was staring at her.

"I am Anima. I am life," she said, her voice seeming to echo around them.

Vanessa found her own voice did the same. "Am I dead?" she asked.

Anima nodded. "Yes.," she said.

Instead of feeling panicked, Vanessa felt a peace like never before. "Then why am I here? It's like I am still alive. I expected nothing—oblivion," she noted.

Anima laughed. "You think everything ends when you die? No. Death is only the beginning. Your body is trapped in that realm, but your spirit is free."

Vanessa suddenly recognized the name. "Anima? Are you like my great-aunt or something?" she asked.

Anima nodded. "Or something. Do you want your life again? You will save all your friends, but there must be a price." Anima waved a hand. "A small one, considering all life of Terra is in danger."

Even though she still felt uncertain, and really loved the peaceful feeling she had, Vanessa accepted the offer with a nod. "OK. Please send me back."

Anima laughed. "Not yet. First, you must gather people to help with the battle. I have a few creatures in mind that may assist you in your . . . quarrel."

Vanessa found she was staring up at a very tall man. He was at least seven feet tall, with broad muscles that bulged from his arms. His long black hair flowed around his shoulders, and his eyes were a chocolate brown. The upper half of his body was almost normal; the beastly muscles were the only abnormal part. But his bottom half was that of a large dappled gray draft horse. The centaur swished his tail impatiently.

"Will we be going?" he said in such a deep voice that Vanessa felt her teeth rattle. His shoulder-length black hair was a tangled mess, and his deeply tanned skin was etched with battle scars.

Anima flowed next to Vanessa, her wispy form a delicate reminder that Vanessa was dead. "Soon, be patient," she said to the centaur.

A hundred or more other centaurs were formed behind their leader, but the one in front of Vanessa seemed to be the buffest. Vanessa decided that she should be brave. "Hi. My name is Vanessa. What's yours?" she asked in a small voice.

The centaur snorted, "*Hola*. My name is Toro. I am captain of the eastern area."

Vanessa cocked her head. "*Hola*? Toro? You sound Spanish, unless your name is a fatty piece of sushi."

Toro frowned, not understanding what sushi was, but before he could say anything, Anima whispered into Vanessa's ear, "Child, you may be dead now, but remember that you will live once more. I would hate for your life to be taken away so quickly after it's been returned."

Vanessa caught the hint. "OK," she said reluctantly.

Anima waved her hands. "Go now! You may have a chance to save your friends!"

Vanessa's vision faded.

Vanessa woke and found she was lying on soft grass next to Toro. He was lying on his side and looked very uncomfortable. Vanessa came to her feet with ease but noticed the centaur was stuck in his reclining position. The other centaurs were standing but were too far away to notice their leader. Toro looked humiliated.

Vanessa smiled and put a hand on her hip, reading his mind. "Only if you say please," she said.

The centaur was at a loss for words but eventually sighed grumpily. "Please."

Vanessa went to the other side and pushed him to a sitting position, surprised by her own strength. The centaur sighed once he was up and thanked Vanessa profusely.

"I would look like a fool if I had stayed on the ground much longer," he conveyed.

Vanessa waved the thanks off, saying it was her pleasure. The hundred other warriors galloped up to them.

"Captain, we will rush to the center of the island with ease, but what of the elf? They are fast but not *that* fast," said one man with a muscular piebald horse as his bottom half. Toro nodded, "She must be carried, Pedro."

The centaur called Pedro scoffed, "None of ours should be downtrodden enough to carry another creature on our backs as if we were some common beast of burden!" He spoke scornfully.

Toro's eyes blazed. "Well—" he began, but Vanessa stepped in.

"Sorry to make you feel 'downtrodden,' but if you haven't noticed, your people are also in danger. Since you think you are so high and mighty, perhaps you could use a bit of humbling! Why don't you carry me yourself, buster?" she said.

Pedro looked appalled. "Do you have any idea who I am?"

Vanessa fearlessly stepped in front of him. "Do you have any idea who *I* am?" she shot back. Pedro scowled, but before he could say anything, Vanessa continued, "I am Vanessa Regina Nox, princess of the elves, dragon elf, shape-shifter, and recently, I have added Prowler slayer, malus killer, and shadow titan destroyer. Listen up, my little pony, I have died twice, seen my friends turned against me, I've been dumped into a magical world with creatures that have mouths full of teeth and bad attitudes, and I have missed several showers. Long story short, I have had a bad month, and if you keep up this bratty attitude, I will be forced to add centaur spanker on my list of names. Now shut up and do your job!"

Pedro stopped in his tracks. "Yes, Your Highness," he said with a submissive bow. Vanessa thought she saw a smile on the other centaurs' faces, but they became serious every time Vanessa shot glares at them.

"Well, let's be going," Toro said, offering a hand to help Vanessa up. She swung up and held to his shoulders as he took off at a swift gallop. That gallop turned into real speed. They raced along, and hardly a minute passed before they reached the war zone. Vanessa caught a few faces of her friends: Neal, Astrum, Syringa (in dragon form), Avis, and her father's dragon form.

They were fighting massive waves of goblins, malus, shadow titans, and other creatures that looked as if they had stepped out of a fiendish nightmare. She also caught the faces of sprites in elf form. They had the advantage of being able to fly without wings, enabling them to squeeze through cracks and have less of their bodies be targeted.

Toro sent his centaurs into the battle, while he and Vanessa galloped to a tent at the top of a high hill. Near the tent's entrance was a flag that showed a lamb next to a lion and a dove flying next to them.

Vanessa recognized the person at the entrance of the tent as Truncus. He ran out to greet her, and she swung down from Toro to hug him. His wooden body was covered in even rougher bark, obviously as armor. Truncus led the two into the tent, and Vanessa ran to hug her mother. Regina's hair smelled of anise, and Vanessa smiled as she shoved her face in it when she hugged her.

Regina looked at Vanessa. "You were actually dead this time. I reckon since you are now standing before me that you met my aunt Anima? Well, you are the princess that I knew I'd have," she said.

Suddenly, Abigail appeared. She looked disheveled, and her eyes were swollen and red. "Vanessa? You are alive!" Abigail said in surprise.

Vanessa held her arms out to hug Abigail, but Abigail didn't come to hug her. She just stared. "Let me guess. You went on another adventure without me. How am I surprised? Tell me . . . Did you make friends with a unicorn? Or are you dating a fairy-tale prince?" she asked, her eyebrows coming together in a resentful scowl.

Vanessa's heart plummeted. "Abigail? I—I thought you would be happy to see me . . ."

Abigail just shook her head. "Never mind. See you later. Just try not to 'fly away,'" she said and dashed out of the tent. Vanessa was furious and distressed, but Regina calmed her and told her the plans.

Nero appeared and smiled at Vanessa, lifting her heart a little. "Hey! You really need to stop making enemies. Abigail just ran away, obviously mad at you . . . And Rex . . . He is really . . . Well, you should see him. By the way, we have stopped fighting for now. The Dark Forces have retreated. We won again, at least this battle." He directed his attention to Regina.

Vanessa felt panicked, and she ran out of the tent in search of Rex. She searched among the sprites and other warriors, greeting her father and aunt before finally getting the information she needed. Rex was in a forest, going with a healer to fetch water.

She ran to the forest and found him sitting by a beautiful blonde on a mossy log along a gurgling stream. Rex shyly handed the girl a pretty blue wildflower, and she blinked and kissed him on the cheek, laughing as Rex made a face.

As Vanessa just stood there, watching them, the girl was the first to notice her. Her eyes locked on Vanessa's, and she seemed to be shaking her head. Rex looked up, almost as if he would go into shock. Vanessa's eyes reached Rex's, and then they welled with tears of anger at herself

for feeling hurt. She turned into a falcon and swooped away not looking
back.

Vanessa was sitting calmly atop a high cliff when Rex found her. She
took one look at him and was about to turn into a bird and leap off the
cliff, but before she could, Rex snatched her hand, pulling it.

She glared, pulling back her hand. "Let go of me. I just need
some air."

Rex shook his head. "No. I am tired of losing you. We need to talk,"
he said adamantly.

Vanessa stared daggers at him, hating herself for being so delicate.
"Fine."

Rex sat down on a stump and motioned for Vanessa to do likewise.
She chose the spot farthest from him and waited.

Rex sighed. "Is there something you want to talk about?"

Vanessa stood and scowled, "There isn't anything to say. You made
that pretty clear."

Rex raised an eyebrow. "Why?" he asked.

Vanessa laughed, but there was no humor in it. "Um, how about
the fact that you and that pretty healer of yours were just sitting there
ignoring that I was there?"

"Vanessa! I would never do that to you! I did not ignore you! And
technically, even if I were 'hanging out with her,' I'd have a right! I am
sick and tired of you 'dying.'"

Vanessa was outraged. "You think I liked being dead? Maybe you're
right! I come back to life and Abigail is being a brat and thinks I am
having fun without her, and you, Rex, are hanging out with some very
pretty girl!" she said angrily.

Suddenly, a soft voice came from her left. "Well, all thanks to you,
Vanessa, though I think you meant to bring someone else back," said
the blond healer.

Vanessa yelped and scrambled back. The girl had a hand on her hip,
and Vanessa could see that the girl had one green eye and one blue. The

colors were beautifully abnormal. The girl had on a silvery dress, and she was staring at Vanessa through almost catlike eyes.

Vanessa stared. "What do you mean?" she asked.

The girl smiled. "You brought me back from the dead . . . which you can only do once."

Vanessa suddenly remembered the time she had done so. "Oh, but then you are—" She stopped. She realized her mistake and felt the blood rush to her face.

"Yes, I am Olea Noctis, eldest daughter of the Dark Lord. I can't exactly date my bother. Talk about *gross*! Besides, I am *much* older than he is! It is a bit ironic, don't you think, Rex? When you showed up, we were just talking about Vanessa. Rex was telling me how loyal you were," she said with a smile. Vanessa felt her anger turn to outright embarrassment.

Olea waved a hand. "Oh, don't be embarrassed! I would've done the same as you! Actually, I would've walked up and said, 'You are the biggest jerk I have ever seen!' Then I would've punched him! You handled that much better!"

Vanessa felt a little better. "OK. By the way, how did you get up here, Rex?" she asked casually, glancing down at the sharp rocks a hundred feet below.

Olea's eyes widened. Rex suddenly looked lost for words. He was about to say something, but Olea broke in, "Oh, I have a pet roc! He is so sweet. His name is Rocky. Now don't mind the name, I was eight when I got him," she said and trotted down the steep hill.

Vanessa turned to Rex. "Sorry. I hate when I am wrong." She smiled sheepishly.

Rex laughed slightly. "Don't worry, Olea was right . . . Even though I think she was just saying that to get back at me for putting a cochlea in her bed once."

"A what?" Vanessa asked.

Rex smiled guiltily. "A cochlea is a giant snail. They smell really bad and have an attraction to hair."

Vanessa could just imagine what horrors Rex had brought to his family as a child. It made her feel happy inside to think that Rex could have such humor. It was a nice difference to what he could be.

Vanessa laughed and hugged Rex, hoping her change of mood would change any bad feelings Rex might have toward her. She inwardly berated herself for being so jealous.

"What a jokester!" she said with a giggle.

Rex grinned. "Yep." Then he looked sad. "Sorry about Abigail. I didn't realize that she was in a bad mood. She does have a reason though."

Vanessa looked at him. "What?" she asked in surprise.

Rex gave her his silly grin. "You did get the cutest elf there is in town for a boyfriend!" he said, knowing this would trigger a punch of some kind.

Vanessa elbowed him lightly in the shoulder, surprising Rex. "Yeah, but she is probably grateful that she didn't get the most annoying boy ever. Anyway, I think she is just really anxious about the battle. She'll cool down soon."

They turned to Olea and met her roc. The giant bird was slate gray and had an eagle's beak. It had a saddle that could sit four people, so Vanessa figured they would be fine. She sat behind Rex and thought about what had transpired. She enjoyed a fresh breeze while she pondered.

The roc took off. As they rode on him, Vanessa remembered the line in the prophecy, "*At the cost of your hardest strife, the Olive will return to life.*" She said this aloud.

Rex nodded, and Olea smiled from her position at the head of the roc. She looked at the nearby island so Vanessa wouldn't catch her expression of relief that the princess was calming down and would not be mad at her brother anymore.

Rex nodded with a grand smile. "All thanks to you." He reached over and grasped Vanessa's hand. It was icy. He almost withdrew, but his instincts told him it would be a big mistake. Instead, he put both hands on it to warm her and grinned at Vanessa.

Olea looked back at them. "You're all smiles!" she chirped. The roc let out a roar, and they glanced ahead as the a separate batch of the Dark Army's camp came into view. It had come to surround the Heroes army. Olea shot down some of them with a bow, and Rex rained hail balls on them, while Vanessa muttered a few Draconic phrases and set the tents on fire.

She called up lightning, and massive bolts fried the masses of goblins and malus. Vanessa caught a few gargoyles but not many of them. Looking at the stone creatures, she shattered them instantly. Rex's hail balls had summoned fifty of them into the air, and eventually, they had destroyed them. They then flew off without a sound.

Rex leaned back into Vanessa. "Phew! That was hard work! You know, when my fire friends ask me what I did on Friday, I am going to say, 'Well, I destroyed a hundred goblins and everything—nothing big,' and I'll act like nothing happened."

Vanessa enjoyed the breeze as they glided through the sky. She smiled at Rex curiously and raised an eyebrow. *"Fire friends?"*

Olea laughed and leaned back to whisper in her ear, "He has a boys' club called that, Really 'secret' is what Rex claims. Sometimes they are doing good things, and sometimes they are just hanging out, but they are just a bunch of pranksters!"

Rex raised an eyebrow of his own. "Oh yeah? Is Tror 'just a prankster'?"

Olea blushed and smacked his arm. Vanessa laughed, but her cheerfulness faded as she stared ahead. They were getting close—close to the battle. Vanessa felt the sinking sensation grow worse. She knew that only one side could win.

CHAPTER 44

THE BATTLE

When the trio finally reached the camp, they found Toro and Nero head to head in a fight. Vanessa and Rex a knowing were certain who started the fight. They closed in to hear more.

"My name is a what?"

"A white, fatty piece of sushi," Nero confirmed.

Toro's eyes blazed. "Again, what is this thing, sushi?" he asked.

Brecon Bellum leaned in and whispered the answer. Vanessa leaned over and whispered into Rex's ear, "Uh oh. Brecon is no friend of Nero's."

Rex smiled and nodded. "I know, but Nero is seriously asking for it! He could get killed!"

Vanessa agreed with enthusiasm. "At first I thought he was trying to die early, but I eventually realized that my brother was more than capable of handling himself. He made a mistake, though, when he chose Brecon as an enemy," she said this just as Nero had to dodge Toro's furious sword stroke.

"I AM NOT A FATTY PIECE OF SUSHI!" the centaur roared. Nero giggled and turned invisible. Suddenly, he appeared on Toro's back. The centaur tried to buck Nero off, but Vanessa's brother stood up and danced. The centaur stopped, and his waist twisted so he could face Nero.

Nero stopped. "Oops," he said then sprang off and rolled on the ground to a stop.

The centaur prepared to charge Nero, but Regina stepped out of the tent. "That is enough!" she scolded.

Several of the watching sprites said, "Aw," and "What?"

But Regina held her stern face. "A scout just reported that the Dark Army is coming for a final attack. We are to meet their attack on that hill," she said, pointing in the distance. "Then we should be good . . . unless they surround us."

In response, everyone suddenly scrambled to get the armor and weapons. The sprites flew to positions to be ready. A few of them had close combat weapons, but some of them had sorts that Vanessa had never seen before. The rest of the sprites took to the air with long-range weapons, such as bows, slings, crossbows, spears, and throwing knives. Each of the flying sprites had a small close-combat weapon. Each also carried a paralyzing liquid which could be dropped on the enemy.

Meanwhile, all the other soldiers were preparing the army. Fairies fluttered about, healing wounds. Pedro came up to Vanessa.

"I would be honored to carry you into battle," he said shyly.

Vanessa smiled and reached up to hug the shaggy-haired man. "Thanks for offering! It would be an honor to ride such a magnificent being." She said this knowing that Toro had "suggested" it to him and was trying to make him feel better.

Pedro smiled, a bit of his former pride returning at the comment. He trotted over to the makeshift armory and got out a breastplate. He strapped it to his bare chest and slung two short swords to his back. Then he strapped on a crossbow and grabbed a mace.

Vanessa raised an eyebrow and asked, "You know how to use all those weapons?"

Pedro grinned proudly. "We are trained to use all weapons of war. I believe your mother has your armor."

Vanessa was surprised by this comment, and hastened to her mother's tent. She ran into Avis before she went in. Her aunt was in silver armor that had designs on it like feathers, and her helmet was shaped to resemble a bird head. She was talking with a beautiful woman with a stomach protruding so enough that Vanessa knew there was a baby in there. The woman had auburn hair and bright green eyes. Vanessa shrieked and hugged the woman.

"Filix! Are you pregnant?" she asked in astonishment.

Filix made a mock frown. "No, I have been filling up on cookies. OF COURSE, I AM PREGNANT!" She said the last part with a grin.

Avis told the princess to go to her mother. Vanessa smiled and went into the tent obediently.

Regina was waiting for her and held up a shining armor carved with Elvish symbols. "Here you are, Filia."

Vanessa strapped the Elfish armor on and went over to Pedro. She gracefully swung onto him and realized she had her sword in her hand. She smiled as she held up the wondrous blade of Ensis. She saw her father motion her to the head of the army. He waved his hand toward the army, and as Vanessa looked at the faces of her friends, she wanted to cry. Then she caught Rex's eye, and he gave an encouraging nod. She felt a new surge of valor and winced when she heard Truncus telling a sprite that this would be the beginning of the final war.

She looked at her father, who did not have a horse, and watched him step forward and change into his natural state. Drake, now in his dragon form, told her she should be ready to do the same.

She readied herself then and looked at the barren hill that spanned in front of the army. Suddenly, the crest of the broad hill was topped with an endless amount of dark creatures. Vanessa gasped and looked at the number of beings that were advancing.

At the front of the army, a lone horse carried a cloaked figure. Only when Vanessa tapped into her dragon sight did she realize that the horse was skeletal. It had a mane of crimson fire, and the dark saddle was embellished with carvings of skulls.

The figure threw back its cloak, and Vanessa was astonished to find a regular-looking man with blond hair staring at them. His grin was ruthlessly evil, and Vanessa heard Gemma and Rex gasp, while Septimus and Olea groaned.

The man at the front of the army stepped forward with his steed. His armor was coppery, and he had a crown of pure blackness. The horse turned into a six-headed dragon, and Vanessa shivered. "Hydra," she muttered.

A silky voice next to her answered. "Yes, except this Hydra has seven tails," said a flying sprite that walked next to her.

Vanessa noticed this sprite had a waterfall carved on to her silvery sprite armor. Vanessa squinted at the helmet, trying to see who had spoken. The sprite lifted her helmet and smiled, showing brilliant white teeth.

Vanessa gasped, "Stream!"

The sprite floated up and hugged Vanessa. "Syringa brought my brother . . . You expected me to sit back at that sprite city and do nothing? What a friend!" she said sarcastically.

Vanessa looked back at the Hydra and shuddered when she realized Stream was right. She turned back to the sprite to study her armor. "I thought you all had the same armor."

Stream snorted. "No! We are each unique. We have our names carved into a picture on our armor. For example, my brother Thorn has thorn branches on his, and Gemma has gems on hers . . . And they are actually real gems. I will live though this we can talk about it more. For now, we need to focus on the army that is charging us," she said and pointed to the man at the front of the army. He raised his hand, and the dark creatures charged. Umbra let these go before him and watched as the millions of magical beasts enveloped the small army.

Vanessa and Pedro met their first attacker with an easy swing of the sword, but soon they were overwhelmed. Vanessa caught a glimpse of her brother Nero and watched as he sprayed hot white flames on his enemies. Vanessa dismounted Pedro, leaping off his back and crashing into several goblins. She looked up and saw that more dark creatures were coming. Then a shadowy hand caught her shoulder and wrenched out her arm from its socket. She gasped in pain but whirled around to face the next attacker.

She whimpered as she beheld her mother or—she stopped. "Alauda?" She beheld Aqua and another woman that she guessed was Prati. She shrieked when she saw that Aqua's blue eyes had turned black as had the eyes of her other aunts. And their skins had turned a ghostly pale. Vanessa realized that it was Umbra who had made them this way, as well as many other sprites. The good sprites that flew above them began picking up their friends that had turned evil and spiraled away to Regina's tent to be healed.

Vanessa saw Olea and went to help her. They stood back to back and cut down the creatures. Vanessa glanced at Olea and spoke while fighting. "So do you know what Umbra did to our friends?" She had to yell over the clashing of weapons.

Olea grimaced. "Yes, and only something very pure would heal them."

Vanessa sliced a Prowler to ribbons. "Like?"

Olea seemed thoughtful as she stabbed a gargoyle, reducing it to rubble, making Vanessa smile despite herself. Olea shattered another gargoyle.

"Well, maybe mandrake flower powder or Pegasus feather, but that would take a whole lot of them, and we don't have that much time. There is also dragon tears, Corpia shell; silver and gold powder mixed with griffin bone, unicorn horn, and—"

But Vanessa cut her off. "Unicorn horn?" she asked, smashing a gargoyle with the hilt of her sword.

Olea nodded as she dodged a dark sprite and smacked him on the head, knocking him out so his friends could take him to the tent.

She glanced back at Vanessa. "Yes, but the unicorn would probably have to be there and heal them itself. And we don't have one."

Vanessa mentally called the unicorn with all her might, barely missing the blow of a goblin. She took Olea by the hand, and they raced to the tent. Vanessa yelped as a Prowler's blade caught her shoulder, slicing through it. Blood gushed from the wound, and she stumbled to a stop, accidently slamming into a small boulder. Blood poured from her nose.

Olea looked back and stopped, but Vanessa motioned for her to keep going. Olea looked toward the tent and ran back toward Vanessa. She stopped some of the bleeding in her shoulder and healed Vanessa's broken nose. She ran toward the tent at Vanessa's command and entered in a flash.

Vanessa rolled to the side as a malus crashed into the ground next to her. It moaned in pain and looked at Vanessa. She felt a pang of pity for it and spotted a slash next to its throat. She realized that she was going to be sapped of strength, but she leaned over and touched the bloody scratch, and it healed. The malus got up and looked at her. Vanessa expected it to kill her, but it didn't. A cry came from Vanessa's left, and she looked over to find Gemma trapped underneath another giant malus's arm. She cried out again, and Vanessa tried to stand, but she was too weak. Instead, the malus that Vanessa had healed raced over and pushed Gemma's attacker to one side, and they started fighting. The malus Vanessa healed quickly dispatched the other malus and ran to help other friends.

The wound in Vanessa's shoulder was pounding blood again, and she gasped in pain. She caught a goblin that was attacking a sprite by the foot and tripped it, allowing the sprite to kill it before helping fight off a Prowler. Blood was rushing from Vanessa, and she ripped a piece of her shirt to stop the blood flow. She managed to stand up and hold her sword in her other hand while fighting off a few short attacks. Managing to reach a tree, she slumped beside it and then fainted.

She snapped to wakefulness five minutes later to find a brunette in a green gossamer dress next to her. The brunette looked worried. "I healed you. Are you OK?"

Vanessa nodded and looked around. She was sitting in a small wooden room.

"Time has stopped for you for a moment. I am Maple."

Vanessa recognized that she was a wood nymph, and suddenly, a verse in her prophecy came to mind.

"Will you be able to keep time stopped while I am out of the tree?" she asked.

The girl grinned. "I might be able to do so for a minute or more, but your friends are losing."

Vanessa grimaced. "I know. Will you do this for me?"

Maple smiled thoughtfully. "Only for three minutes. Smash a malus for me!"

Vanessa ducked out of a small hole and realized she had been in a tree. She raced over to the battle and saw that time had stopped. She picked out the people that needed help and killed their enemies. She saved Rex from a deadly blow and dispatched a few shadow titans, gaining eight more pearls. She killed a few more in a minute and sighed once she was finished. She still had a little less than minute left. Vanessa decided to go to the tent.

Once she arrived, she noticed a dark sprite had a knife to Olea's throat. She was screaming. Vanessa pulled the sprite away and realized that time was up. The sprite came alive in her hands. He twisted and then knocked her to the ground. The dagger he had had to Olea's throat was in his hand. As he pressed it to Vanessa's neck, she closed her eyes. Suddenly, the knife fell away. She opened her eyes to find a normal sprite looking at her. He yelped and scrambled away. She looked over his shoulder to find Alba staring back. She whinnied as her horn gleamed. Vanessa thanked her.

Olea ran over. "That was our guard!" Vanessa looked at her confused, and Olea cleared her throat. "One of the dark sprites bit him, so he turned into one of them. Our army is in big trouble!"

Regina guided Alba to where the rest of the dark sprites were tied up, and Vanessa and Olea raced outside. They told several sprites, who ran to tell others. Some sprites carried their fallen friends to Alba and made sure to not let them bite anyone, including them.

Vanessa saw that the army mobilize into action, and she looked toward the front of the battle where the Dark Lord was casually swinging a sword, cutting down the brave sprites that tried to get in his way. She knew what she had to do. Vanessa ran to the front of the battle to face Umbra. He smiled, and fiery darts sprang from his hand. They raced to Vanessa, but at the last moment, she held up a hand.

"Deflecto!" she said, and they bounced harmlessly away from her.

Umbra held out his hands. "What do you think, Princessa? This is what every second of every day of every year would be with your reign."

Vanessa fought off the feeling of despair that his words conjured. "You want to know what I think? You *really* want to know what I think? I THINK THAT I SHOULD DECAPITATE YOU!" she said in absolute rage and swung Ensis into Umbra with her anger turning into power for her blow.

He deftly caught it with his black adamant shield and rolled away. Vanessa had put so much strength into that blow that the sword had sliced clean through Umbra's shield.

Umbra growled, "You think that you can defeat me? Well, your arrogance is your weakness!"

Rex shouted distantly from the battle for Vanessa to duck. She did so without hesitation and yelped when a sword swung from *behind* her. She looked back and realized that Umbra had teleported back behind her. She growled and stabbed at him. It caught his hand and sliced it clean off. He groaned and said "Curo!" to heal himself. Instantly, his hand grew back. She noticed that he somehow looked smaller, and she had an idea. She started hacking at him, her sword a blur of pure destruction.

Umbra was much more careful now, and she only managed to cut off two fingers of which he healed with ease. She noticed that he kept getting smaller with every wound he had to heal. Suddenly, he grinned and turned into a huge malus. Caught in surprise, she scrambled away.

Umbra had become twice the size of an adult malus, and he roared, "You don't know anything about me! My children only barely knew I could place-shift. Vanessa realized that she needed to get to her mother. Suddenly, Filix appeared next to Vanessa. "Go. We'll hold him off," she said.

Vanessa tried to argue, but Filix held up a hand and pointed behind her. Avis, Regina, the newly purified Prati, Aqua, and Alauda sat behind her. Vanessa looked at Alauda with uncertainty.

"You're on the good side?" she asked.

Alauda gave her an evil grin. "There is no true 'good side' on this planet. Nor on the one you call earth. I am fighting with my sisters. They are fighting with you, and so shall I. Herba is fighting with us too. She was poisoned before, but now we are united." She said this just before Herba sneaked close to them.

The Dark Lord grinned at the boulder and advanced toward it. Just in time, the sisters flew on top of him. Filix pulled a jagged whip out of thin air, and the other sisters followed suit, except each had a different weapon. Their weapons were made from different metals, some Vanessa didn't recognize. Vanessa realized they were missing one sister—Nebula.

At that moment, a fog rolled in behind the Dark Lord, and a striking warrior flew from the mist. Her armor matched the gray fog, and she held a mace in her hand. She swung it around and put a dent into Umbra's arm. He roared in pain and, with his anger, grew a foot larger.

Vanessa gasped and ran for the camp. Behind her, Alauda lashed out with a wicked javelin and stabbed Umbra in the foot. Regina now held two short swords in her hands and sliced a finger off, which grew back instantly. Unfortunately, Umbra's monster grew larger still, and he now towered over the battlefield.

Avis grinned and looked back at Vanessa. "I must tell you a secret that shall be no longer kept. My name was never Avis. At first, it was Bella. Then I was renamed. Can you guess why?" she asked. Vanessa shook her head, and Avis smiled. "Then watch and learn!" she said, holding out her hands. Umbra was busy bellowing at Herba who had shot a crossbow bolt through his ear..

"You should thank me! Now you won't have to spend any money paying for piercings! And I think this is a lovely earring! Need a match?" the ex-traitor called.

Aqua snickered and dove out of the way, firing her bow and putting an arrow through the malus's nose. "Oh, but these days nose piercings are much more popular! Say, I can even see why! This is *very* becoming! Don't you think so, Avis?"

Avis smiled and winked at Vanessa, a spear shining in her hand.

Falcon wings sprouted from her back and sent her soaring into the air. She made a shooing gesture to Vanessa, and Vanessa took her chance to run.

Avis grinned at the retreating figure of her niece. "Isn't she lucky to have such great aunts?" she asked Nebula as her sister floated next to her.

Nebula yelled and pulled Avis to the right as an arrow flew through the air in. Nebula glared at Avis as the arrow passed. "Pity she won't have much time with us all since one of them is trying to get herself killed!"

"Puh-lease! I can last for a while!" She threw the spear, and it stuck straight into Umbra's skull, hardly doing anything but infuriating the beast. She grinned. "Nice barrette!" He roared in pain and tried to swat her out of the sky, but she was faster than a falcon and swooped away. Now her wings had changed into humming bird wings, giving her more agility than a hoverfly.

Nebula laughed. "Oh, but with a barrette, you must have hair . . ."

She shaped fog into a million little arrows and flung them into Umbra's head, giving him the appearance of having fuzzy hair. This only served to enrage the Dark Lord's creature more.

Alauda giggled and ran daintily up his back, walking vertically with ease. Laughing when she reached his shoulder, a chain appeared in her hand. "Oh, you must try on this fabulous necklace though!"

She pulled it tight around his throat, pinning it there with her javelin. She leaped off just in time, and Avis caught her as the Dark Lord's beast tried to smash her with his fist. Alauda and Avis landed on top of his head and found a place he could not reach. Alauda grinned at Avis.

"I have always wanted a pet, haven't you?" she asked happily.

Prati's sickle slashed through the air, and she grinned. "Here, I know what will make this all better: a bracelet!"

She grabbed a large rope from Nebula and swung it like a lasso, bringing it over his two hands, and as she pulled with brutal force, he lurched to one side, sending Avis and Alauda into the air. Avis caught Alauda, and they flew off unharmed. Prati and Nebula continued to battle the grotesque creature but could find no way to kill it. Umbra was growing tired of the exchange melted out of the beast.

"So long little girls... enjoy battling my beast," he said as he trod off into the fray.

CHAPTER 45

GIANTS

Rex scrambled to one side as a malus crashed into the spot he had just been standing. With his sword, he cut the beast's head off and kicked another attacker away. He looked around for Olea, but she was nowhere to be found. He then caught sight of Abigail dodging aside as a shadow titan ran toward her. Oddly, the shadow titan didn't hurt her; he just ran away.

Rex frowned. "I wonder what she is doing," he said, flipping up his sword to catch a rat-faced goblin by its spear.

He gave Rat-face a look and talked to him conversationally as he blocked the slashes and asked the frustrated goblin, "Hmm. What do you think she is up to?"

And Rat-face shrieked with a gurgled cry. Rex nodded. "You're right. How 'bout I finish off you and find out?" With that he sliced the goblin's head off and bounded toward Abigail.

He used a bucking malus to spring himself into the air and catapult across part of the battlefield. He landed on a shadow titan, and it threw him off its back. He let out a painful moan as he slammed into an armored person and gasped as a sword came to his throat.

Suddenly, a familiar voice came from above him. "Rex?" And the sword fell away.

Vanessa, covered in dirt and blood, stared at him. Rex stared at her. He was momentarily speechless because, for a second, he thought she was glowing with an intense white light. Then the light was gone, and he was looking at his friend again.

Vanessa grabbed his arm and pulled him out of the way as a gargoyle lunged at him. Vanessa held her Prowler blade up, and when the gargoyle looked at it, he shattered.

Rex gasped with awe but managed to look somewhat composed. "Nice trick! Why don't you turn into your dragon?"

Suddenly, Vanessa's head became that of a white dragon, and it bit off the head of a nearby malus. Her head turned back to normal, and she looked at Rex with a face of disgust. "It takes more energy to do so than just turning a part of my body into one. Besides, I hate the taste of malus!"

Dodging foes, they ran toward the tent. Rex became aware of something missing in Umbra's army. He looked at Vanessa as she killed a shadow titan with her sword. She sensed his confusion and gave him a questioning glance. He looked at her.

"Where are the giants? Aren't we supposed to fight them?" he asked.

Vanessa raised an eyebrow. "*Giants*? You have got to be kidding me!"

Rex shook his head. "Nope. They are mentioned in your prophecy. Dragons are supposed to kill them."

Vanessa quietly cursed her prophecy in Elvish. Rex raised an eyebrow.

"Very polite! Great language for an elf princess! Who taught you that one?"

Vanessa glared at him. "Aurora!"

Rex looked stunned for a second. "Well, nothing like the queen of the elves to teach you how to call your own prophecy unsavory names in a celestial form of Latin."

Vanessa grabbed Rex. "Come on, magna ore!" she said as she turned into a rhinoceros and, with Rex on her back, ran to the where one of the generals was.

Rex glared at her as they rode through the chaos. *"Big mouth?* REALLY? Maybe Elvish is not so celestial," he exclaimed as she ran to Astrum.

She had barely reached a full run when she skidded to a stop next to him. She shape-shifted into her elf form and told Astrum about her prophecy.

He shook his head and laughed. "Sorry, but giants were extinct. There is no way there could be even one giant here!"

ROOOOAAAARRRRR!

A monstrous bellow sounded across the entire island. Vanessa gulped as huge shapes loomed out of the fog Nebula had created. Three giants swung clubs at the army, smashing sprites and satyrs and even killing those that were on their own side. More shapes loomed out of nowhere, and they began to form a line to the west.

As she raised an eyebrow at Astrum who was now regretting every word he had uttered, Vanessa ran to help the generals guide the army out of the way. She called a group of ten sprites to go to the healing tent. She helped a female sprite with a badly bashed head to the one of the nearby healers. Suddenly, a gigantic hand grabbed Vanessa, and she shrieked when it pulled her up into the sky. She wriggled in his grasp, but he only tightened his grip, crushing her ribs in the process. She focused her attention on herself, making her skin turn into pure heat with an Elvish word. The giant dropped her, clutching its hand, and Vanessa plummeted. She tried to change into something to slow her fall, but she could not since she was momentarily depleted of magic. Suddenly, strong hands grabbed her waist and flew her gently to the ground.

A male sprite smiled kindly at her and rested her against a boulder. She gazed weakly at his face as he healed her wounds from the giant's strong grip. He had a short beard, and his face was etched with years of smiling. She also noticed he had a long scar across his face, and she nodded her thanks. He took off into battle. Vanessa stood as strength flooded back into her.

Then something got her attention. The gleam in the giant's eyes was a slight orange. That was familiar, she thought; that looks like someone else's eyes, someone who was commanding the third part of the sprites. Vanessa gasped and grabbed the nearest sprite. His injuries were slight, and Vanessa quickly glanced at his armor to see what his emblem was. His breastplate had the carving of a thundercloud. She guessed it was Elvish by fancy way it was carved.

"Your name is Tono?" she asked. He nodded, surprised. She pointed to the retreating Terrians. "I need you to lead them away from the tents. Get a party of fifty or so, and leave them to protect the tents. I need the army to start edging further and further to the south. There will be a high hill there that will make it easier for you to defend yourselves. Remember, don't retreat too quickly, or they will realize that you are drawing them away from their target. Go!" she said.

The young sprite looked a bit overwhelmed but nodded. Then he cocked his head. "Who is their target?" he asked.

Vanessa grimaced but decided to tell him. "Me."

CHAPTER 46

THE TRAITOR

Vanessa rounded the corner of the sick tent and came face to face with the traitor. Her heart skipped a beat when she saw he was carrying a club, but she forced a calm expression and managed to look quite regal. She saw a momentary look of surprise flash across the traitor's face, but he covered it up skillfully.

Truncus smiled at her cheerfully. "My princess! How are you? I thought—"

Vanessa cut him short with an angry look. "I know what you are up to! You are the traitor!" she said calmly.

Truncus didn't look surprised. "Of course, I am. Well, at least, I am *a* traitor. There are more."

Vanessa was momentarily off guard at his confident manner in the way he admitted it. Truncus lunged, a knife in his hand, and swept Vanessa's feet out from under. She cried out and landed with a thump. He pinned her to the ground with the knife to her throat. She choked in surprise, and he gave her an evil look.

"So that means I have to kill you!" he purred. Vanessa's gurgling cry was halted when the knife pressed further into her throat.

Truncus smiled. "Tsk, Tsk. You don't want anyone to hear you! You might get hurt. Now come with me." As he hauled her up, he knocked her out with a club.

Vanessa woke up on a horse. They had been galloping for only five minutes when they stopped suddenly at a cliff. Truncus had her tied up with an enchanted chain, and she could hardly move. Now he untied her and left her on the ground. Her head throbbed, and blood tricked down her forehead. She snarled weakly at Truncus but could not move her body an inch. Her strength was slowly coming back, but the cramps from her bonds were too great for her to stand, so she just sat sprawled on the grass. She tried to move again and found she could only twitch a finger without the pain surging back into her veins.

Truncus was grinning at the helpless form when a scraggly crow landed on his shoulder. It carried a scroll in its jagged black beak and now dropped it in Truncus's hand. He untied it, and his orange eyes widened. He crumpled the paper and threw it off the cliff. He then turned to Vanessa.

"The Dark Lord has made his will known. We are going to kill most of your sprite and satyr friends and save the rest to turn into our own soldiers. Whether by pain or by evil, they will fall to us. Your family will be killed . . . except for your little sister. She will be important in the days to come. You are to be killed now, even though my Excellence wishes he could be here to do so himself," he said with a wicked grin on his face.

Hopelessness clouded the princess's thoughts, and Vanessa felt the cold hand of fear clutch her heart. She had to try to escape. Vanessa tried to wiggle away but got only a few centimeters before Truncus raised his sword above her head. Vanessa stared at the blade. She realized she was about to die, and she silently prayed for her family to be protected. Then just as her prayer met its end, the blade came down in an arc of silvery death.

CHAPTER 47

VICTORY FOR A PRICE

But not her death: She waited for the blade to end her, but instead, she heard a gurgled cry. Septimus stood over her, the sword buried deep in his chest. Vanessa cried out but was unable to move. Septimus, though mortally wounded, reeled around and sliced Truncus's head off clean before pulling the sword out of his chest. Blood gushed from the wound, and Septimus muttered a phrase. Though the bleeding had stopped, but both of them knew Septimus was doomed to die. Vanessa managed to crawl over. Septimus looked up at her, blue eyes pained but also relieved. Vanessa looked at him with eyes full of sorrow, tears threatening.

"Septimus. Why? You shouldn't have," she said softly.

Septimus smiled weakly. "But who would've? Rex? No. My brother has a life of his own to complete. I am joining my love. After this war, he should join his," Septimus said, pointing a bloodied finger at Vanessa.

Vanessa felt hollow. Deep down inside of her, she knew it was true. Vanessa looked at Septimus. "I will never see you again?" she whispered.

Septimus smiled. "We all will see each other again. It is only a matter of when."

Vanessa whimpered. "But surely I can heal you! Let me use Draconic! Elvish! Something!" she pleaded.

Septimus shook his head slowly. "Vanessa, remember! Magic is not the only way to victory."

His breathing stopped and his body still. *It's over*, Vanessa thought. Her grief halted when his body suddenly dissolved into tiny twinkling objects and flew into the sky. She then saw all the stars as they shone brightly, and Vanessa picked out one that shone brightest—Candentia. There next to her shone Septimus.

The emptiness now surged through her, and the tears that had threatened flowed without end. She didn't know how long she was there, her face in her hands, mourning but after some time, she felt a hand on her shoulder.

Rex crouched beside her. Vanessa buried her face in his shoulder and cried her heart out. She felt Rex shake a bit and realized he was crying too. While still overcome with her own grief, she could not bear to see his. She looked at him, and he looked at her. Both of them had tear-stained faces, and Vanessa let out a little chuckle.

"You look awful!" she said.

Rex laughed too. "You look worse!" And they laughed a bit.

Rex stood, putting out his hand to lift her. Vanessa stared at the hand. It was worn, many scratches lined it, and she felt something lurch within her.

How could I give him false hope? He is the son of the Dark Lord! Why would I dare be friends *with him?* But then the other half of her said, *He didn't pick his father's fate! Why would you dare* not *be friends with him? He is a worthy prince. He is a worthy friend.* And Vanessa took his hand.

As he pulled her up, Vanessa swayed a bit, her muscles still aching. But she kept her balance and managed to stand straight. She grinned at Rex, and he grinned back.

Then a sarcastic voice came from a little ways beside them. "OK, enough with the mourning and hugging and whatnot! It gives me a headache!" Vanessa nearly jumped out of her skin. She turned to find Brecon, Nero, Luna Flask, Astrum, Neal, Drake, Regina, and her sisters. They stood in front of Vanessa and Rex, and Vanessa saw that it was Brecon who had spoken. She smiled to show that she was not trying to be rude. Vanessa gave her a tired little smile in return.

Now it was Nero who spoke. "We have a giant problem," he said then smiled at his own wit. Before anyone could say anything, he added, "It seems our 'Dark Lord' has disappeared. Don't ask me how a huge malus-like beast could disappear, but he managed it. Also, the army has been surrounded, and so have the tents."

Vanessa suddenly felt an awful sensation at her back. She turned around to look at the cliff. Then she whirled around. "Wait! I know Truncus was controlling the giants and did that, but who told the Dark Lord that our army was slipping away?" She looked at each of them carefully. One of them must be a traitor.

Rex seemed to get that impression too. He stood straight. "Who was it?"

Then a small voice answered from behind them all. "Me."

All turned. Abigail stood uncomfortably facing them. She had tears of anger and sadness in her eyes. She glared at them and turned to leave.

Regina suddenly cried out. "Abigail, come back! Please, you must listen—"

But Abigail cut her off. "No one wanted to awaken me! No one wanted to send me on a quest! No one made a prophecy about me!" she said as she stormed away.

Suddenly, Filix stepped forward, her auburn hair flowing into her face. She looked at Abigail. "You are already awakened!" she said fiercely.

Abigail took a step back, fingering her own auburn hair. "But . . . but what about my hair color? Why aren't my eyes blue like theirs? I don't look like Regina!" she asked angrily.

"That's because you aren't *her* daughter! You are *mine*!" Felix exclaimed. Everyone was in silent shock.

Abigail had her jaw to the ground. "What?" she asked.

Filix lowered her head, and her husband came to hold her hand, looking shocked himself. Filix stiffened, trying to be strong. "You see, being a first-born child of an oracle is dangerous. They always seem to

die. So I hid you with Regina. Maybe that way you would live long.
Then when I had my second child, he or she would live too. I had hope
for a good life for you with Regina and Drake, but here we are," she said.

Rex stepped forward. "Abigail, she foresaw your death, and instead
of you dying, another chose to . . . for you."

Vanessa muttered, "Olea." She looked to Rex.

Rex nodded. "Yes. She offered to. I tried to stop her, but nothing
I said did anything to change her mind," and he sighed. "She is 'the
healer' in the prophecy." They all understood.

Avis stepped forward. "Hate to break it to you guys, but we have
a bunch of goblins and things coming toward us. We need to—" But
she broke off as a giant hand came crawling up the huge cliff. It was
followed by another hand, and those pulled up the huge Dark Lord. He
bellowed at them and growled.

Rex stepped up. "You killed your very own son! I revoke you from
being my father! I am free of your evil from now on!"

A figure suddenly stepped free of the skin of the malus. He had
blond hair and pale skin. He wore a scowl, and his eyes were fluttering.
Vanessa thought he looked like he was fighting himself when he reached
out his hand. Rex seemed to realize something and took the hand. He
spoke in a voice that was not his. It was deeper and stronger. Rex's eyes
had now turned a deep, glowing green and were shining intensely as he
looked into Umbra's eyes,

"Umbra Noctis, I hereby remove the evil that has taken you. I,
Nimbus, the father who you murdered, command the iniquity from you
depart! *Purgo!*" And Umbra and Rex slumped to the ground. Vanessa
and Brecon, being the closest, ran forward and caught the men.

A black shadow slipped from Umbra and went back into the beast.
Rex and Umbra both looked up at the beast, and the huge malus-like
creature bellowed in rage. It suddenly grew larger, black horns and
spikes grew out of it from nowhere, and Vanessa gulped.

Umbra got up. His hair had turned pure white, but his face remained
surprisingly youthful. Umbra growled back at the beast, "Malum! You

are responsible for my eldest son's death! You must die also!" The awful beast bellowed a ghastly sound resembling a laugh.

"Umbra, Umbra! You are very amusing! But remember, evil will never die!"

Vanessa looked up with defiance. "Never say never! But even if you are right, there will always be those to fight it! Yes, some may die. Yes, some may fall to your wickedness! But we will always fight you! Now be rid of us!" And it howled and clawed as some force dragged it to the edge of the cliff.

Vanessa realized that the edge dropped of into a pit of endless darkness. At that moment, she also realized that they were all standing on a peak that protruded into the pit. The malum clawed at the ground, shaking the earth and rocks beneath them. Realizing the cliff was beginning to crumble, Vanessa screamed for everyone to run.

Abigail, being the smallest, tripped. The ground crumbled out from beneath her, and Vanessa was too far away to help. As Abigail fell, Rex turned, ran to the edge of the pit, and leapt after her. Vanessa screamed, too shocked to move. Just like that, they were gone… or not… a gasp was ripped from Vanessa as a blur of movement shot out of the pit. Rex and Abigail landed next to Vanessa. Vanessa wrapped her arms around them both and hugged them with all of her strength. She was *not* going to loose them again. Rex was laughing, and Abigail was crying tears of joy.

"Rex! You can fly?" Vanessa asked letting go of them. Rex smiled.

"Yes. I'm half sprite. I can even shrink!" he said. Drake ran forward and hugged them.

"Thank goodness you're alive!" he said. Then Luna Flask stepped forward.

"We still have a war to finish," she declared.

EPILOGUE

Five years later,

Vanessa sat in the forested park, watching the swans drift across the glassy pond. The grass was incredibly soft, and there was a gentle summer breeze blowing. On the gray stone bench, Vanessa felt like a queen…. In fact, she was. After the war, Aurora had given up her place as queen, allowing Vanessa to step forward and take the throne. It was grueling work rooting out the rest of Umbra's minions, but with the help of Umbra himself, she got most of them. She still couldn't find Sperno, and the thought worried her.

She already had had several assassination tries, but with the help of Peregrin, her pug, she had gotten away safely. Peregrin, in fact, was actually a werepug. At any time, the pug could shift into a dwarf-like person. Of course, Peregrin delighted in being a dog.

He had persuaded Vanessa to make a special velvet pillow beside her throne, that had his name embroidered on it with golden thread. Vanessa now was petting the pug, enjoying the feel of her hands running along his black fur.

She thought often of Abigail and missed having her around. Though she was able to visit with her from time to time, Abigail was busy learning the healer's art from her real mother, Filix. Filix had given birth to a baby girl and had named her Stella, and even at her young age, Stella was learning the ways of a healer.

Astrum and Avis had gotten married, and now had four little hellions…. with wings! Nero and Brecon had gotten married, and now Brecon was expecting. Olea, Aqua, Luna Flask, Gold-storm, and Gemma had started their own band. The name of the band was (hilariously) the Pack of Wolves. Prati and Herba had died in battle from the king of the giants, and Luna had fulfilled the prophecy by drinking the giant's blood. The dragons and the kapacki had come together, also fulfilling another line. Vanessa was still waiting for the last line that said something about she and a young man forever ruling… Vanessa was thinking about it just as Rex said, "Boo." Vanessa jumped. Rex sauntered over and sat beside Vanessa,

"So… cool swans…" he began. Vanessa tried to keep her hopes down. Vanessa felt ready to marry, and she had deliberately given Rex many chances to propose, but he still had waited. Rex sat back, staring at the park,

"Nice place, really," he said. Vanessa nodded, "Of course," she said. Rex sighed, "Perfect place to start families… right?" he asked. Vanessa raised an eyebrow, "That was subtle," she noted. Rex shrugged, "I'm a subtle guy… so…." Rex rummaged around in his pocket,

"Vanessa… remember this?" he asked, pulling out a conch from his Pera. Vanessa gasped. This was the one that had told her to go to Pearl Water… Vanessa put it to her ear. The only sound she could hear was a strange tinkling. She frowned at the conch, shaking it slightly.

"That's weird…" she reached her hand as far as she could inside the conch. Her fingers touched something… something cold and metal. Barely keeping in her excitement, she pulled the ring out. It was so delicate, picture of a dragons entwined around a shining diamond. Rex suddenly knelt,

"Will you be my jewel?" he asked. Vanessa kissed him, holding tightly to the ring. She pulled back, "Forever." she breathed.

THE END

GLOSSARY OF LATIN WORDS

adsurgo	to arise
alauda	lark
alba	white
altus	high
anima	life/soul
aqua	water
argentum	silver
aro	to cultivate
astrum	constellation
aurora	dawn
aurum	gold
bellum	war
australis	southern
ave	hello
avis	bird
canis	dog
candentia	shine/radiance
capitulus	chapter
celestis	celestial
celsus	noble

cetus	whale/dolphin
chama	clam
citra	without/on this side of
claudius	lame
cochlea	snail
compono	calm
curo	heal
deflecto	divert
elisium	paradise
ensis	sword/blade
fael/felis	cat
filia	daughter
filix	fern
flumen	river
fulmen	lightning
gemma	gem
gnatus	to be born
gracula	crow
haedus	kid (goat)
herba	herb
ignis	flame
ipsum	very much
lapis	stone
lilia lilies	
luna	moon
lupus	wolf
lux	light
lyra	lyre
margarita	pearl
magna	big
malum	evil
malus	bad

mons	mountain
nascor	to increase
nebula	fog/mist/cloud
nimbus	cloud
niger	black
nisi	unless/except
nox/noctis	night
octavius	eigth
olea	olive
ore	mouth
ossis	bone
pardus	leopard
pater	father
pax	peace
pera	wallet/sack
peregrinus	stranger
prata	meadow
pravis	depraved/corrupt
purgo	clean/purge
pyra	pyre/bonfire
quid	what
regina	queen
rex	king
scire	know/learn
scutum	shield
septimus	seventh
silex	flint/stone
silva	forest
sol	sun
spemo	hope
stella	star
surgo	to grow

syringa	lilac
te/tu	you
tempestas	storm
tenebra	darkness
terra	earth
tonitrus	thunder
tono	thunder
truncus	trunk
ultra	more
umbra	shadow
ursa	bear
pera	void
vecors	mad/crazy
ventus	wind
vero	yes
vesper	evening
ventus	wind

Edwards Brothers Malloy
Oxnard, CA USA
October 17, 2014